The Enemy's a Son

JAMES JOHNSON

The Enemy's a Son

To my mad, mental, Glaswegean friend – Karen, Lots of love –
R Johnnn.

- NWㅜㅗ⊓ ⅃ᴇⱤᴛ н сн Ⱨᴏɴɪᴄʟᴇꜱ ∞ ⅃ ᴏ̄ ⅃ Ñ w̄

BOOK I

THE ENEMY'S SON: ERTH CHRONICLES BOOK I

www.erthchronicles.com   info@erthchronicles.com

This first edition published 2008 by Mam Tor Publishing Ltd.
PO Box 6785, Derby DE22 1XT. United Kingdom

www.terminalcondition.com   info@terminalcondition.com

Inside back cover and postcard credits:
Leonardo M. Giron, Jennifer Reagles, Ado Ceric and Alan Lathwell
copyright © 2007

ISBN 13: 978-0-9549998-4-1

Printed by RPM Printing, Chichester, UK

www.mamtor.com   mamtor@mac.com

**MAM
T⬛R**
Publishing

F.W. Chaplin
1919-2003

Husband, Father, Grandfather

All Nature is but art, unknown to thee
All chance, direction, that thou canst not see;
All discord, harmony not understood;
All partial evil, universal good:
And, spite of pride, in erring reason's spite,
One truth is clear, 'Whatever is, is right.'

Alexander Pope: *Essay on Man*, Epistle I

One

This was no game, other than a sick and twisted one.

He had been awoken by the distant chaos - a boy, frightened and alone, stumbling through the dense undergrowth. His tear stained eyes could barely make out what was in front of him, as the smoke slowly engulfed the forest.

A single word echoed in the distance:

"Horncastle!"

Hearing his name, Pirian Horncastle paused briefly, coughing and spluttering as he attempted to catch his breath. Gripped by fear, all he could think about was the raging inferno and the icy hatred in the eyes of those hunting him. Wiping his eyes, he ran on, his hammering heart crying out for more oxygen.

Ancient timbers were devoured by the blazing heat, a faint orange glow lighting the night sky as trees groaned and cracked in the distance. Ahead of the fire his pursuers had started, the deathly grey smoke continued to seep through the once verdant foliage, strangling and suffocating all in its path.

Every creature in the forest surged forward. Wild-eyed hares pelted through the smouldering bracken, mice scurried between scorched roots, and glistening reptiles crawled and slithered over the lifeless bodies of those too slow to outrun the encroaching hell.

"There's no one here to save you now…not even your own pathetic father!" a voice called.

There was a painful truth to the harsh tone, driving a knife into Pirian's heart as much as the dying air. This was no longer a place for an eleven year old; even though he had been raised in Greenhouse One, the size of the habitat had now outgrown him; he'd never locate his father without a comlink...if he was here at all.

For once, you should have listened to your parents and never have come back here, he thought to himself in frustration.

Laughter and hollering interrupted his thoughts. They were closer now.

As Pirian and the rest of the creatures raced on, the trees became denser. He was buffeted by larger animals and branches whipped across his face, while small thickets grabbed at his ankles, causing Pirian to trip and fall. Immediately he covered his head, in fear of being trampled. Once the larger animals had passed, he waited and wiped his streaming eyes again. There was a temptation to hide from his pursuers amongst the undergrowth and keep below the smoke.

A targeting laser flashed onto a fallen tree trunk next to him. Pirian followed the red dot as it moved downwards, aligning on his chest.

They were toying with him.

Laughter followed once again as another voice called out, "We'll promise to make it quick and painless. The same way we've put the rest of the Erth scum out of their misery."

The dot disappeared and Pirian scrabbled forward.

He didn't move far.

It was the smell of the dead kyber that pulled him to his feet, more so than its bloody remains. Its mouth hung open, revealing broken, canine teeth; clawed legs twisted under the weight of its body, caked in blood. Clutching his mouth, Pirian ran on; lungs aching and burning, stomach churning, his head pounding.

The kyber wasn't the first slaughtered animal he had come across; there were many littered across the valley. Those which were still alive continued to run with him - they knew as well as he did what 'quick and painless' meant.

Cornelius! Pirian prayed his pursuers hadn't reached his friend. His only friend; one who listened and shared the very same pain he was feeling right now as the fire slowly engulfed the last Greenhouse.

"Where are you going?" a voice shouted.

The voices drew ever closer as he finally broke ahead of the smoke.

Pirian was no runner at the best of times. His body was weak and with no Guild training, he was in poor condition. His legs burned with fatigue as his pace slowed rapidly. Coming up to a steep ravine, his foot caught a vine. There was no floor to catch him this time and he tumbled downwards, crashing through tree canopies as he cartwheeled over and over.

No rocks, please no rocks, he thought.

As he fell, more vines coiled round his body slowing his descent. Finally he rolled out into a clearing. Many of the animals that followed had reached the bottom safely, jumping over him as he lay on the floor in a tangled heap.

Pirian lifted back his hood and pulled away the knotted vines. He then wiped his eyes once again, along with his scratched and grubby face, a mixture of blood, sweat and mud smearing his overcoat sleeve.

Panting, he attempted to catch his breath.

Fresh air.

The smoke hadn't reached the clearing. It continued to rise high above the canopy's orange glow, but it was only a matter of time before the fire engulfed everything in its path. A roaring sound filled his ears as the heat steadily increased.

A waterfall tumbled down the left side of the ravine, feeding a small lake. The river was the main source of life within the habitat. It hadn't been that long since all three of his father's

Greenhouses were as vibrant as this. The lake was one of many scattered throughout its habitat, settling on the outer rim. The cycle washed away the autumn leaves that clung to the banks. It had become a natural ecosystem supplying water to the rain system, helping to prevent any potential fire. But something had been tampered with.

Pirian could make out the breaking of dawn, the approaching fire only emphasising the warm glow.

Butterflies and hummingbirds scattered as most of the animals dived into the water, attempting to reach the opposite side of the lake as quickly as possible.

His pursuers howled.

They were closer than ever and he could barely move.

He had felt the Greenhouse's pain the moment the fire had begun. As its envirocontrol had malfunctioned, its power over him had grown weaker. The nausea spread, pulling at his insides, his guts twisting, before he finally vomited. His altitude sickness had intensified as an unseen force pulled his body downwards.

Wiping his mouth, he dumped his backpack and opened it. Removing a fashioned stick that resembled a wooden sword, he jabbed it into the ground and fought against the gravity. Finally pulling himself up, he clutched his arm and made his way slowly to the edge of the lake. Amongst the commotion he rolled up his sleeve, revealing a small mark that was beginning to change shape.

Although Pirian wasn't a strong swimmer, he was still tempted to jump in. Instead, he simply scooped up water with his free hand, soothed his raw throat and splashed the irritated mark.

The undergrowth parted nearby, and a slow moving animal, the size of a large serving tray, made its way towards him. Before the creature stopped in front of him, a long neck extended from its shell

Gradually, the creature edged towards an apple that had fallen from his backpack.

Pirian took one last gulp of water and pulled his marked arm from the lake.

"This...isn't the time to eat, Cornelius."

Filled with deep grooves and scratches, a small rock was embedded in the creature's shell; a mark of the harsh world in which it lived. The act of cruel pleasure had happened when the creature was younger; the shell now having grown around the rock. Munching the apple, the tortoise sniffed the air, the creature's slow pace at odds with Pirian's frantic worry about his situation.

Cornelius didn't keep the food down for long. The fact that he shared Pirian's sickness only bound them further together. The slow, harmless animal was his only friend. Neither of them relied on the Dosage, and had never felt the need to harm and destroy lives and the work of others. Pirian understood what feelings were, along with every other animal in the habitat.

The smoke hung high above. Pirian flinched as he heard another firebomb go off nearby. There was a sound of trampled undergrowth as three silhouettes appeared through the billowing cloud of smoke.

Flames furled upwards with an intense ferocity, eating everything in their path. Pirian's eyes stayed locked on the figures walking out of the fire.

"Ahhh, there you are," said the leader of the group, masked and hooded. "Wallowing in the dirt. Anyone would think you were Erth born."

It was Viktor Jakahn. Although Pirian couldn't make out his features underneath the hood and gas mask, his tormentor's eyes were all too clear in his mind; the image of the brutish face and sadistic grin had been beaten into him many times before. Seven years older than Pirian, Viktor took full advantage as he towered over him.

Viktor's accomplices were of the same build. Newtonians were bred to physical perfection; the slightest defect eradicated. Even A-class females were built for fighting - Loran in particular easily mistaken for any male counterpart. All that distinguished Neel was the gel cast attached to his broken arm.

As they surrounded him, Pirian held out his wooden sword. He steadied himself as best he could, while the fire closed in.

Viktor swaggered up to him, pushing the sword aside with the back of his left hand. He followed through with the back of his right, striking Pirian square across the face and knocking him to the ground.

Shaking his head, Pirian wiped the blood from his nose.

Standing above him, Viktor tapped his temple, his gas mask flipping down to his chest plate.

An all too familiar glow of amber lit his eyes. Zetameen; Newton's precious Dosage, a controlling drug that had brainwashed society for centuries; turning most into weak, single minded individuals who only knew how to follow the orders of the Hierarchy, Newton's government. The Dosage helped most people forget their true emotions; but for a few it enhanced their psychopathic nature.

Pirian noticed its effects were also apparent in their posture. They had all clearly taken far more of the Dosage than necessary; Loran and Neel's shoulders were relaxed, their arms swinging as they lumbered forwards. Pirian almost felt optimistic that their Dosage-induced state may have relaxed them too much to cause any further harm.

But Viktor was in full control as he loomed in, cocking his head. "Why on Erth do you still come here?"

"To try and get away from people like you," snapped Pirian. He could hear the click and whir of Viktor's retinal implant. The sadistic piece of work was recording the whole ordeal, more than likely to sell as further entertainment.

"Is that right?" replied Viktor, picking up Pirian's backpack and pulling out a book. "You know it's a crime to own one of these," he sneered, and threw it at his accomplices.

"Hardly matters now." replied Pirian.

"I guess not. But we can always have you flogged instead." Viktor looked over his victim's shoulder at the tortoise. Distracted by the burning smell and the intensity of the surrounding heat, Pirian was still concerned for Cornelius' safety.

He held up his wooden sword once again as Viktor stared back. Snatching the piece of wood from Pirian's grasp, he continued to taunt him.

"You know, we could find a much sharper sword to play with," he said as he snapped the wooden replica over his knee, throwing it into the hungry flames. Looking back at Pirian, he pushed him further to the ground with his foot, clicking his fingers and gesturing towards the tortoise.

Loran and Neel immediately set about stamping on the animal's shell.

"Knock, knock!" Loran taunted.

Viktor placed more pressure on a struggling Pirian. "Stop it!" he shouted, almost suffocating under Viktor's weight.

"Keep your mouth shut, Horncastle," snapped Viktor.

"Dad…" he tried to catch his breath, "Dad will have you all strung up if you harm him."

"I'm sure he would…" sneered Viktor, "But your Daddy's not here is he?"

"He's…he's here. Just…"

Victor smiled smugly. "If he was here, there is no way we'd have broken in so easily and caused our little fire."

"No. He…" Pirian began to reply, before thinking of his father's whereabouts.

Viktor grinned, "I'd have thought the Horncastles would

have had a more worthy pet than a decrepit looking tortoise. What good is it?" he paused. "What good is any animal?"

"What good are you?" shouted Pirian, goaded beyond endurance.

Removing his foot, Viktor grabbed Pirian by the scruff of the neck and lifted him from the ground, "You really are asking for trouble."

Hanging limply from Viktor's arm, Pirian wiped his bleeding nose once again. "I've never needed to ask for it."

Viktor grinned with satisfaction, buzzing with zetameen.

"What are you going to do to him?" asked Neel.

Victor released his grip slightly and lowered Pirian, "Nothing..."

"Nothing?" repeated Loran

He sneered over at her and Neel then turned and looked at the tortoise. "But seeing if a tortoise can fly...that might be fun."

The fire raged. Viktor grabbed his victim once again, proceeding to drag him around the lake. Loran and Neel followed carrying Cornelius.

Pirian could see the frantic animals in the distance. Viktor removed his plasma gun, the laser sighting training in on a target. The gun recoiled and in the distance another victim fell.

At first it looked as though most of the animals were hiding in the surrounding undergrowth as the flames crept forward. Then, as Pirian was dragged closer, he could make out a distortion, as though his surroundings were bending in the light of the flames.

A further distortion quickly followed, then a flickering.

It was the Greenhouse's hologram. Projected onto the outer walls, it helped maintain a more natural environment. Usually the technology was impenetrable, but the fire had affected the electrical systems, which was the main reason the water supply hadn't been triggered to kill the fire.

As Pirian and Cornelius were dragged through the projection, what appeared to be a high cliff face and surrounding trees continued to flicker. As it vanished, the hologram finally revealed a cold geodesic structure of steel and glass walls.

Viktor proceeded to smash a nearby console fastened to the wall, then pulled several safety levers, all the while his free arm still wrapped around Pirian's neck. A large, heavy door slowly rose and cold air began to rush into the habitat. Several animals pushed their way through. The opening door slowly revealed a maintenance veranda circling the entire structure, where an angled, transparent barrier with inset steps either side led up to a rail system.

Viktor threw Pirian to the ground.

Dawn's light had taken hold. Transfixed by the expanse of open sky and surrounding clouds, Pirian was reminded further of how high up they were. As the gravity pulled at his guts, he knew all too well how dangerous it was to be on the very outer limits of a flying city.

I

The last thing he remembered was an intense light.

His mind was so scattered he couldn't even remember the word 'death', let alone the meaning of the brightness before him.

Then it vanished into shadow. Darkness was becoming all too familiar, until he felt the heat of the fire.

He could see the light and the dark, or maybe he couldn't see at all?

Pain.

Aware of this, he finally opened his eyes. The cruel sensation was coming from the palms of his hands. They felt as though they had been burnt somehow.

Black.

Two

Defying every rule of gravity, Newton drew the clouds around its majestic structure, its silent pride protected by the elements. At the centre of the flying city stood the silver and bronze towers of its capital, Ivar, dominating every other structure in sight and crowning the Erth below. It was shaped in a circle, and surrounded by three more. These cities, Alva, Beda and Gam, broke away from the central structure, a sign of gradual expansion - for the city was now more like a small country. The once brightly coloured foliage that had sought sunlight now burned brightly within the remaining Greenhouse, resembling an open wound across the gleaming architecture of Newton.

The wind howled and although the fresh air filled Pirian's lungs, the altitude sickness continued to overwhelm him. "Gi… give me back the tortoise," he pleaded, raising his hand to his mouth as he gagged once more.

Viktor's eyes narrowed, savouring the moment. "I don't think so Horncastle, it'll spoil the fun."

Pirian watched in horror as Loran and Neel handed Viktor the tortoise, before climbing the steps of the barrier.

Running the entire circumference of the Greenhouse exterior, the maintenance veranda was strictly out of bounds. Anyone who strayed outside of the maintenance car without a safety harness risked being torn away by the strong winds. Yet Viktor seemed invincible as he stood confidently above everyone.

Becoming more distraught by the second, Pirian shouted out

once again, "Give me back Cornelius... please!"

"'Give me back Cornelius, give me back Cornelius'. What are you going to do about it?" Viktor mocked, balancing precariously along the barrier as Loran and Neel laughed. "I think you're going to have to climb up here and get him off me. If you dare."

Pirian's fear of heights went hand in hand with the altitude sickness; a cruel punishment for being born on a flying city. There was very little he could do about it; the cackles of Loran and Neel taunting him further.

"Throw it over, Viktor, go on!" shouted Loran.

"Yeah, do it!" followed Neel.

"You...d...dare, Viktor!" stuttered Pirian.

"D...d...duh, duh, duh," Viktor taunted. "I told you, come and get him!"

Pirian knew deep down it was the only chance he had of retrieving Cornelius. If it meant confronting his fear of heights, then so be it. The cackling laughter of Loran and Neel ceased as soon as he staggered over to the barrier and began to climb the steps. Not for a moment did he take his eyes off Viktor.

Once he had finally managed to reach the top, there was nothing to hold onto other than the tracks of the rail system running along the surface of the barrier. The tracks were no wider than the maintenance cars themselves, with very little width to crawl along.

He didn't stand immediately. Frozen, he had caught a glimpse of the nothingness below. The clouds were an endless white landscape of cotton wool, blocking out any hint of land. He could make out what looked like more Newtonian cruisers approaching the city, and the wind battered at his body as he held on for dear life. The twirling white and blue was both magnificent and horrific, as everything around him began to spin and spiral out of control.

His stomach rose to the back of his throat, his altitude sickness taking hold once again. Retching, he heard the blood pumping in his head, a deafening thud as he looked up at Viktor. Pirian couldn't hear a word he was saying, nor could he hear Loran and Neel laughing anymore.

Petrified, he gripped the freezing metal tracks. Turning his head away from view, the thumping in his head began to calm as the laughter and jeering of his tormentors slowly rose.

"Get up, Horncastle!" shouted Viktor. "You snivelling little rat! If you want the tortoise to live, get up!"

Closing his eyes, he struggled to calm his breathing. His whole body shook as he dragged himself up onto his knees. Eventually, he managed to stand upright, his legs trembling. Finally, he opened his eyes again, glaring at Viktor. The sadist held Cornelius casually under one arm as though he weighed nothing, while his tormentor swayed in slow motion.

"That's it. Not that hard when you put your mind to it. Even a wimp like you can do it."

"L...le...let him...go," begged Pirian reaching out his arms, his own voice slowing in his head.

"Oooh, I'm not sure," Viktor replied as he spun the tortoise around between both hands, holding him out in front of Pirian.

Pirian looked at Cornelius' shell, but the animal was barely visible inside. There was no telling if it had already died, until gradually its head began to poke out, eyes slowly opening.

"P...put him down."

"I think you should make more of an effort and come and get him off me."

Pirian tried to place a foot forward. It might as well have been glued to the barrier. He was rigid, frozen from fear as well as the cold winds.

"I...I ca...can't." he looked at the helpless creature still held out in front of him. It blinked. He almost thought there was a smile from the tortoise as Viktor held him over the barrier.

"That's too bad, Horncastle," he said, letting go.

"No!" wailed Pirian, slumping forward to his knees, as he watched Cornelius fall from view. Losing his balance, he almost fell himself, gripping the barrier with one hand as he reached out with the other. The cold metal stung his chest, his arm stretched over the barrier in a hopeless effort to catch his friend. As everything began to spin once again, he closed his eyes. Shaking, he gripped the barrier harder than ever. Then he felt himself being lifted up, his throat being squeezed as Viktor lifted him clear off the ground. Keeping his eyes closed, he prayed for Viktor to end it now. There was no strength left in him, as Viktor threw him down the sloping barrier.

Sliding downwards, Pirian hit the veranda floor, rolling over onto his back. He was too numb with cold to feel any more pain.

Jumping down from the barrier, Viktor landed with a slam in front of him. He nodded to his accomplices, and they lifted him off the ground, as Viktor rammed his fist into Pirian's stomach.

He doubled over, the wind momentarily knocked out of him. Managing to regain his breath, he looked up.

Viktor drew his plasma gun and placed it against Pirian's head.

The plasma cells charged.

Pirian quivered uncontrollably as a warm, wet sensation filled his leggings.

"POW!" taunted Viktor as Loran and Neel howled with laughter.

Then the barrier began to shake.

Distracted, Viktor frowned and lowered his head slightly, concentrating on the approaching sound.

"The maintenance car?" said Loran.

Viktor looked back at Pirian and grabbed his face. "Looks

like Daddy's finally arrived. Better late than never, hey?"

Pirian clenched his teeth. He let out an uncontrollable breath, and his bottom lip trembled.

Viktor shoved Pirian's head away as Loran and Neel dropped him to the floor. Then, Viktor made his way over to a mechanism known as a jettison lever - a contingency programmed into most structures on Newton, in case they caught fire or systems failed. With no care for the state of the world below, all structures jettisoned were condemned to destruction - becoming no more than another dangerous obstacle.

Loran and Neel helped to shift the weight of the lever. As they brought it down with a rusty clang, the Greenhouse lurched.

On the huge jettison arm, the whole habitat slowly began to move away from Newton.

There was nowhere for Pirian to go. Even if he had the strength, or even the guts to brave the fire raging inside the Greenhouse, the door was now firmly shut. He couldn't even stand, and prayed for the imminent arrival of his father.

He watched as Loran and Neel climbed the barrier. Viktor approached one final time. "You want to see Erth so much, so be it. You can both go down with your precious Greenhouse." He paused savouring the moment. "I always said this would be the death of your father. Now the great Jeradon Horncastle can watch his son die with him."

Quickly pulling up his hood, Viktor's mask snapped back up into place. Then he ran up the barrier, jumping from view. Loran and Neel followed and within seconds they soared upwards, wings extended from their Guild training suits.

Caked blood surrounded Pirian's nose and mouth, his tears having almost frozen his eyelids shut. As he hugged himself for warmth, his nausea continued to pull at his guts. He shivered from the cold and sickness, as he noticed a few animals nervously scamper past.

Pausing for a moment, he dragged himself to the door. Looking through, he could see the Greenhouse ablaze

He slumped down, waiting for the inevitable.

Jeradon Horncastle had no time to wait for the maintenance car to stop. Pirian watched as his father jumped from the doors directly onto the veranda.

"Pirian!...My boy..."

Pirian trembled, placing his hand to his mouth in an attempt to stop himself from being sick once again

"I have to get you onboard. Before the Greenhouse is jettisoned."

In no time at all Pirian was lifted and carried back up to the car.

"H...he, he k...killed him Dad. He...he threw him away like he was nothing."

"Killed who?" asked his father as he threw the accelerator forward.

Pirian couldn't bear to look him in the eyes. "Cornelius. Viktor...th...threw him over the side. Like he was...was a piece of rubbish."

"You're safe. For the time being that's all that matters." Jeradon was obviously controlling his frustration. "You fell asleep again, didn't you? Your mother and I, we told you not to come here. We kept telling you."

"I...I'm sorry." replied Pirian.

His father concentrated on what was ahead as an explosion surged outwards from the Greenhouse, throwing glass and metal across the veranda and track. "Good job I know where you hide at night. Just hold on, son."

The car shook as it hit the debris. Luckily it remained fastened to the track.

Several more explosions erupted behind them, flames licking

at the car. In the distance, Pirian and his father could make out the fringes of the city, as the Greenhouse continued to move outwards, revealing its jettison arm more and more.

As the docking station approached, Jeradon attempted to slow the car down but it continued to accelerate.

Pirian could see the broken track ahead, tangled up with the station's platform.

His father grabbed hold of him, diving to the far end of the car to avoid the impact. As they approached the platform, the car was hurled upwards across the station, and carried on through.

Crashing through walls of glass and metal, Pirian and his father were thrown to the side as the car turned over, falling away from the Greenhouse station and down onto the jettison arm.

Cradled in his father's arms, Pirian had escaped any serious injury. Jeradon was on his feet before the car had even finished sliding to a halt. Lifting his son, he made his way out.

Pirian flinched as more explosions followed, debris falling all around them.

The colossus tracks that the Greenhouse moved along resembled gigantic metallic trenches, reaching back towards Newton. Pirian looked on helplessly as his father slung him over his shoulder and began to run.

Due to the arm moving the opposite way, they weren't getting any closer to the city, but they were still moving away from the Greenhouse. Pirian watched as the habitat came to a halt. He could see the titanic mechanisms underneath the habitat unlock. With an almighty roar the flaming Greenhouse fell away from the flying city.

Jeradon turned briefly, watching his life's work disappear. The Greenhouses had taken him over a decade to build and nurture. Erth's answers were lost; secrets of the Newtonian's enemy now nothing more than ash and twisted metal.

They could both feel the entire jettison arm tremble. Pirian looked on as the claspers closed and rotated and his father turned and started to run again. Then the empty arm slowly began to move back.

Although the arm was now moving in the same direction as them, helping them cover more ground, Pirian realised that there was the danger of being crushed as the huge mechanism moved closer towards the city.

Noticing the service ladders hanging down at the end of the trench, Jeradon increased his pace.

As Jeradon raced up the ladder, he swapped Pirian to his other shoulder and began the ascent.

The huge mechanism continued to close in on them.

All Pirian could do was watch as the trench began to engulf them. He twisted his neck around, in an attempt to see how far up the ladder they were.

They reached the top and his father opened the hatch. As Jeradon raced further up the ladder, Pirian hung helplessly, watching the trench finally close beneath them.

Another hatch opened out into a maintenance room. Before long Pirian and his father had reached the glass doors of the inner docking station. It had once looked out across the valley of the Greenhouse, now it had been replaced by open sky.

Pirian was gently lowered to the ground. As his father steadied himself, he gripped his chest with exhaustion. Jeradon then turned and rested his head against the glass doors, his spirits crushed and his energy depleted.

"All your work, Dad."

Pirian could see the tension in his father as Jeradon clenched his fists, then raised one in an effort to pound the glass door. He knew his father was controlling the anger as best he could, resting his fist against the glass instead. "Why couldn't you listen?"

Pirian could sense his father's disappointment, having

mistaken it for anger. Under the circumstances, he felt his father had every right to be angry. Tears streamed from Pirian's eyes. "I…I've s…said I was sorry Dad. I was trying to find you. I didn't mean…I didn't mean to get into trouble. The Greenhouse, it just felt so safe there. My sickness…"

Turning his head, Jeradon looked at his only child.

Pirian watched as his father removed his dirty overcoat, placing it around his shivering son. "I know. You're safe. That's all that matters now."

Jeradon then continued to stare through the glass doors. The Greenhouse having vanished from view.

Pirian caught his own reflection. A dirty bruised face stared back. He watched his father slowly move his hands across his shaven head; his trousers were stained, along with his white, bloodied tunic.

Pirian felt as cold looking at the interior of Newton as he did out on the veranda.

The sound of marching footsteps approached. He noticed his father clench his fist once again as the footsteps grew louder.

Several Guildsmen appeared in perfect alignment, holding large rifles at their sides.

The Emperor's Guard wore chrome lightweight ceremonial armour with matching helmets to conceal most of their faces. There were five of them - four guards and a Commander who wore a regimental blue-grey uniform, instead of his own armour. A crimson red cape hung down from one shoulder, the Newtonian symbol holding it in place.

Pirian's stomach turned as the adrenaline rushed through his body. The pressure set him more and more on edge as the intimidating figures surrounded them. He could feel his heart rate increase once again, as he attempted to pull himself up from the floor. Giving up, he shuffled closer to his father for protection.

Something was wrong.

The guards and Commander came to a standstill.

Pirian noticed his father's blank expression as he turned to face them, addressing the Commander much like an old friend. "Bendarick."

"I'm sorry, Jeradon."

Holding out his arms, as though he knew what was coming next, Jeradon reluctantly replied, "Yes...so am I."

Bendarick raised his right hand and a guard stepped forward to cuff Jeradon's wrists. Then, with no hesitation, his old friend formally addressed him.

"Jeradon Horncastle III, the Newtonian Guild hereby arrests you..."

Pirian was speechless. It wasn't his father who had started the fire.

"For the murder of Lord Surel, Emperor of Newton."

II

Black. Cold.

Beat. Beating.

His mind was trying to fight the darkness, but the slow pounding inside his head wasn't enough to keep him conscious. The dull thud was like an explosion growing louder and louder. Feeling the heat of the fire once more, he thought he was in the very depths of the inferno.

Beating.

Feel? Feeling…

Open.

No. Yes, feeling cold. Open, try to open.

Noise, hear.

See…to see, seeing…open…eyes.

White. Cold. Open.

He remembered nothing. His head was nothing but a box of broken toys; a jig-saw puzzle.

A white canvas lay before him. Piecing together his thoughts, he attempted to come up with a distinct picture.

Feet?…No. Hands…my hands.

Beating. Pain.

His head was now pounding like a drum. He remembered now that the surrounding whiteness had a name. It was no longer a metaphor.

Hands sunk into the coldness as he attempted to hold his own weight.

Snow.

Nearly losing consciousness again, the man pushed himself up and swayed for a moment in the snowstorm. Stumbling forward, he clutched at his chest. He was fully clothed, but lacked the warm garments for the harshness of winter.

Snow, ice, cold. Warmth, fire, heat, food.

Then, through the white, he saw the outline of a building. As he continued forward, more shapes came into view and before long the man was standing before a small bridge stretching over a frozen moat.

His own breath was the last thing he noticed, before he fell into darkness.

Three

From her high-rise quarters, Neeve Horncastle looked across the expanse of Newton, her eyes fixed on the news blimps slowly passing by. Hanging from the surrounding skyscrapers, huge crimson banners rippled in the breeze. The Newtonian symbol rested at their base, casting its presence over the city; an imposing design resembling a crimson 'w', capped by a small dash, resting perfectly within a pristine white circle.

The synthetic relay of the news blimps added to the insult of her husband's arrest with the announcement of Rayal Jakahn's self appointed position of Emperor. Overlaying voices became a high pitched hum - she couldn't listen to the brainwashing anymore, her ears having become far more sensitive than any User's.

After her husband's detention and the state her son was left in, Neeve could barely control her anger. It had taken her all day to calm Pirian, having not left his side for one moment.

"My Dad's a good man."

"We know that, Pirian." assured Neeve, turning to tend his bruised face.

"I want to see him."

"The dungeons are no place for a child."

"I don't care, I have to see him!"

Neeve stood up from the bed. "I know you mean no harm by upsetting your father and me, but you must listen to us, Pirian. It's for your own good." she placed a hand to her mouth, "Just look at what's happened when you wandered off to the Greenhouse again. If you had not been there, Jakahn's thug of a son wouldn't have done this to you."

"They'd have done it to me anyway. Alva Greenhouse One was the only place left that I could hide from them. Now they've destroyed that. Destroyed Dad's hard work, once and for all."

"Houses can be rebuilt, even Greenhouses. But lives can't. You should be resting; you're lucky to be alive. If your father hadn't been there..."

"Exactly. That's why I have to be there for him. Tell him... tell him I'm sorry."

"I'm sure he knows. A son should never have to apologise to his father."

Neeve looked at her son, he reminded her so much of Jeradon. She was thankful he had at least been brought back to her in one piece, but there was still nothing to smile about. She rolled up his sleeve and injected his serum. It was the last Jeradon had concocted. Without the Greenhouse, there was no way of creating any more.

She knew that her son would die without it. Although it certainly wasn't the Dosage, it was a mild drug all the same, concocted from medicinal plants and herbs from the Greenhouses. Jeradon and Neeve had discovered early on that Pirian was reliant on their natural environment and the only way to prevent him slipping into a coma, or worse, was to inject him with a part of his birthplace.

Before long they were being flown low over the city by car.

Pirian was glad his mother had finally agreed that he could visit his father. However, he wasn't so pleased at having to fly; his stomach turning as he attempted to take in the approaching capital. Newton was an immense place, the traffic as loud and busy as any other day. The buildings became grander the closer they flew to the centre; tall, striking monoliths bathed in sunlight, harsh shadows cast upon their ominous structure.

Eventually the car touched down in Ivar, the capital of Newton, where the dungeons were located at the core of the flying city. Untouched by modern design and technology, they were the oldest remaining remnants of the world below; dilapidated prison cells left to decay along with their prisoners over thousands of years. These cells, deep within the dungeon, were dark and grimy, dampness and lack of sanitation causing an unbearable stench. Newton's belly had always been a dungeon, even before it took to the sky. Dug out of the rock, it still remained rooted to the base of the city, like a rotting core.

Torches hung every so often from the walls, several extinguished by the water and slime dripping from the ceiling, only adding to the gloom of the dank, descending tunnel. Pirian and his mother were escorted down the winding stairs by two guards who took up most of the width with their sheer bulk. Covering her shaven head, Neeve wore a pale nondescript gown, the hood resting delicately on top of a uniformed headdress, which hung down over her shoulders. Her blue eyes were dulled by the darkness of the surroundings and by her husband's fate.

Holding his mother's hand tightly, Pirian was careful not to slip on the slimy steps as they reached the bottom. Turning a corner they came to a row of caged cells. Pirian couldn't help but look into each one as he walked by. The groans from some of the Prisoners were unsettling. There was a murmuring, as one repeatedly banged his head against the bars. The torchlight caught his eyeless face, cavernous, unblinking holes pleading for sight.

Burying his head in his mother's dress, they walked on.

They finally stopped before a cell door and a guard proceeded to unlock it. The heavy door swung open with a rusty clank. There stood Jeradon with his back to them, hands clasped behind his back, posture like a rod of iron. Pirian expected nothing less from his father; Jeradon was holding onto something deep inside, refusing to show any signs of weakness. Jeradon hadn't even been given the privilege of a wash after the ordeal at the Greenhouse. His coat had been removed, revealing his torn and dirty shirt, bloodied further from his lashings. If he had been mentally tortured, he certainly didn't show it to his family.

The guards left without a word. Pirian's mother walked into the cell with her son and the door was closed behind them.

Jeradon continued to stand with his back to them as he began to speak. "Seems the final part of his plan has worked," he said. Then turning round to face his wife and son, he sighed. "Things can only get worse."

"Jeradon...?" Neeve clasped her hand to her mouth. "I don't believe for one second that you killed Lord Surel. But please, for your son...."

"He is dead, Neeve...I saw him with my own eyes...lying there, like..."

Neeve inhaled and held her breath, tears welling. "But I..." She struggled to speak. "You were there?"

"I was called to his quarters. Seems I was the last to be in his company." He stepped forward and held his wife. "There is no point saying I did or didn't cut his throat. I'm condemned either way. We both know that. I...we, have to protect our son. He's all that matters."

"What are you talking about?! We all matter, we're a family!" Neeve paused, as a cloud of doubt infected her mind. "It's him, isn't it? He's had it worked out all along, waiting for the right moment." She looked down at Pirian. "And the fire, it's all connected? They tried to kill our son as well?!"

"Dad...?" asked a concerned Pirian.

Jeradon looked down at him. "I'm sorry son, sorry for placing you in so much danger. But...we must be strong...we must be prepared for what is to come. All of this is beginning to make more sense - Jakahn has longed to be Emperor and his power as Advisor has done nothing more than poison this city further. It's given him a solid grounding and his voice *is* heard. He knows that we're a threat, free of the Dosage." He paused, shaking his head. "Removing me from the picture has been well timed. I'm such a fool...I walked right into it."

"But what about Pirian, he's only a boy?"

"He doesn't want any of the underclass clean. The Dosage is law. The fact we are Horncastles just makes things worse. We are a huge threat."

"I'm a Horncastle, does that mean he's planning to kill me as well?" asked Neeve.

"I think we both know that's not going to happen."

"Please...Jeradon..." she pleaded, looking down at their son.

"Pirian knows, Neeve. Jakahn's son has taunted him about it long enough. It's not just Newton he has wanted...we've always known that."

It was true. For months now Viktor had taunted Pirian about getting rid of him and his father. He knew that Victor's own father had other motives towards his mother.

"I'd rather die," sobbed Neeve, holding her husband's hand to her cheek. "I can't go back to that."

"Neeve, listen to me. You must be strong. Take Pirian with you and contact the Resistance, before it's too late. You must warn them about Jakahn's intentions. There are no rogue Guildsmen left to support the cause, they've even got to Bendarick. There is so much to tell and I am running out of time. Most of the prisoners here are the people that had faith in me. They no longer rely on the Dosage and they'd have supported my actions. This New Order will be through *his* eyes now, and with the city as brainwashed as it has ever been, he'll be unstoppable."

"How will contacting the Resistance help you?"

Jeradon held her close. "It won't, but I am hoping they will help you and Pirian. He's already Emperor and now there is no one to oppose him. Myself and the rest of the prisoners will be executed."

Pirian rushed forward, lashing out with his fists. "Dad! No! Say you didn't do it! Say it!"

Jeradon grabbed his wrists then knelt down holding him close in an attempt to comfort his son. "Pirian..."

The cell opened and two guards walked in, standing either side of the heavy door. Dampened footsteps approached, then a man stood in the doorway for a brief moment before entering the cell. Torchlight caught his sharp features, casting harsh shadows on a ghostly white face. His ginger hair was tied back and receded, revealing a sharp hairline. Coils of teased hair hung down over his sideburns, which feathered outwards, while an equally groomed goatee decorated his chin.

The newly, self-appointed, Emperor was in traditional attire; pristine crimson suit, black pin stripe down the trouser leg; zig-zagging above knee high boots. A long robe hung down from his shoulders, the Newtonian symbol clipping it around his neck. Wrapped over one arm, he held the robe from the slimy floor.

Pirian immediately noticed the glance Rayal Jakahn gave his mother.

Relishing the moment, he then gave Jeradon a wholly satisfied look. "How quaint to have a family get together," he said smugly, pulling at his beard. "Touching. Still I'm not one to split up families in their time of need. A man needs his wife for that little extra support; especially one who has committed such a terrible crime."

He looked down at Pirian, "Ouch. Looks as though your boy's been in the wars."

"What do you want, Jakahn?" snapped Jeradon.

Pirian flinched as Rayal raised his hand, snapping his fingers. The two guards left the cell, closing the door behind them, while Rayal moved one step closer to Jeradon. "I think we both know the answer to that."

"No...you can't do this!" shouted Neeve.

"Oh? I think you will find, dear, that I can do what I want. I'm the Emperor now and I wish for many things to be changed around here. The first being public execution for your husband..." he paused, "...and son."

Neeve began to shake uncontrollably. She opened her mouth, but no sound came out. Pirian gave out a scream and held onto his father.

"Leave Pirian out of this, Rayal, he's just a boy. Do you think executing a child will do you any favours? This is about you and me!"

"Oh please...your son is as much a problem to me as you are. You know as well as I do that you have no more of your precious serum for his sickness."

"That doesn't condone execution you heartless bas..." Jeradon bit his tongue, his rage swelling inside. Taking a quick breath he continued. "Newton will wake up to killing a child."

"Perhaps, perhaps not. I can always increase the Dosage. Besides, we all know the punishment for owning one of these." Rayal held out the book that Viktor had taken from Pirian. "So you continue to encourage independent thought to a child - rebellious youth born out of the written word. Newton isn't about inspiring our people to climb trees and look towards a promised land. I guess that doesn't matter to you, so why should any of this matter to me? The thing is, I don't need a reason. Nothing shocks Newton. The Dosage even blinds them to murder...it clouds everything and controls everyone; the true beauty of cutting off emotion. None of these people need to read, or communicate at all to eachother - just listen and do as they are told."

"Your little Empire." added Jeradon.

Jakahn sneered, "If Viktor had done his little job properly, you'd be none the wiser about the death of your son."

Jeradon lurched forward with ferocious speed. Grasping Rayal by the throat he pushed him against the cell door. Jeradon grunted, clenching his teeth.

Pirian had never seen so much fury from his father; as if he had suddenly tapped into something dark and channelled. "I knew it! You really are something, Jakahn!" shouted Jeradon.

Gagging, Rayal stared directly into Jeradon's eyes. "You see...you see emotion my friend; it's a real killer." He raised his hand. "I only have to snap my fingers...and you'll be torn apart before your family. Would you really want them to see that?"

Pirian and Neeve watched in horror as Jeradon's grip tightened around Rayal's throat. "Dad...don't..."

Even without the Dosage, Jeradon's Guild training was an automatic reflex. From the age of five, all Newtonians who measured up to A-class, began to channel and focus their enhanced strength and ferocity. Newton had created the perfect killing machine; one that only knew how to answer to the Hierarchy.

"Newton may have always had the Guild brainwashed, Rayal, but they will only protect you for so long. One day they will wake up."

"They'll be gone before it comes to that. I have other plans. In the meantime, they can continue with the crusade. As long as they believe they are looking for something of importance on Erth, there is no need for any Guildsman to return home. This way I can have them securing all the protronium we need; our precious fuel."

Jeradon slammed him against the cell wall one last time. "I knew it! There is no artefact! It's just an excuse!"

Rayal shrugged, as though he didn't care either way. But the mysterious artefact; the object for which Newton had searched across an eternity, held more answers than Jeradon's Greenhouses had ever offered. Rayal hoped controlling the protronium fields one by one, would eventually point him to the artefact. There were still thousands of outposts scattered across Erth that belonged to their enemy, the Rojin - outposts that, could still lead to their capital city and the very artefact Newton was looking for.

There was a silence as Rayal looked over at Neeve. "There is one thing that could save you and your son."

Jeradon caught Rayal's eye.

Neeve took her hands away from her mouth. *How easy it would be*, she thought, *to stab out your eyes and be done with you.* At least then she could join her family in death. But she knew all too well what was coming. They all knew.

"You'd release them...for me?" asked Neeve.

"Oh my dear, no. I'd give them a choice other than trial and execution."

"A choice," muttered Jeradon under his breath, as he slowly released his grip on Rayal's throat. He pondered for a moment on how a trial would make no difference, then placed both hands up against the wall, shaking his head slowly in desperation.

"Neeve stays with me and becomes Empress. In return I will spare your lives. There will be no trial - you will simply be outcast with the rest of the scum. Kind of a 'cleansing of Newton' if you will. You'll become Fallen," answered Rayal, flattening his hair after Jeradon's assault.

"Then you may as well execute us. If we become Fallen, the chance of survival is a thousand to one."

"Mmmm. Well, at least you get to see Erth again. Perhaps the Rojin will welcome you with as much affection as my good self; especially as you're responsible for killing so many of their people. Those were the days, hey old friend?"

Pirian's stomach turned at the thought of Rayal and his father side by side. Jeradon was no longer a killer and no one could convince Pirian otherwise. Even if it came from his father's mouth.

"I've changed."

"So I noticed. Just look where it's got you. Lord Surel was a fool to allow you to be clean."

Neeve detested seeing her husband tormented like this. Sensing his pain, she couldn't stand the ridicule of the man she loved any longer. "I'll do it," she interrupted glancing at her husband. "I'll go with you."

Jeradon pushed himself away from the wall and looked his wife in the eye. "No." he whispered.

"I have no choice. At least if you are outcast there is a chance you'll survive."

Pirian was speechless, burying his head further. What was his mother saying?

"Then it's settled," added Rayal.

Jeradon slackened his tense fists. He continued to look across at Neeve as she knelt and held their son. She knew as well as her husband that this was the only chance of survival Pirian had. Without his serum, he would die anyway.

"Mum, I don't want to leave, I can't..."

"Pirian, it's the only way. You must go with your father, he'll look after you. I'll be alright, I'll be safe here on Newton. You must be brave...both of you."

The thought of his mother with Rayal, brainwashed once again by the Dosage, sent a chill down Pirian's spine.

With her back to Rayal, Neeve looked her husband in the eye. The pain was unbearable.

"Neeve..." whispered Jeradon.

She put a finger to his mouth and whispered, "Don't say anything. Just look after our boy. You know as well as I do, he's dead either way. There is more chance for him on Erth. Keep him safe, I can take care of myself. Just don't forget me, Jeradon Horncastle, one of us has to keep our memory alive."

Tears welled in her eyes.

Jeradon felt his throat constrict, preventing him from saying anything.

Neeve addressed Rayal while still looking her husband in the eye. "When are they to be outcast?"

The tension was unbearable while she awaited his answer.

"This evening."

III

"Get away from him child, he could be diseased."

"No, he's healthy. I think he may be from…"

Voices.

Open your…eyes.

"Praise the Erth. He's awake, father!"

The warmth of a touch.

He thought his eyes were playing tricks on him. Before there was only white, now a serene face looked down upon him. If only he could speak. If only he could think of a word that could describe…

Beau…

He tried to say the word, but it remained locked within his mind.

Was he still a boy? Or was he a man?

He didn't know anything. He couldn't remember anything.

The few words that rattled around in his head were the first thoughts of his mind crying out.

Awake, only asleep. Found, yet still lost.

It was her eyes that pierced his very soul. Blue eyes. The first he had ever seen, or at least the first he could ever remember. Her skin was fair, delicate and untouched. Her dark hair was tied back, a wisp hanging down over her face.

She tucked it behind her ear.

He tried to speak once again, but his head pounded once more. Turning his head away and closing his eyes tightly, he attempted to block the pain.

She placed her hand on his forehead as he fell into darkness once more.

Green.

   Blue.

   The Sky...falling.

And then he saw something else he couldn't describe. What was it? Words almost familiar.

"F...Father." he murmured.

The young woman had sat at his bedside the whole day. Startled at the man's voice, she leant in closer.

"Yes...?" she whispered in reply, unsure of what he'd just said. "It's ok, you're safe."

"Rrrr...." he could barely catch his breath. "Jrrr...J... Jinnnn

"Jinn...? puzzled the woman. "Your name?"

"Jrr...Jinn." He could see the bright light once again, so bright it was blinding. Briefly he saw something flash before him, something he couldn't recognise. Then the light became a woman's face. As he slowly opened his eyes he no longer saw anything. "My...name?"

She looked down at his unfocussed eyes and realised the man was blind.

Four

Hundreds of prisoners were marched out onto the old industrial complex of Newton's under belly. There was a fierce storm; winds pulling at the old gantry as heavy rain washed the savage, rusting metal. Precariously, they made their way down onto a huge open platform and awaited scanning.

Jeradon shielded his eyes from the stinging rain with his arm, the other wrapped around his son. Pirian held on as best he could to his father, frightened of being dragged away and lost amongst the prisoners. He was in a bad state; his nausea had returned and his head had begun to pound once again. Without his medication, it was only a matter of time before he lost consciousness. His body could feel Newton's change in altitude as it descended slowly, now hovering as low as it could above the sea - the largest of spires already submerged at their tips, like claws attempting to grasp at water.

The strength of the gale tore at the surrounding structure, prisoners and guards battling to stand still as they leant into the wind. The platform was located at the lowest portion of central Newton, constructed around the bare rock, hardly visible under the sprawling city. Exits from the overcrowded dungeon were close by for the 'Fallen' prisoners to be outcast. Newton's underbelly was an upturned landscape of weathered spires and upturned skyscrapers, each one arching down and inwards towards the capital's central axis. Huge battleships and cruisers escorted by smaller aircraft flew past, between the raging sea and upturned towers of the city - they headed towards their docking stations, a deafening roar shaking the platform further.

On the edges of the platform were a number of old rusty skiffs, which had been thrown together using crude metal from the surrounding complex. There were twenty in total and each held around one hundred prisoners - those lucky enough to be given the chance of survival. Jeradon had seen it before, yet still watched in horror as those more unfortunate were being lined up and thrown from the platform in the same way waste was discarded. The skiffs, however, would not hold together in the raging storms and the prisoners' 'chance' of survival was slim. It was simply another way of herding the prisoners to their doom. Rings and poles attached to the skiffs were used to tether the prisoners, further limiting their possibility of survival. It was only a matter of time until Jakahn's rule found a far more efficient way of discarding Fallen - if any were left to discard.

After scanning the remaining prisoners, the guards continued to march them onto the skiffs, Jeradon looked up to the sheltered gantry that loomed over them. He could see the silhouetted figure of his wife. Sheltering his eyes from the rain, he looked on as Rayal Jakahn walked into view. The Emperor had finally got what he wanted. Jeradon only wished that one day he might make it back to Newton and wipe the smug look from his face.

"Father...I'm scared, I feel sick...so sick...I need, I need to..." Pirian coughed and held his hands to his mouth as he vomited. Jeradon knew there was nothing he could do for his son, only keep him from harm as he had promised his wife.

Just look after our boy, keep him safe.

Jeradon helped to wipe his son's mouth with his own sleeve. "Just stick close, Pirian," he said watching Jakahn make his way down the gantry towards them. It was his final chance to dig the knife even deeper.

Two guards walked forward, pushing Pirian aside, and

grabbed hold of Jeradon to take him away.

"I'm sorry it's had to come to this," Rayal shouted through the storm. He wore a ceremonial Guild helmet, sculpted specifically for such a slender face and to protect his groomed hair from the wind and rain.

As he clutched onto his father, Pirian was unable to pick up on what was being said through the howling storm.

But Jeradon could hear every word, even when Rayal had lowered his tone, leaning closer to speak directly into his ear. "Just be at peace, knowing your loving wife will live…" He held up a dosage of zetameen in view of Jeradon, "…and in time, learn to love your enemy in many ways."

Jeradon's rage was almost impossible to control. It swept through his body, like a time bomb waiting to explode. He clenched both fists so tightly, his hands bled as his nails dug into his palms. Controlling himself, he breathed slowly looking up at Rayal as he sneered back at him.

Leaning even closer towards Jeradon, he toyed with the vial in his hand. "There are a privileged few that may not need this anymore, my friend - including your family and I. But everyone must learn control at some point. I can see the hate…but the pain you feel inside can be made easier."

Nothing. Jeradon wasn't biting.

Nor was he swallowing anything like that ever again. He never wanted to forget. Rayal knew and simply gave the guards a nod, spinning round and making his way back up the gantry to stand beside his new Empress and out of imminent danger.

Pirian held tightly onto his father as they were escorted to the edge of the skiffs. Held aloft by large rusty chains they awaited to be lowered into the raging sea below, now Newton had reached the correct altitude.

Jeradon could feel the platform moving beneath his feet and feared that it would be torn away from the flying city at any moment. Just as the guards were about to secure Jeradon and Pirian to the raft, a powerful gust of wind tore a gantry support loose. As it flew across the platform, the support sliced into a crowd of guards and prisoners.

The lucky ones were knocked to the floor, while others were torn in two or sent hurtling over the side of the platform in to the stormy seas below. The support continued to smash into the platform's surface, tearing huge portions of the floor into spiralling, razor-sharp metal. Debris, prisoners and guards continued to fall from view; their screams unheard in the deafening storm.

Jeradon looked up at the sheltered gantry one final time. He caught sight of Neeve. The last image he had of his wife was her silhouetted figure reaching out as she shouted and screamed for her husband and child - all the while Jakahn dragging her away from her family's fate.

The platform lurched to one side. Four guards who had been securing prisoners hesitated to jump from the skiff. A delirious Pirian made an attempt to shout out, but his father couldn't hear a thing. They both watched helplessly through the deafening storm.

Several guards on the platform threw the levers to the winch, releasing a number of skiffs that immediately fell from view.

Then the platform lurched once more.

Jeradon caught the guards looking at each other. Still hesitating, they didn't know whether to risk jumping from the twisted platform or remain where they were. One of the guards held onto a nearby pole. In a split second decision he drew his gun, shooting the winch that held the chains to the skiff. Jeradon quickly grabbed his son, sandwiching him against a pole the rest of the Fallen were tethered to as it plummeted towards the raging sea below. One guard, caught by surprise, fell backwards into a crowd of chained prisoners, rolling further overboard.

Jeradon's stomach lurched as the descent accelerated. The fall seemed to last a lifetime, the noise and chaos unbearable.

Pirian clutched his father, while Jeradon held onto him, protecting him at all costs.

The skiff hit the water with such force that it immediately broke in two. Each half stayed afloat, as the huge waves rolled in front of the night sky. Lightning struck and for a brief second caught the chaos in slow motion, as the sea lit up around them.

There was a fierce howl. Jeradon looked up - Newton had begun to ascend as the platform simultaneaously ripped away and began to fall towards them. Two skiffs were immediately wiped out by the structure, a mountainous explosion of water pouring down after the impact, the tangled mess sinking without a trace.

A guard jumped into the sea as more debris continued to rain down from above.

There were screams all around. Pirian saw the frantic prisoners on the remaining skiffs, still secured to the platform by their chains. As they were dragged under, he looked around deliriously in the water for the guard, assuming he had sunk with the weight of his armour. He noticed the other guards' blank expressions, the Dosage cutting off any fear of the situation.

Moments later, the guard surfaced. He had stripped his armour so he could make it to the surface and the other guards reached out to pull him onboard as he slumped in front of Jeradon.

Everything had happened so fast, no one had time to breathe. Pirian shivered uncontrollably, grasping the pole. He was in a state of shock; the storm's chilling bite gnawed at his bones and the icy cold water did nothing to ease the pressure building in his head.

The broken skiff lurched and then heeled upwards in a sudden squall. All the Fallen who were not holding onto their bindings, hung uncomfortably from their wrists as the skiff approached an almost ninety degree angle.

Jeradon could hear the skiff moan as it attempted to hold itself together. Then it righted itself as the storm pushed them on towards the black horizon.

After several hours the winds died down and the rain turned to drizzle. The heaving beast that was once the sea had gradually began to calm, but she had no intention of releasing those that had been offered to her just yet.

Jeradon looked at the guards. They avoided catching his eye in shameful recognition. If they did survive, they would soon wish they hadn't as their addiction kicked in. These were men that had once served under Jeradon and, over time, forgotten themselves. Luckily Jeradon wasn't shackled, but he may as well have been. He wiped the water from his face, working out how many prisoners there were: thirty-six in total. Most of them would be innocent; people who had stopped their Dosage and slowly began to voice their own opinions. Opinions were dangerous on Newton and a threat to the Emperor. Jeradon was still aware that some Fallen could still be cold-blooded killers. Struggling to keep warm, he noticed Pirian had passed out long ago and was worried that his son was falling into a deep fever.

He placed his hand on Pirian's forehead, expecting his eyes to open from the shock of his cold palm.

A kaleidoscope of images was filtering through Pirian's mind.

*Be brave. Be my brave little man. I'm so sorry, Pirian...
please forgive me.*

He could clearly see his mother's face, then Rayal Jakahn's, his red hair turning into barren wastelands. Then there was the sound of the sea. Ships, he could see hundreds of ships; some small and rickety with ragged sails, others larger, churning out black smoke from their huge funnels.

Nameless faces invaded his dream...

"Pirates," was all he murmured, "P...Pir..."

Jeradon pulled his hand away from Pirian's forehead, watching him drift off, contemplating what his son had said.

Looking at the guards, he could see them attempting to contact Newton for pick-up as their communication gauntlets sparked and let out a small whisp of smoke. Jeradon shouted over to them. "It seems like we're all going to die together! This storm...it's the least of our worries!"

Two of the guards looked at each other, while the third - the one who had shed his armour - gripped his body in the cold.

"Wh...what do you mean?" he asked, shivering.

"Even if your communications worked, Jakahn would never give an order to have you picked up - you're as disposable as the rest of us. From here it gets better - if the sea doesn't claim us in the next few hours, then the cold will. And when the storm settles, there is no food and no protection from the sun." Jeradon didn't even want to think of the beasts roaming the depths of the ocean beneath them. All that was important was that he and his son survived. No matter what Erth threw at him. "There is a way out of this, but it means your co-operation. Any time now, you are all going to have withdrawal symptoms, then you'll be of no use to anyone. I'm hoping that the zetameen is already wearing off enough for you to see some sense. You will have to make your own decisions and the first one you make, will be to trust me." Jeradon stood up and moved closer to the Guards.

One of them stood up quickly and drew his sword, holding it outstretched to Jeradon's throat. "Sit down!"

"This will get us nowhere," said Jeradon calmly, "Put the sword down."

"If we die...we die."

Jeradon lowered his head and sighed. The lack of emotion

was all he needed to confirm the Dosage was still working.

His movement was a blur. Before the Guard knew it, Jeradon had spun, disarming his sword arm in one fluid movement. He brought the weapon up and across his aggressor's neck, using his body as a shield. Prisoners reacted in an agitated fashion, roused by Jeradon's sudden action.

Standing up, the other armed Guard began to make a move as he drew his gun. Jeradon knew that he wouldn't fire in case he hit his colleague. It was all the time he needed to make the first shot, pulling the plasma gun from the Guard's belt with his free hand. The shot was barely audible, but the scream of the Guard dropping his gun and clutching his shoulder was enough to grab the attention of the rest of the Fallen.

"Dad...?!"

Jeradon quickly glanced at his son. The screaming Guard and chattering chains of the prisoners had woken him.

Focusing on the Guard, Jeradon attempted to put Pirian at ease. "It's okay, son. How are we feeling?"

"I'm...I'm okay. I'm...I feel..." he squinted, puzzled, "... warm."

Jeradon was worried that he had indeed broken a fever, but didn't make sense with him sounding so alert. "Good...good. Feeling strong enough to get over here and pick that gun up?"

His father never allowed him to pick up any weapon. But it seemed Jeradon had no choice. Pirian didn't ask any questions, he simply crawled over in front of his father, keeping his eye on the other wounded Guard, and picked up the gun. He felt uncomfortable as he held it out with both hands.

Jeradon quickly looked down at his son, surprised at how alert he was. It seemed as though the cold had no effect on him at all. Still holding the Guard, he shoved the gun into the back of his trousers, unclipped the Guard's utility belt, then pushed him to the floor. "Hurts, doesn't it?" he said to the other Guard clutching his shoulder. "That burning pain you are feeling right now is the first sign of the zetameen wearing off. You can forget the cold - your bullet wound will distract you from that."

Slinging the belt over his shoulder, Jeradon sheathed the sword and then proceeded to empty the plasma cell to see how much power was left along with a quick count on the ammunition. Keeping a clear focus on the Guards, he held the cell up in front of his face. With a quick snapping action he reloaded the gun and continued to address them through the distraction of the prisoners still banging their chains.

"As I mentioned, getting out of this situation is going to require your cooperation. But since you're still clearly under the influence, I'm going to have to try again." Jeradon knelt down in front of one of the guards, and proceeded to remove his broken communication gauntlet. "Not all outcasts have died out here. In fact, prisoners often used to make deals with you...for these." He pressed a button on the gauntlet and a panel slid out revealing a small red disc the size of a coin. Switching it on he continued, "Transmitters - they'll survive pretty much anything, it's the gauntlets that break first. It used to be that prisoners would simply try and hide them in their clothing, until they were found out. Then they would swallow them or place them under their skin. Now every prisoner is scanned before they are boarded or tossed into the sea."

"They were signalling?" queried the wounded Guard.

Pirian was thinking back to his dream and some of the illustrations he had seen in his old book. There were ships that roamed the dangerous seas.

"Correct. Anything that happened to be nearby," said Jeradon.

"Pirates." mused Pirian.

The guards all looked at the boy and then back at Jeradon. "Indeed. Newton is where they come from in the first place and they're always looking for Fallen to increase their ranks. It's happened for centuries - Pirates *are* Fallen."

"You're signalling them? They'll cut our throats!" cried out the injured Guard, his emotions finally taking hold.

"Wrong. They'll cut *your* throats." Jeradon tilted his head. "Besides, if you die... you die."

IV

From the ashes of the Inferno, only twelve cities remained. Adapting to their new environment, many people of Erth had evolved in different ways - the burnt and broken land that hid them from the outside world having shaped them into something else entirely. Many battles followed as they fought for control over what little was left of their past. Some cities fell, others were lost along with their history and people - for some, not even a name remained, only a number on parchments and scrolls.

New Town, the Twelfth City had gained immense power and wealth - having seized control of all protronium; a fuel source which had evolved from the cracked Erth. Claiming to be the oldest, yet certainly not the first to be written about in scripture, the people of the Eighth City, Old Town treated protronium as the very blood of the planet; yet it was slowly being drained by their enemies. There had been no leadership amongst its people for decades. Their great Castle having fallen long ago - now nothing but an abandoned monument, haunted by former glory and the roaming spirits that had vowed to protect it. Still standing strong, its ominous presence held the town in shadow. It was only a reminder of what could happen to all of them, if they once again defied the power of New Town. They had put up with the undermining of their land and people long enough, as smaller cities and protronium wells were slowly taken over.

Bled dry, Old Town, had nothing until the blind man opened

their eyes of its residents.

People had said the man with no memory had walked a thousand years; that with every step his past had slowly, but surely vanished. Who he was and where he had come from was a complete mystery.

Jinn's visions were crystal clear, though. He could almost touch the future with his scarred hands, although he couldn't remember his past. In his visions he witnessed the dark times and the light, the taste of Erth lingering in his mouth. He knew that a vital part of Old Town's growth still needed to be found.

A seed needed to be planted.

Many settlements made an attempt to band together and suppress New Town's control, including Old Town itself.

Sixty thousand men were sent from New Town to perform the will of their Emperor. Their claim was simple; relinquish all supplies of protronium, or die.

There were few from Old Town that had been trained to fight, yet their spirits told them otherwise as Jinn led them into battle. For his name only, they would slaughter and die. They had seen what he was capable of, yet there was no time to be trained. It was enough to believe in one man.

The blind leading the blind.

As everyone died around him Jinn's will began to dwindle. Yet instead of leaving the rain-soaked mountainside, he pushed on into battle. As he reached the top, a misplaced footfall led him away from certain death. After his fall from the mountain, he awoke to find himself in a drowned wilderness. For the second time he was lost. Feeling himself through the swamp he sensed those that looked on. They took him into their homes as they hid away from the war.

He spread his word for the first time. Asking for help, he marched back to the Eighth City with thousands of followers to help rebuild what was lost. Old Town's survivors looked on in disbelief; not just at the miraculous return of their leader, but the strange manner of beasts that entered their town - those of which had been hiding for too long.

Indeed Jinn was blind and for once so were his own people. They didn't judge, instead they welcomed the strange looking creatures, for they had brought all kinds of secrets.

Seeds of knowledge, as well as seeds to plant.

Five

All that remained of the passing storm was a calm breeze; the sea having become nothing more than a billowing blanket under the moon's light. Jeradon no longer had the fierce score of the harsh winds to prevent his mind from wandering. To fall asleep now could be disastrous; he had his son to protect, as well as carefully watching the guards and fellow Fallen. To him, the Guards were more dangerous than any prisoner aboard while they were still under the influence of the Dosage.

He stretched his arms, easing his cramped muscles.

Pirian rested the gun on his knees, still pointing it at the guards. All he could do was think of his mother; his determination to get back to her was as strong as his father's. A part of him felt guilty for having the book in his possession, but he knew he had been outcast for other reasons.

He questioned how miserable his life would be if he had been left on Newton. Rayal Jakahn wouldn't just be his Emperor, but a sadistic replacement for his father. Then there would be Viktor as his stepbrother. His life would have been miserable, he was glad he was with his own father; safe and secure even on the dangerous seas.

Considering his circumstances, Pirian felt far better than he had back on Newton. He didn't feel the cold, yet was aware of the throbbing in his arm. He held the gun in one hand, clamping his other hand around his arm, slowly massaging it. Under his wet tunic sleeve, he could feel that his irritated mark had become raised. Briefly distracted by the change, he quickly remembered to keep his concentration on the Guard.

Although it didn't hurt, it was uncomfortable.

Up until now, no prisoner had said a word.

"Ship!...There's a ship!"

Most of them were still shackled and although one of the guards had the key, Jeradon was not about to unlock them for fear of mutiny aboard the skiff. Control was all-important. He followed the gaze of the Guards as they reacted to the prisoner's pointing finger. Pirian, wide-eyed, looked into the darkness, eager to witness what he had only seen in books.

The prisoner was right. On the distant horizon there was a silhouette. It was too far to detect it moving towards them, but as time progressed the ship's engines could be heard.

Before long Pirian could almost smell it.

The closer the ship approached, the more the Guards began to fidget. The one Jeradon had shot was already losing consciousness, resting in a pool of his own vomit. The other two were aware enough to react to the ship as it approached head on. It was colossal, and seemed to be currently unladen, its huge bulk standing high in the water.

"It's mercenary class," stated Jeradon as the ship's engines became louder. "These guys are pirates alright, and judging by the ship they're protronium barons."

The prisoners started to become nervous as they noticed the ship was heading straight for them. Jeradon lowered his gun slowly as another prisoner piped up.

"They're going to sink us!"

Closer the ship loomed.

There was no change in engine pitch and no sign of the vessel slowing. The only thing to do was jump. Jeradon stood his ground as Pirian waited quietly behind him.

Closer.

There was a jangling as prisoners began to pull at their chains, then a splash as one of guards shed his armour and jumped overboard.

Closer still.

Just as Jeradon closed his eyes, expecting to be sunk by the leviathan, there was an almighty roar of metal, followed by gushing water as the front of the ship split in two. Jeradon and Pirian held onto one of the securing poles as the prisoners began to panic. The bow continued to open swallowing up the skiff. No sooner had it opened than it began to close behind them, one final deafening roar of the ship's mouth as they were swallowed whole.

Lights.

They were deep in the bowels of the ship.

Jeradon, placed the plasma gun in its holster, studying the gigantic emblems painted on the inner hull. They had peeled and faded over time, but the large, rust stained images were still recognisable, reminding Jeradon he may have made a mistake. The wolf's skull he saw identified a pirate who went by the apt name of 'The Sea Wolf'. Like any pirate, he would increase his numbers by picking up Fallen, and he'd earned an unsavoury reputation for killing many Newtonians and destroying their protronium rigs.

The Sea Wolf's ship had been crudely maintained using various raw materials. Jeradon noticed that it was mainly old skiff wreckage, along with other Newtonian debris. The ship was a scavenger's nest.

Mechanical noise reverberated from underneath them. The skiff was jolted upwards as the water was released from the inside of the ship. Two large arms clamped the skiff, carrying it forwards to walkway level. As it came to a halt, pirates clambered through several doors, crowding the walkway and glaring at the castaways in an unsavoury manner.

To call them a 'motley crew' would have been generous. These men and women were outcasts themselves; Fallen given a second chance at life aboard the pirate ship. They resembled people Erth had broken and rebuilt, both mentally and physically.

Fear struck Pirian as the pirates made their way aboard the skiff. Although there was a strange sense of excitement, he was overwhelmed by his surroundings and the intimidating atmosphere.

The pirates' first priority were the two Newtonian guards. Stripping the conscious one of his armour, they dragged him away, while their shipmates followed with the injured guard.

Several more surrounded Jeradon and Pirian. They were intimidating to say the least - their stench preceded them by ten paces. It would have been foolish to do so much as flinch.

It would be obvious to the pirates that he was Fallen, yet they would be unsure why he and his son were the only ones unchained and in the possession of Newtonian weapons.

Jeradon held his ground.

An unfamiliar sound approached. A rasping sound, much like a tombstone dragged across the floor. Wings flapped amongst the sound of footsteps on clanking metal. All he could make out was a mass of dirty, silver hair moving behind the pirates. They stepped aside and the prisoners began to twitch once again.

Jeradon wasn't fazed at all.

Pirian, however, couldn't believe his eyes. He was seeing his first mutant, not counting the other strange looking creature sitting on its shoulder stretching stone-like wings.

The Sea Wolf quietly looked down at the Newtonian guards with his piercing blue eye, and then at the rest of the Fallen. What resembled tarnished silver fur, flecked with darker patches, flowed down past his shoulders. Upright tattered ears carried a number of piercings; beaded plaits of hair and leather figure-of-eight strips were tied and knotted into what resembled a mane. The creature's face was also covered with similar ill groomed fur, its protruding snout tipped by a jet-black nose, which was dry and chapped. A patch covered one eye. Underneath the scuffed, brown leather waistcoat was a beige shirt, open at the neck and embroidered with gold flex forming subltle hexagonal patterns and the already familiar figure-of-eights. His trousers were a similar design, turned over at the knee - powerful, bootless hind legs raising him above most of his comrades. An antique handgun was at his side along with a curious looking object, much like the hilt of a sword, minus the blade.

Protruding from his mouth was a large half smoked cigar. He held it between his teeth, black lips curled round it as he took a drag, then pulled it away from his mouth and exhaled.

There was a tension as the Sea Wolf pondered and then placed the cigar back in his mouth.

Jeradon recognised the creature on his shoulder right away - a Gargoyle. With a grey, stone texture, the creature was roughly the size of a large parrot, which any ordinary Fallen would have had perched on their shoulder. Its hide was shifting and solidifying every so often and around its waste were a number of small markings that resembled an upturned 'L'. Jeradon realised the gargoyle's owner wasn't just called the Sea Wolf as a nickname, it described him perfectly.

Two pirates were signalled to take away the weapons that Jeradon and his son had commandeered. As one of the pirates approached to grab Pirian's arm, Jeradon raised his weapon in a split second as the pirate pulled his son closer. "Take your hand off the boy." He cocked his thumb, charging the plasma gun. "Now!" he snapped.

The rest of the pirates raised their weapons as Jeradon stood his ground, and he heard the sound of a dozen guns cocking.

Pirian could make out his father's steely expression, knowing full well he meant to fire, whatever the consequence.

"The first pickup via transmitter in over five years," the Sea Wolf said as he signed to his crew to lower their weapons, "We gather from what others have told us, that 'transmission' has become impossible. A Newtonian guard under the influence would die before having enough sense to signal. I'm curious as to how you have managed to commandeer a weapon or two, while having two Newtonian guards onboard in the first place?"

Jeradon watched as the delirious guards in question were pushed into a crowd of pirates. Their bodies had begun to shake uncontrollably, sweat streaming from their faces, bloodshot eyes rolling back in their sockets. They had already entered the second stage of 'going cold'. Kneeling down on the floor, they twitched their heads as they bobbed against each other. The Sea Wolf stepped forward, pulling the obscure handle from his side and taking another drag from his cigar in preparation.

A swift sound cut through the air, and the decapitated head of the injured Guard rolled under the feet of the surrounding pirates. There was no reaction at all from the surviving Guard, his delirium making him oblivious.

Jeradon saw that, with his back still to the pirate who held onto him, Pirian couldn't make out what had happened, fortunately. Craning his neck round, all he could see was the fallen body of one of the guards as several pirates kicked it into the shallow, remaining pool of water below in the ship's hull.

The Sea Wolf signalled several crew as they removed the remaining Guard.

Jeradon had seen the act carried out many times before. He calmly lowered the weapon he held to the face of the pirate as the Sea Wolf nodded. Jeradon was seriously outnumbered and was of no use to his son without a head.

"There was no need to demonstrate your reputation. If you have no use for us, then allow the sea to decide our fate rather than your blade."

"Reputation? Everyone has a reputation. I just hope no one has been giving you the wrong impression of me. I was just simply putting a sick dog out of its misery. Perhaps the other won't be so lucky."

"The only sick dog I see is you," snapped Jeradon.

The Wolf stepped forward, the gargoyle snarling as much as he was. "You are in no position to judge me, Newtonian! I should have you licking the blood off my paws for such insolence. Only then would you taste my so called *reputation*."

"Except you want me to answer your questions," mused Jeradon.

"Hmph...indeed." Composing himself, the Sea Wolf addressed the rest of the prisoners. "Welcome to the *The General*. It seems you should thank the man who stands before me for saving your lives. You are no longer Newtonian, you're bottom feeders now - 'Fallen'. Get used to it. This ship is your General and and you may address me as your Captain - Captain Lomax. The appearance is a permanent feature I'm afraid. Eat, drink... there will be much to talk about once you have had some rest."

Prisoners were escorted into the belly of *The General*, rubbing their bleeding wrists, their stomachs rumbling just from the mention of food. Jeradon placed an arm around his son and looked at Lomax.

The Sea Wolf looked down at Pirian as the gargoyle fidgeted on his shoulder, "This is no place for a child," he said before walking on.

"This is no place for anyone," stated Jeradon as Lomax's pirates escorted them away.

The General was somewhat of a mongrel, its makeshift appearance adding to its character. Yet Lomax's own quarters were entirely different. Dawn was breaking and the sun shone through two large windows, flooding the panelled room with a warm orange glow. It seemed to Pirian that there was more to this pirate than met the eye. This was reflected in the antique weapons hanging from the walls and odd looking weaponry of a far more organic nature - which looked very much alive. Most, if not all of the items were more than likely stolen and quite possibly in the process of being smuggled - Lomax after all was a pirate. Smuggling was what they did best.

A wooden desk and leather chair sat at the back of the room. At its side was a food cart. Pirian could smell the meat, his stomach growling in response. A selection of fruit and vegetables lay on plates, a jug of water and carafe of wine standing either side.

Lomax stubbed out a smouldering cigar ember in the palm of his hand as he entered his quarters. The gargoyle dropped down from his shoulder onto his desk. Opening a beautifully carved wooden box, it proceeded to pull out a fresh cigar, so big it took both of its hands to hold it. Jumping back onto the Sea Wolf's shoulder, the gargoyle pulled out the lighter from Lomax's breast pocket and lit the cigar. The creature took a drag, before eventually passing it to his Captain.

"I try not to teach Vagabond here any bad habits." Lomax placed the cigar between his teeth. "He usually eats them instead. Gargoyles will eat anything."

Jeradon was simply weighing up his surroundings, but he could see that Pirian was still in awe of both Lomax and his strange pet. Jeradon knew that the Wolf might decide to take his own head at any minute. All that mattered to him was to get his son to safety.

"Wolves tend to be more selective?" replied Jeradon.

Lomax scowled. "Perhaps I should have been more selective when I decided to bring you all onboard."

"No. I appreciate you picking us up...Captain."

"You're welcome, Newtonian. Now please, sit down." He beckoned. "You must be hungry. Eat." Jeradon and Pirian sat down on two high back chairs as Lomax gestured towards the food.

Jeradon was still weary enough to tuck in, the quality of food making him all the more suspicious. The food must have been smuggled or stolen from Newtonian rigs, unless the Sea Wolf had deeper connections. Although he and his son were both hungry and needed to quench their thirst, Jeradon longed for sleep more than anything.

Vagabond flew over the food cart and grabbed an apple, perching himself on the windowsill. He devoured it in seconds.

"I have no intention of poisoning new crew members and certainly no reason to poison my little companion here," Lomax said, obviously assuming Jeradon and his son would become part of his crew.

"I need rest just as much as the other prisoners. I can eat later," replied Jeradon.

"How about the boy...?"

Pirian looked at Lomax. There was something a little unnerving about his remaining, steely-blue eye. He looked at his father, who nodded his permission, and Pirian immediately leant over and grabbed some food.

Lomax eyed Jeradon and his son.

"I think both of you will fit in here. Out of all the ships that could have picked up your signal first, you were lucky it was *The General*. Not all pirates take onboard Fallen and there are more deadly things in the sea than all the pirates on Erth. You will need your wits about you. I am just concerned for the boy and even more curious how on Erth he got here. In all my years, I've never come across a Fallen child. He must have committed a serious crime."

"He's committed no crime. He is part of my own

punishment,"

"I see. Seems your Emperor has become even more heartless."

"You could say that. He's dead."

Lomax removed the cigar from his mouth and blew out a cloud of smoke. "Interesting."

"I killed him," added Jeradon.

Pirian didn't even blink. *Dad is bluffing*, he thought, *just establishing what he is capable of in case the pirates turn out to be cannibals*. At least that is what he hoped. He gulped down some water and placed the glass back down on the cart.

"You killed the Emperor of Newton?" Lomax repeated in disbelief.

"That's right…and although I appreciate the thought of you integrating my son and I into your pack of wolves, I would be very grateful if you would leave us ashore."

"It's really no hair off my back what you've done. But at least allow me to know the name of the man that killed the Emperor of Newton."

He thought for a moment. There was no point lying, there were far too many prisoners that would tell Lomax the truth if he didn't. "My name is Jeradon Horncastle the Third and this is my son Pirian."

Lomax sat up straight almost choking on his cigar. Suddenly there was an ounce of recognition, "Horncastle…?" He stood and made his way over to the window. Dawn's light had become a soft yellow by now, highlighting the wolf's fur in a pale hue. "I know of your name." He turned, pondering some more. "Death is what I associate it with."

"The same as I recognise the emblem on your ship. I think this all boils down to reputation again. You're an outcast, the same as me. If you are the original owner of the gargoyle and the katanac symbiont blade you have on your belt, you can only be from one place." Jeradon paused. "You're Rojin."

Lomax stroked his mane. "What I may be or may have been is of no importance. Vagabond will show you to your quarters. Feel free to take some of the food and drink back with you. There will be dry clothes waiting. We shall talk more once you have had some rest."

In the depths of the ocean, beneath *The General*, a true leviathan awoke. As it shook itself free of the silt and decay that covered it in the darkness of the deep-sea trench, a groan echoed through the chasm. A rotting whale carcass was lit and overshadowed by the beast's inner glow. It shuddered one final time as it slowly made its way up towards the surface.

V

With every seed planted, Jinn began to teach a handful of men and mutants his discipline.

In time, they too began to teach and before long the blind man had turned the majority of Old Town into warriors. All ages embraced their new discipline; as soon as the young could walk, Jinn's philosophy and training were imprinted on them, gradually becoming instinct.

Years passed. Jinn had finally taken the woman who had woken him as his wife. With the help of the town, he rebuilt the old castle of Vhan Hoarne, becoming central to his teachings. He began to write and print his teachings in the form of scrolls and books - and before long the most talented of his students travelled the Erth as missionaries spreading his beliefs further throughout the land.

A son and a daughter followed. The blind man had become a great leader, a teacher and now a father. His firstborn was named after the fallen King of the Eighth City and Vhan Hoarne was to grow into a noble warrior and missionary.

One day, while travelling Erth, he was captured by New Town's Guild.

Vhan Hoarne was interrogated and tortured by the Twelfth City, finally succumbing to a new and far more controlling power than his faith. A poison was spreading through the land, which influenced the people of Erth just as much as Jinn's teachings. This poison, this 'Dosage', was what the people of New Town had found amongst their streets. An all-controlling power helping their people forget about their problems, their loss; how to feel, even how to love.

It was the last Jinn would see of the man he knew as his son.

Finally, Vhan Hoarne had forgotten his own name. But not before he had told New Town's ruler about the man he called 'Father'.

Six

Promise you'll come back for me, Jeradon. I'm so frightened my love, frightened that he will make me forget. Please don't hate me for what I've done...you must live. Look after our brave little man and bring him back to me. I will always love you both so very much.

Keep me alive in your thoughts. Don't forget me.

The howling wind tore at the overcrowded platform. Her delicate hand was on his cheek and as her face slowly faded, he realised it was his own as he awoke from the tormenting dream.

For a brief second Jeradon wondered where he was.

Then the continual hum of *The General's* engines reminded him. He had fallen asleep as soon as his head hit the pillow and as usual his mind was full of cruel, vivid memories. He wasn't sure if they were real or not. But one thing he *was* certain of was Neeve. Glad that he hadn't been robbed of her memory, Jeradon smiled to himself; it was comforting she still occupied his mind when he closed his eyes. *Hold onto this and don't lose hope*, he thought. Biding time aboard the pirate vessel, he would have to make it to shore and survive as best he could, while protecting Pirian.

No problem.

Feeling the coarseness of his face, as several days stubble had taken hold, he felt free of the flying city already.

Pirian was still awake. He and his father had left their own clothes to dry, but had also grabbed a couple of extra shirts and waistcoats for warmth. They were a tad on the large side for him, so he fastened a belt around his waist. Jeradon could see the agitation in his son - his arm obviously still bothering him.

Rolling up his sleeve Pirian inspected it properly. The birthmark had become darker in colour and was still prominent, pulsating as he held his hand over it. In the past, back on Newton when he visited the Greenhouses, he could remember having a similar sensation. The mark had changed shape and size slightly, but it had never been like this.

"Your arm still bothering you?" asked his father.

"It's the birthmark, I noticed it back on the skiff but I didn't get chance to look at it properly."

"Does it hurt?"

"Not really, just feels like…like it's alive. I can't describe it. But it seems to be changing shape again. It itches." he replied scratching his arm.

Jeradon moved closer. "I've not seen this before. Might just be a reaction to the salt water. It's not something you've been exposed to before."

"I don't feel sick, not even sea sick."

"Good. Considering all that's happened you're doing fine. I was worried about you, without the medication I…" Jeradon paused, he didn't even want to think of what would have happened. "The Greenhouses seemed to do you some good. They were just a taste of this place."

Pirian pondered at what his father was saying. There was a great deal he still didn't understand. He had questions, but more importantly he wanted to get back to his mother.

"Will we see her again, Dad?"

"In time, yes. We both have to be positive. You'll just have to trust me, Pirian, I promised your Mother I would take care of you and that is the most important thing right now. I won't lie to you son, getting back to Newton is going to be difficult. Difficult, but not impossible. It's just going to take a little patience and a lot more courage."

"I'm sorry Dad. I shouldn't have taken the book to the Greenhouse. I shouldn't have gone there at all. If I'd have listened to you and mum in the first place, I wouldn't be such a hindrance."

Jeradon held his son's shoulders and looked him in the eye. "Pirian, you are not a hindrance to me, you are my son and I am glad you are with me. Stop apologising when you have nothing to apologise for, you hear me? Nothing. We are here because of me, and this situation has come out of something far deeper than you realise. Whether you took the book or not, whether you kept visiting the Greenhouse - it's irrelevant. Jakahn would still have done the same."

"I just can't stop thinking of mum left alone with him... brainwashed."

Jeradon seethed at the thought, but maintained his positive words for Pirian's sake, as much as his own. "She's a strong woman, she can take care of herself. She'll be ok, Pirian."

"What makes a man like that Dad?"

"I'm afraid some people are just born evil, where as others are misguided and led astray by Newton and its methods."

"You mean zetameen?"

"Yes. It's a powerful drug and awakening from it can kill you. The adjustment leads to memory relapses that can send a person over the edge. We were some of the few people left who were free of the Dosage. At least those that the Emperor knew about."

"Do you think being born zetameen-free is why I'm sick?"

"More than likely. The drug started off as a necessity, people became dependent, until generations were born with it in their systems. Your sickness seems too much of a coincidence."

"Jakahn…he doesn't take the drug, does he?"

"Not anymore, but he remains just as twisted. Which proves to me he was born the way he is - or at least shaped. Men like him are brought into this world with a hole right through them, so no need for zetameen in the first place. So he's ended up more in control and in turn strives to be the controller. It was the same with the Emperor. I think these are the men you have to watch; the controllers; the puppet masters. There are none better than Rayal Jakahn. He even overshadows Surel's methods."

"The Emperor…earlier with Lomax, that wasn't…" Pirian's question was interrupted by a knock on the door as a pirate entered.

"The Captain would like to see you down in the mess, he's reserved two places at his table."

Jeradon nodded in acknowledgement.

Pirian looked at his father, irritated by the badly timed intrusion. He was all the more eager to know what his father was planning.

He would have to be patient - in this as in all things.

It was early afternoon in *The General's* mess. Captain Lomax's crew were already over two-hundred strong and once the new members had adjusted, he would put them to good use in the engine room, cooking, cleaning and making sure they knew how to fend for themselves.

The crew were all tucking into their food. The ship wouldn't have been a pirate ship, and the pirates wouldn't have been pirates, without a good quantity of alcohol too. Yet Lomax seemed to run a tight ship and kept drinking to a limit during the day when there was work to be done.

Pirian was still intimidated by the crew. He was the only child onboard and from what Lomax had stated, perhaps the only child to have ever fallen from Newton. The pirates stared at him and his father as they made their way to the Captain's table. Their attire left much to be desired, most of it heavy-duty hide and leather and the only splash of colour were their tattoos and graffiti on their shirts; those that wore any.

The women were as tough as the men and certainly appeared as though they could look after themselves. There was an abundance of characters covered in piercings, scars and tattoos. Some of them were quite literally walking illustrations. Others had false mechanical limbs; crudely made and adapted from the materials at hand.

Before they had chance to sit down, Lomax's coarse voice bellowed across the mess. "My fellow crewmembers, this is a time to embrace our new guests, may they strengthen our numbers. I am most honoured to have found you all, but may I share the toast with your true saviour; Jeradon Horncastle! Fill your guts and bladder! You are free from Newton. Free to celebrate!"

There was an almighty boom as the crew cheered at Jeradon. Pirian could see that this was not something his father was expecting, and he wasn't entirely comfortable with it.

Jeradon recognised some of the faces that were on the skiff as he sat down with his son at Captain Lomax's table. There were three pirates in Lomax's company, and Jeradon assumed these were his right hand men.

There was already a sense of uneasiness as Lomax introduced them.

"Jeradon, these men are the very first I sailed with on this cursed ocean. We have travelled many years and miles together. Gutso at the far end of the table is my second in command…" Gutso wasn't one for acknowledgements and continued to fill his face. "Hileen here is the one responsible for the fine cooking…" The hardened woman nodded at Jeradon and Pirian. Then Lomax placed a firm hand on the man's back sitting next to him. "Finally Kochek. He's my Head Engineer, responsible for keeping *The*

General fit and healthy."

Pirian found Kochek the most intimidating out of all the pirates he had come across. The man was huge and towered above everyone at the table. His protruding brow shadowed his eyes and his neck prevented any visible jaw line. "The Captain here thought it was fitting that the Emperor's killer ate with us," said the Engineer.

Jeradon smiled coldly at Kochek. "A real icebreaker. But I'd appreciate it if you didn't bring that up again, especially in front of my son."

Kochek looked at his Captain and crewmembers and then back at Jeradon. "Maybe you should have kept it to yourself, if your son still hasn't come to terms with such a tragic loss."

"Pirian has nothing to come to terms with. He is aware of my past, I just don't feel he has to be reminded."

Lomax knocked back a glass of whiskey and then stuffed a cigar back in his mouth. "That's fine, Jeradon...isn't it, Kochek?"

"The surviving guard, what have you done with him?" Jeradon asked Lomax.

"Dead of course." Lomax quickly replied as he casually blew cigar smoke.

"You put him out of his misery."

"I did consider it, yes. Perhaps beheading the other was too honourable. I was far too hasty there, but I had to know if the other would react or not. Just confirmed to me he was too far gone. I felt it would be more fitting to allow the new crewmembers to do what they had to."

"Which was?"

"Fish bait."

Jeradon didn't want to hear anymore. If more time was given to both the guards, Lomax could have eventually had two extra crewmembers. "I'm sure the sea will appreciate your generosity."

"They were of no use in their state, dangerous and unstable to have around. That one in particular had a rather nasty plasma wound; not just a turkey, but a crippled one at that." added Lomax, knowing full well Jeradon was responsible. "I've never seen withdrawal like that before. It was as though he'd been sucked dry. I'm assuming the Dosage has become stronger?"

"Very much so…and so has Newton." Before Lomax had the chance to ask anymore, Jeradon added, "Will you be dropping us ashore?"

"If that is what you wish. We are making our run off the coast and picking up supplies. We should arrive by night fall."

"You mean rig running? You're taking down more of Newton's protronium wells?"

"You could have your first taste of life aboard *The General*."

No. I've had my fare share of Newtonian blood. You will drop us ashore before you make your hit."

"Very well."

Jeradon could see members of the crew glaring at him.

"Thank you."

Vagabond belched and continued to stuff his face as Jeradon began to eat. He needed to build his strength back up; his stomach ached as he poured a glass of water to wash down his first bite in three days.

"I'm assuming this is Newtonian?" Jeradon asked as he held the meat out.

"It is. On top of the protronium, we scavenge as much as possible from the rigs and intercept their communications. *The General* is a thirsty beast and protronium brings us all a good price."

Pirates would often attack the rigs to hinder supply to Newton. There were thousands of them all over Erth, both at sea and on land. However, most of them inland had now run dry. Jeradon was fully aware of the effects it was having on Erth, only turning up the heat of war. New protronium fields were claimed and reclaimed all the time by the Guild. Nothing stood in their way.

For pirates there was no 'side'. They simply added fuel to the fire.

Pirian looked around, the sound of voices and jeers filling the mess. He could see plenty of pirates staring at him and his father, which made him more nervous. He hadn't noticed any other mutants onboard. At least none with physical deformities "Are you the only mutant on the ship, Captain?"

Lomax was taken by surprise. "That's right. Mutant born and bred, the Rojin blood is strong in my veins."

"What about the gargoyle?"

Finishing off a strip of meat, Vagabond looked over at Pirian.

"Gargoyles are from the Seventh City, Gargoy. Long story, but I wouldn't consider them mutants, although I guess some people would. They've been around ever since man built the first roof over his head."

Pirian only knew a little about Gargoy from his book, a time in history before the flying city, a time that led to much bloodshed. "Demons?"

Vagabond's stone hide rippled with moss, as though the mention of the word sent a shiver down his spine.

"I think that may be more plausible." Lomax threw his companion a wry smile. "But it's not exactly something they like to be labelled. You have a curious eye."

"All of this is very new to him," said Jeradon.

"Of course, of course. The boy's first visit down here, it's understandable."

"I have read about it, though. I've read about Erth and its

stories." said Pirian.

"Have you now?" Lomax poured himself another whiskey. Pirian could almost taste its potency. "Hear this fellas, the boy's read about Erth. How'd you manage that then? I hear books are banned on Newton?"

"They are," answered Jeradon as he looked his son in the eye. "That's why he's here."

"So you're here to tell us a story." said Hileen.

Pirian looked at his father who gave an approving nod.

"Ok…If you like."

Vagabond jumped up onto his Captain's shoulder, waiting for Pirian to start.

Giving a moment of thought, he remembered one of his favourites, hoping he would do it justice.

"Men that were outcast to the ocean hadn't always become pirates. Long ago, the sea welcomed Yarna…It was said that before the inferno, there was a woman thief. She had grown up in a small village by the sea. She was an orphan who had learnt to fend for herself from a very young age and was often caught stealing food from the nearby stalls and fishermen. She discovered she could sing and would often try to make money from her voice. Alas, the villagers were not interested in her songs and Yarna had to revert back to becoming a thief.

"Although she didn't mean any harm, the village became tired of Yarna stealing and placed a curse on the woman. It was said that whatever she stole next would infect her.

"Unfortunately this happened to be fish.

"With her body gradually transforming and the village labelling her a freak, she was banished to the ocean. It was this new home that spoke to her, and making a deal with the sea she was able to infect the very minds of sailors with her voice. She drew them closer to the rocks and consumed everyone onboard. It was said that she bred with the very sea itself, her offspring increasing in numbers over the centuries

"Siren were mutations, their stories twisted through time as much as their bodies.

"Only the females sing.

"Siran however, their male counterparts, never need a voice to lure their prey."

The afternoon heat is at its most deadly as *The General* ploughs through the water, churning crests of white in its wake. Underneath the ship a large shadow rises. What could have been mistaken for one giant beast slowly starts to dissipate, a shoal driving upwards and breaking the surface.

Sun light catches their glittering sickly green scales and the hint of fins.

This is their realm and no ship has out run them yet. Bobbing and diving, the creatures submerge one final time before propelling themselves into the air, grabbing hold of the hull's raggedy surface.

The Siran wail and screech as they clamber over one another, and in minutes they are aboard.

"…Her call is answered." concluded Pirian.

Distracted, Lomax's ears twitched.

Pirian received no answer to his story, just silence as Lomax looked blankly across the mess.

"I've heard that one before." stated Gutso.

"What is it, Captain?" asked another.

Jeradon smiled. "Well I enjoyed it, son. It was always my favourite."

The clattering overhead became louder. Most of the crew were already out of the mess before Lomax said a word. "All hands armed and on deck!"

Pirian's stomach sank.

Vagabond took off as Jeradon grabbed Lomax's shoulder, looking him in the eye.

"Seems your boy's story may have paid a visit. Out of all the tales he could have told he picks 'Old Yarna.'"

VI

New Town's power had grown over the quiet years following the capture of Jinn's son. Throwing himself into his teachings, his influence had taken hold of Old Town on higher levels, becoming one with the symbiont known as the katanac. Its gift to them was the very blade they would come to depend on.

Flying machines from New Town had taken to the sky. They began to travel the further reaches of Erth for protronium supplies, swallowing many settlements. It was only a matter of time before Old Town was attacked once again.

However, New Town was not expecting such resistance. Jinn's people fought with all their strength, pushing the Guild back. Jinn led his people into another fierce battle against a new leader; a man who had grown in rank very swiftly. A man who seemed to know every move they made.

They had not pushed them back at all but were being pulled into a trap.

As Jinn battled their Guild Commander he discovered it was his own son; twisted and brainwashed. The son he had once loved drove his blade into Old Town's Messiah. As Jinn fell from the Twelfth City, it rose above the Erth for the first time, bringing down all of its power and destruction.

Centuries passed.

New Town had renamed itself Newton; The Thirteenth City

of Erth.

A scarred landscape was left behind in the wake of the Great War. Cracked and wounded; the vast protronium source that Newton had generated taking to the sky, along with its sheer firepower, had polluted the Erth further.

From the ruins of Old Town grew Jinn's order, known as the People *of Jinn,* 'Rojin' in respect to their great leader. Once the city was rebuilt and renamed 'Yodann', missionaries continued their journeys; spreading their teachings to the people that had evolved into something else entirely.

Hidden deep underground three surviving gargoyles of the Seventh City, Gargoy, had ventured above ground hearing of Jinn's influence and acceptance of those who were 'marked'. Once a home to man, giant and gargoyle - winged creatures who were the true protectors of Erth - they protected Gana, which they believed to be Erth's spirit, a godlike creature cast in stone. Feeling that Jinn shared Erth's spirit and Gana's power, the gargoyles helped him to further his teachings and beliefs, entrusting the Rojin leader with Gana itself. Their destiny was was to become one, yet these beliefs had slowly begun to divide Jinn's people. With talk of traitors in their midst, the Rojin began to slowly fracture and lose touch with their leader - something of which Gargoy had predicted within their own scriptures. It was believed that the Rojin would be led underground by a new leader, a leader who would rule on what was known as the 'Traitor's Throne'. Many had become despondent and yearned for a better life on Newton, embracing the temptation of zetameen and forgetting their Rojin origins. No one with a mutation, or 'mark' as it was now referred to, was allowed on the city. Only those refugees who had been conditioned with the Dosage were accepted.

While every book and reference to Erth's cultures were collected and destroyed, from fear that they would harbour independent thought and rebellion, Newton and its drug induced population continued to rape and pillage the Erth as it replenished its protronium supply, growing in power and size. Generations were born with zetameen already in their systems; controlled from birth.

A plague thought to be spread by Rojin extremists caused a great sickness and during this time many Newtonians rejected their Dosage. Rojin refugees remembered their origins, growing into an influential movement known as the Resistance, shaking the foundations of the flying city.

Only Emperors and those within the Hierarchy were allowed to remain clean. *Their* drug was simply power and control. Newton had lost its history through polluted minds and only whispers of Rojin beliefs remained. Each new ruler of Newton became obsessed with finding a man known only as The Father, a man who held the secret of immortality; an artefact known as the Clock of Ages.

Seven

At nearly thirty-two thousand tons and half a mile in length, *The General* was an awesome ship. Its original structure had been salvaged from a grounded tanker, and over the years the modification to the bow included cannons and various other riggings from scavenged war ships. *The General* had, over time, become something of a deformity itself.

Even though Fallen had recently been taken onboard, Captain Lomax still wished he had a larger crew. Crewmembers were lost all the time. Guilt lay heavily on his mind; he'd lost count of how many people had died at sea since he was in charge. Erth's seas were a dangerous place, he had encountered many obstacles and fought many times for his ship and crew's safety. The Siran had become an all-too-familiar foe.

Gutso was the first to the bridge. Looking out across the expanse of the ship, he could see the remains of the day shift ripped apart and scattered across the deck. In the distance, there was a mass of green, swarming over *The General's* surface like a disease.

Crewmembers made their way topside. The screams hadn't lasted long, and the scraping sound above them was growing louder by the second.

With night approaching, the sea remained calm. Too calm. Pirates armed themselves with rifles, pistols and swords, while the newly initiated Fallen were being given the perfect opportunity to fight. They were eager to prove themselves as they stood behind the iron doors, awaiting their orders.

"Fifteen years I've been with this ship, I don't take kindly to unwelcome visitors," Lomax said entering his quarters, Jeradon and Pirian following behind. Opening an ornate cabinet, he pulled out the weapons he had confiscated from Jeradon when he arrived. "You'll be needing these back." He handed them over, addressing him once again. "I suggest the boy remains here. He'll be safer."

"No. He stays with me."

Lomax sighed, grabbed a small sword from the wall and held it out for Pirian. "In case you need it." Pirian looked to his father.

Jeradon reached his hand out to prevent Lomax handing it over. "There's no need for that. I'll take care of him."

Pirian grew agitated at the fact his father wouldn't allow him to have the sword. He was sure he would have said the same even if Lomax had handed him a wooden one.

Jeradon noticed Lomax poised over one of the organic-looking guns mounted on the wall, as though tempted to use it.

"You're not thinking of using that?" asked Jeradon.

Lomax pulled the gun down from the shelf, its twisted beauty cradled in his hands, "No…no, it would only make things worse. But it's worth a small fortune on the Black Market. I can't allow it to go down with the ship."

"That's the pirate in you talking."

"Piracy is all I have left," Lomax emptied the seed-like bullets from the gun and placed them in his waistcoat pocket. "I guess the bullets will pay a high enough price."

Lomax was aware that his crew had been caught off guard. A

fair amount of alcohol had been consumed and although they'd certainly have some Arbain courage, their ability to fight would certainly be hindered. Even he was beginning to feel the effects of ten double whiskies.

A comlink sparked to life.

"Captain, the day shift has been wiped out. Siran are massing on deck," stated Gutso.

"How many?"

"Four, maybe five hundred strong. We are seriously outnumbered and they're already attempting to get in via the trap doors."

"I want men armed and ready inside the ship in case they break through. The rest of us will engage them above deck and keep them distracted." Lomax glanced round at Kochek. "Gather engineering and the Fallen, give them weapons and take care of the docking bay." He pressed the comlink button once again, "Gutso, keep Kochek and his men posted if they break through."

Jeradon grew agitated. "What do you want me to do?"

"I suggest you look after your boy. Go with Kochek, it's safer. If the hull is breached you'll have no choice but to help prevent them coming through."

The General was still travelling at a top speed of twenty-three knots. The Bridge towered above the deck and rested towards the back end of the ship. Quarters and corridors took up one sixth of the ship's length. Surrounding the bridge were a series of armed walkways and heavy iron doors.

A door opened as Lomax led twenty of his crew out onto the decks.

He flicked his cigar away, looking down the length of his ship and then up at Gutso standing at the bridge. Vagabond weighed up the situation as much as his Captain. The rest of the pirates made their way on deck from the opposite side, keeping their eyes on the Siran gathered around the docking bay trap doors.

Lomax could taste the sea breeze and smell the hint of land - they were not far from shore.

Yet there was a more potent aroma in the air. Rotting fish so rancid it stung his nostrils. No one else could sense it, they didn't have such a keen sense of smell. He led his crew further down the deck shouting out more commands. "I want a man on each harpooning arm and cannon, right now!"

Pirates volunteered themselves, climbing onto the harpoon's rigging as soon as possible and awaiting further orders. The rest of Lomax's crew spread out as they approached the Siran tearing at the trapdoors, who stopped as soon as they noticed the pirates approaching and immediately rushed them, three hundred strong. The crew were outnumbered eight to one, but at least they had some firepower.

The sky was becoming darker.

Siran flashed a sickly green under the gunfire as they fell to the deck. Lomax almost wished he could hear the Siren lulling him towards the rocks, instead of the ear-piercing screech of their male counterparts, cutting the air around him. His crew fanned out, the majority using their guns at long range. Siran and his crew were falling all around, the deck becoming a precarious mixture of crimson and green fluids.

The hideous creatures had begun to swarm over the bridge. Some were more mutated than others and hindered by severe wounds and loss of limbs - their bodies pierced by broken harpoons and wire netting that had gouged their flesh. Powerful arms drove their sharp, webbed talons further and further into the metal with each powerful punch. Their blind, contorted faces hissed - row upon row of razor sharp teeth breaking on the hard metal as they frantically bit down on the decking. Fuelled by a mindless frenzy, they didn't stop until they were cut down.

Despite his size, the gargoyle Vagabond was entirely capable of looking after himself. He had taken to the air and morphing to a harder stone, plummeted from the sky, cannon balling as many Siran as he could. It was impossible for them to harm him. Siran attempted to take a bite out of him or swallow him whole, losing their teeth in the process. Vagabond was strong and although he couldn't lift a creature of their size, he was capable of knocking them clean off their webbed feet. If need be, he could even take a bite out of *them* instead; but contrary to the belief that gargoyles eat anything, Vagabond passed at the taste of rotting fish.

One by one the pirates fell as they became more outnumbered by the minute. Lomax was back to back with three of his crew as they continued to fire upon the onslaught of Siran. The agile creatures leapt from view, avoiding the barrage of bullets and blades.

Lomax trained two handguns, howling as he fired. Suddenly from nowhere, a Siran rushed them, knocking Lomax to the ground. He watched helplessly as two of his crew were dragged overboard in the blink of an eye. A second Siran turned and approached him with ferocious speed.

Bringing his guns round swiftly, he squeezed the triggers.

Click.

Empty.

The Siran charged, needle teeth bared, lifeless eyes glimmering as it brought its full weight down on Lomax.

The sound above the docking bay echoed throughout *The General*, rust falling from above with every pounding move.

Jeradon could see the trap doors buckling inwards.

Kochek bellowed at his peers. "Conserve your ammunition. Show no mercy!"

"Stick close," Jeradon shouted to his son.

THE ENEMY'S SON

Two trap doors tore open. Helpless, Pirian looked on as Siran dived through the openings above. Some were hit immediately, falling to their deaths on the docking bay floor. The rest crawled down the ceiling and walls, some making use of chains and fittings to help in their descent.

Pirates spread along the walkways and down to the docking bay floor as they approached. The sound of gunfire was deafening. Pirian was surprised how strong and agile these creatures were. Centuries of swimming in the sea had strengthened them; moving out of water was effortless.

Pirian kept his back to his father, acting as the eyes in the back of his head. Jeradon's plasma gun sounded as he began to fire; already the Siran were on top of the crew, their screams cut short in seconds. Pirian shouted out at his father. Jeradon immediately spun round in reaction, blasting one of the creatures square in the face. He could see many more approaching Kochek and fired on the creatures once again to cover the engineer.

Kochek glanced up at Jeradon and nodded.

The bay was a frenzy. Jeradon could clearly see that the crew were sitting ducks; drunk, and caught off guard they were easy pickings to such agile creatures. Looking up he noticed two Siran from above. Swinging his gun arm up, he caught one in freefall. As the second creature descended, the weapon was knocked from his hand, along with his sword. The Siran then swiped Pirian across the floor and grabbed hold of Jeradon.

Skidding to a halt Pirian picked himself up. Catching sight of his father's sword, he grabbed it and rushed to his aid.

Jeradon forced the creature's jaw up and away from his face, as Pirian approached, driving the blade into the creature's back. Screeching in pain, it spun round backhanding him to the floor once again. Pirian hadn't had enough strength to drive the blade deep enough, and the rest of the sword protruded from the Siran's back.

Jeradon sprung to his feet, kicking the blade further in, just as the creature spun round to face his son. It screamed out, twisting away from Jeradon, before he removed the sword, decapitating the creature in one, swift, executed move.

Jeradon caught his breath and gave his son a concerned glance. "You're too young to be playing with swords."

"But…I was trying to help. You were in trouble…"

"I was in control."

"I was trying to help," repeated Pirian under his breath.

The strange looking protrusion that had driven itself into the Siran and out the other side seemed to wither and distort. The dead creature slumped to the side as Lomax pulled himself from under its weight. Releasing the pressure on the hilt, the blade retracted from the creature very slowly. One of the Siran's claws had sunk into his shoulder. He gritted his teeth as he ripped it free.

"Captain! The docking bay has been breached!"

He knew they were in trouble. He'd never seen Siran in these numbers before and the reality of what was happening was being driven in with each sobering moment. He clipped the katanac to his belt, and ducked as two more creatures rushed him. Sliding across the deck he righted himself, pulled a gun from a fallen comrade and fired, hitting one squarely in the chest. It tumbled overboard and he immediately fired on the other, clipping its shoulder. The Siran's claws stretched at Lomax, but he tossed the gun to the floor and threw the creature over his shoulder. Landing on its feet it immediately spun round, its forearm fins flicking up like razor blades and slashing out at the Sea Wolf.

Ducking with each lethal blow, Lomax timed his punch just right, driving the full weight of his upper body into the creature's face. As it fell to its knees it looked up at him hissing as he followed through with another punch. "Stay down!"

∞

Pirian thought he felt *The General* lurch as the remaining crew clustered together, surrounded by Siran. The ship tilted slightly and an almighty boom sounded through the hull of the ship. It was enough to distract the Siran, while the pirates took advantage in striking them down.

All but Jeradon had ran out of ammunition, yet even his plasma cells were low.

There was another boom as the ship lurched once more.

Lomax steadied himself, as Siran stopped in their tracks.

Another boom and Lomax stumbled backwards toward the railings as the ship tilted. It was as though *The General* had run aground. Looking over his shoulder he could see the water below lit up with bright cyan blue.

Siran had already begun to flee.

The General's engine tone changed as the ship raised out of the water, the great twin propellers slowly spinning free. Lomax could hear the straining and creaking of metal. His ship's back was beginning to break.

A torrent of water erupted at the side of the ship, revealing what looked like an enormous tentacle. On closer inspection, as it began to loom over them, Lomax could see that it was a neck leading to a head of horrific proportions. As he looked overboard once more, *The General* was illuminated in a bright light that slowly began to dull.

The monstrous head lashed out at both the Siran and Lomax's crew, picking them off with ease. He hadn't encountered Yarna for over five years. It was rare she fed, but when she did, nothing stood in the way of her enormous appetite. Another two heads erupted, and she took hold of *The General* and squeezed tightly.

The vessel began to buckle.

"This just gets better," muttered Lomax.

∞

Kochek flung a Siran against the wall and immediately grabbed another in a headlock while it attempted to claw at him. They were as slippery as soap, but not even with all the struggling could the creature avoid the snap of its neck. The monstrous engineer was distracted by the disturbance throughout the ship and the sounds *The General* was beginning to make. The very life was being squeezed out of it and Kochek could clearly see the internal structure buckling in on itself. Although the protronium tanks running the length of the hull were empty, they were at their most flammable due to the gas left in them.

If there was a rupture, there could be a deadly explosion.

"We have to make it topside before we're trapped down here!" shouted Kochek.

The survivors all began to make their way back up the walkways as they began to twist and break apart. Siran crawled back up the inner hull and through the trap doors they had entered.

Kochek continued to guide everyone through the doors as they all rushed upwards towards the deck.

Yarna held onto *The General* with all her strength, even as the propellers caught her thick blubbery hide. Yarna's heads tore at the deck and hull as though it was paper. Other appendages lashed out at the crew and remaining Siran; finishing them off with voracious speed.

Unaware of his Captain's injury, Vagabond landed on Lomax's shoulder. The Sea Wolf grimaced slightly, witnessing the slow death of his ship and crew.

Kochek and the surviving crewmembers poured through onto the deck. The night sky was flooded with a frenzy of death and destruction. Wailing serpentine heads lashed out and swayed above, while tentacles wrapped around the length of the ship in a fierce grip.

Pirian couldn't believe his eyes. He wondered if Lomax had got it right, about him cursing the ship with his story. Things just seemed to be getting worse. Jeradon sheathed his sword and held onto his son.

Kochek approached Lomax. "Captain, we have to get off the ship, it could blow any moment!"

Lomax silently looked at the engineer.

"Captain!"

Tentacles ripped away a gun turret and harpooning arm. As it did so, the beast received the full force of both weapons going off automatically. The quadruple harpoons caught one of its serpentine necks, but the cannon hit the bridge square on. Everyone on deck dived for cover as shrapnel flew towards them killing two pirates instantly. Hit in the arm, Kochek unflinchingly tore the sharp metal from his flesh.

The beast roared as one of its tentacles was pierced by a girder, skewering it to the deck.

No one could have survived the bridge being hit.

Kochek gritted his teeth. "There's no way of getting to the life rafts, we're blocked!"

"Then we take our chances overboard!" replied Lomax.

Pirian's heart sank. Not again, he'd already been a victim of the sea once and was lucky enough to survive the ordeal. What was the point of being saved in the first place, only to be left to the will of the sea once again? This time there would be nothing to keep their heads above water.

Jeradon kept his cool. His eyes were fixed on Yarna. She had finished feasting on her children and Lomax's crew trapped at the far end of the ship. Now her attention was fixed on them.

One head lashed out, grabbing Kochek. As he was lifted into the air, Pirian turned his head and covered his ears from his hollering. Jeradon, Lomax and the rest of the crew watched in horror as the man drove his sword into one of the creature's eyes. It dropped the broken engineer, and as he fell from view into the water Yarna's other heads uncoiled upwards, looming over them. Just as they were about to strike out at the remaining crew, there was an almighty groan: *The General's* dying breath, followed by a deafening roar as the lower quarter of the ship exploded.

The thunderous explosion was enough to tear into Yarna's belly and rip her tentacles and gripping spines apart, as the ship suddenly broke in two. Her remaining heads screamed, falling down onto the broken, burning mass of the ship.

The stern, sank downwards into the water with the remaining crew clinging on. There was another explosion. Knocked from his Captain's shoulder, Vagabond caught himself in midair as Lomax landed badly, hitting his head. The Sea Wolf attempted to pull him self up and then lost consciousness. Vagabond landed immediately at his side like a faithful dog, pawing at his face.

There were only another four crewmembers alive now other than Jeradon and Pirian, but they weren't about to leave Lomax behind. The broken half of the ship shook and began to tilt upwards.

They had to jump. Now.

Pirian grabbed hold of the railings as the rest of the crew jumped overboard. Jeradon watched on as Lomax's unconscious body began to slide from view, while Vagabond grabbed his captain, frantically flapped his wings to prevent the Sea Wolf from falling into the flames. Jeradon was more than aware of the safety of his son, finding it difficult to move forward and save Lomax. But before he knew it Pirian had already slid down the deck past Lomax and grabbed hold of the nearest railings.

Jeradon knew that his son would not be able to handle his weight and followed suit, sliding and holding out for the railing. Grabbing Lomax's limp body, Vagabond began to tug upwards as Pirian helped his father lift the Sea Wolf and hold him over the side.

There was no time to think about jumping as they threw themselves overboard. The sheer weight of the dying beast still tangled up in the wreckage of the ship, was enough to ensure the sinking of *The General*. One final deafening explosion resounded and the great ship's broken hull reared up almost ninety degrees as Pirian helped his father pull Lomax through the water, and away from the sinking wreckage.

The rest of the crew who had jumped overboard were nowhere to be seen. Lomax was falling in and out of consciousness as Jeradon held him under his arms, keeping his head above the water. Nearby a large portion of decking floated by as they took hold. With their last ounce of strength, they pulled themselves up, slumping down from exhaustion.

In their death grip, the tangled beasts vanished underneath the surface. Smouldering debris was all that littered the surface as the lone survivors floated on into the night.

VII

The name Horncastle had become synonymous with death throughout the centuries. Their blood was strong, yet it was still controlled by the rulers of Newton. In search of a myth, generations of Horncastles were ordered to search and destroy, as they led their armies across the ravaged Erth. The answer to life itself had become far more important than Newton's precious protronium.

This source of power had become nothing more than an excuse.

The little girl drew a figure of eight in the sand, over and over with her finger.

A doll lay at her side. No older than three, she wore a tanned leather skirt, trousers and top, which were marked with subtle hexagonal patterns. She wore braided leather bracelets around her wrists and ankles. Bleached blonde strands were entwined within the jet-black hair resting on her shoulders.

The girl's skin had been darkened by the sun, her eyes as black as charcoal. In the centre of her forehead was a horizontal mark, resembling a small scar.

All around, a small community farmed dry worms from the desert. A field of wooden poles stuck up from the ground, a foot apart and as far as the eye could see. Men and women collected the worms in baskets - their main source of food and water. Without this sustenance they would simply perish.

Surrounding the fields were their homes, round huts made from the skin and bones of cattle, enclosed by stone walls. The farming outpost was one of many small communities that had been converted by Rojin missionaries and populated by a mix of those that carried marks and those that didn't. One Rojin put himself to good use mending the worm poles, carrying the enormous equipment in arms three times the size of any other's. An older man had lobster coloured skin, blinking his six eyes as he tethered his two-headed dog and patted it on the head.

Other marks often not as obvious. They were concealed deep inside or simply hidden by clothing.

The young girl and other children had no reason to fear their own people, no matter how different they seemed. What they did fear was the Newtonian Guild who scourged the land.

In the distance she could see them approaching. Picking up her wooden doll, she ran to her mother close by.

Panic filled the air as dust began to rise amongst the turmoil.

The Guild entered the village fifty strong.

Their drop ship flew overhead, surveying the farm. Ten men were on foot, while four were mounted on giant Mechats, their metallic roars deafening any villager nearby as they bounded through walls, destroying everything in sight.

The ten Guildsmen carried huge cannons strapped to their back. Holding large broadswords, they walked directly behind their Commander as he gave several signals with his hand. In response, his unit began to fan out.

The Guild's drop ship landed in the centre of the farm as the Commander gave another signal. Sand swirled upwards as a ramp opened and the rest of the Guild spilled out. After months of duty, their rustic, corroded armour had taken on a similar appearance to the harsh barren landscape, helping them blend in

JAMES JOHNSON

to their surroundings.

Villagers were thrown through walls and crushed by metal jaws. Tethered Umah pulled and broke free from their carts and ploughs, galloping to their masters' side in an attempt to save them. The young girl could clearly hear the sound of plasma fire amongst the chaos and dust. Frozen with fear, she held closely to her mother's breast and wailed as they crouched behind one of the walls.

A Guildsman grabbed a farmer, throwing him several yards through the air, he then pulled the cannon from his back, gunning down three other people as they ran from view.

The Commander inspected two nearby huts, his huge sword drawn. Finding nothing, he torched the primitive buildings and began to inspect the worm poles. Two farmers appeared from view, both of whom stood their ground.

The commander moved forward.

Bringing his sword up to his side, he noticed the farmers held out what looked like small, organic looking devices. Blades manifested in a split second. *Rojin missionaries*, thought the commander as he spun forward without hesitation.

The first didn't even have chance to raise his sword as his headless body fell to the ground, the symbiont blade immediately decaying in his dead hand. The second managed to parry a fierce blow. The organic sword was as strong as any Guildsman's, but the Rojin could not stand up against the strength of zetameen coursing through the Commander's veins.

The Rojin's arm buckled. Pushing his sword inwards, the Commander moved in closer and grabbed the Rojin's sword arm. He squeezed and watched the blade retract into its hilt, before his wrist snapped. The Commander then brought his sword back round to finish the job. Shaking his blade free of blood, he stamped on the dying Rojin sword at his feet.

Pulling out his plasma gun he continued his search, while the carnage increased.

Another Guildsman threw a man into an Umah's drinking trough, watching his face turn pale under the water. Just as his victim finished thrashing, two other villagers appeared directly behind him holding forks. Spinning round he drew his sword, cutting them both down in one brutal move, as blood splattered onto his armour. He immediately sheathed his weapon and stepped over the fallen bodies.

The girl's mother picked herself up off the floor. Still holding her daughter, she backed away towards one of the tents.

Unaware, she turned to see a Guildsman approaching from the other side, his plasma gun pointing directly at her head. She gripped her daughter even tighter as she heard the charge of the plasma cell.

Closing her eyes, she awaited the impact of the bullet.

But it never came.

She slowly opened one eye at a time and stared directly at him. His eyes were not visible through his visor, all she could see was her own terrified face looking back.

He was obviously the Commander; his helmet marked by a crest. He wore a heavy crimson cloak, which sprawled over his armoured shoulders.

There was a sudden snap and a hiss as his visor opened. Startled by the noise, the woman flinched. His eyes bore an amber glow, which took her even more by surprise.

The little girl looked around at him, her mother noticing his gaze drift towards her daughter. There was an intense look, a conflict as his eyes wandered down to the girl, squinting slightly as though he recognised her in some way.

The Commander was no longer aware of the village, the smell of death surrounding him and the screams of those who fell at his command. Instead he was standing on a grassy plain, a cool breeze ruffling his cloak and the sun shining against his bloodied, corroding armour. All the while the girl and her mother stood, never taking their eyes off him.

Either this woman's a Rojin witch...or I've overdosed on zetameen, he tried to convince himself. The woman placed her daughter on the grass as he lowered his gun, nausea washing over him like a tidal wave. For a moment he thought he heard a voice. *You will see all...*

A shot rang out and echoed in Jeradon's mind...

Eight

Daylight.

The voices had invaded Pirian's mind the moment his limp body rolled onto shore. It was the inhaling of the seawater that woke him. Panicking, he coughed and spluttered, lashing out his arms as they pushed into the shallows. As soon as his hand touched the red sand, he could hear the whispers. Gradually they became louder while he clawed at the sand, dragging himself onto the beach. The whispers intensified as he pulled himself free of the lapping water.

He couldn't make out anything they were trying to say. It was as though a thousand voices were fighting for space in his head. Pirian opened his eyes wide, rolling onto his back. Unable to blink, he attempted to pull himself up. It was hopeless; his body was a lead weight, heavier than he had ever felt on Newton when the sickness hit him. The resonance in his head was becoming more and more distorted as layers of different sounds began to build.

Then there was silence and all he saw was a great chasm carved into the desolate landscape as his arm shook and was slowly pulled into the sand.

No!...I want to see! he shouted inside his head trying to fight the darkness.

Yet it was his father that the voice answered as he lost consciousness.

You will see all...

∞

Vagabond had flown towards a target one hundred miles inland the moment they had made it ashore. Like a homing device, the gargoyle knew exactly where he was heading. For his Captain, for his master, even the boy and his father, he knew he had to try and seek the help of those he had once been loyal to. Hopefully they would listen.

The sun beat down on the polluted Erth. Following the river away from the sea, Vagabond increased his altitude as he flew over the broken mountain passes. Unaffected by the heat, he swooped directly towards the surface as the struggling river, narrowed from drought, shimmered slightly in the heat and then slowly vanished.

The mirage that covered the chasm seemed weaker than he remembered, almost transparent as he flew underneath it. A sandstorm tore along its walls as he morphed his hide to the same stone texture and colour as the sandy rock.

Vagabond could no longer see below; assuming the river had now vanished underground. The width of the trench became wider the further he flew. Dropping below the storm, he approached the first signs of civilisation. Jutting out from the canyon walls, were what looked like fallen buildings, buried by the sand and time. They resembled giant stone skeletons stitching the canyon together.

Deeper and deeper Vagabond flew. There were walkways and windows amongst the fallen buildings and inner walls, reminding him of his old home, Gargoy. Passing the sandstorm, he landed on the ledge of a protruding roof, surveying his surroundings in more detail.

The canyon finally widened into a valley, less green than he remembered. There was a sickness in the air. In the distance he could make out the Rojin capital, Yodann. It was a magnificent sight, even in its current state - its buildings a combination of carved rock faces and traces of forgotten architecture entwined in giant Rojin vines, twisting upwards towards the sky.

Hidden by the mirage, the city rested thousands of feet below the barren wasteland - unseen caverns and underground rivers opening out into the valley, running for miles. It was a place of many secrets and, to those that sought them, many answers. On the canyon floor lay more buildings, constructed from the surrounding rock and bathed in the reflected sunlight absorbed by strange, sickly looking plants spread throughout the valley.

Swooping down from the rock ledge, Vagabond landed upon a look-out tower that surveyed the valley and the entrance to the canyon in the opposite direction. It was a tall structure, connected to a wall, which grew out of the mouth of the canyon, cutting off the canyon floor from the south and its most narrow point.

The struggling, shallow river had opened up once again, just before it met a huge archway cut into the tower's wall, and spilled over into the valley below, continuing north. Down in the valley were further walls and lookout towers which barricaded the entire city, organic architecture twisted into one ominous presence. The main inner Temple was protected by hundreds of guards and two remaining gargoyles; both of which were older and wiser than Vagabond.

They had become slower in their age. In the old days no one would have even breached the mirage and the sandstorm, let alone made it as far as the canyon's lookout tower; there would have been a gargoyle lining every inch. Vagabond knew there was still no point flying down into the valley; he would be caught either way. So he listened to the grinding of stone and watched as the two swooping shapes in the distance quickly began to fly towards him.

Landing either side of him, Brom and Stone slowly approached.

Where Vagabond resembled a reptile crossed with a goat, his

old acquaintances were pure caricatures. Rom resembled a huge, fat ape. Stone however, was slender, his sharp nose adding to his almost human-like features.

Vagabond knew that giving himself up was the only way of speaking to The Father.

The shot rang out, echoing in Jeradon's mind. Gradually it turned into a distant stampeding as he lifted his head up from the broken decking that had brought him safely to shore. The sound seemed to be approaching from inland. Clutching his head and squinting from the sunlight, he coughed from Erth's acrid taste. He was already beginning to wheeze from the decay and pollution.

The gargoyle was nowhere to be seen and Lomax was still unconscious. Jeradon assumed they had drifted through the night, before coming to rest in a polluted area. A sudden panic hit him. He quickly looked round for Pirian. There he was, lying on his back several feet away. Jeradon stumbled towards him and was about to touch his face when he noticed his eyes were wide open. Panicking, he thought his son was dead, yet Pirian was breathing and warm to the touch.

Distracted by the approaching noise, he held onto his son. Struggling for a moment, it felt as if Pirian was made of stone, or rooted to the ground. Then, gradually as his arm came free of the sand, he was as light as a feather. Pirian's eyes closed as his father held him to his chest.

The stampeding slowed. Several metres inland, on top of the sand dunes, a number of figures on the back of large beasts came to a halt. One rider continued to move forward slowly, his steed cantering as it spluttered. The silhouettes of the dead trees seemed to quadruple their numbers.

Approaching him slowly, the rider and steed moved into Jeradon's view.

The creature, which Jeradon knew as an Umah, resembled

an ancient hoofed animal; its front end built up heavily, while the back portion sloped downwards. Its legs however, resembled something more feline, fast and powerful with no longer any visible sign of hooves. Clad in armour that looked as though it had been fashioned from the bones of many different animals, the saddle, in which its rider sat, was shaped appropriately to its slanting back.

Jumping down in front of Jeradon, the rider wore similar armour. A leather gas mask and goggles hid the rider's face, while a large shield was strapped to its back. A figure of eight turned on its side was burnt into the right shoulder; the mark of the Rojin. Attached to a belt around the waist was a similar looking weapon that Jeradon had noticed Lomax carrying, the hilt of a katanac symbiont blade.

The armoured figure raised his hand, giving a sequence of signals. Immediately the rest of the group approached, dismounted and made their way over to them as a strange looking vehicle floated into view overhead. Each figure's armour seemed to be subtly different in colour and texture, resembling ripening fruit.

Jeradon sat motionless as they sprayed Lomax's unconscious body with a clear liquid, then proceeded to lift him from the decking. The floating object lowered towards the ground like a giant beetle's endoskeleton, held by two enormous balloons. As it touched down, a ramp descended and Lomax was carried aboard.

Making there way over to Jeradon, the armoured warriors paused and looked at each other. There was no communication and Jeradon was far too exhausted to put up any resistance. They continued to spray both his self and Pirian as one of the figures placed masks over their faces.

Inhaling the fresh oxygen, the last thing Jeradon saw was his son being lifted aboard the strange looking airship before he fell into a deep sleep.

∞

"Nothing has been detected in quarantine."

Jeradon's eyes blinked open at the sound of foreign voices. Recognising the Rojin tongue, he attempted to take in his surroundings as the voices continued.

"At least the contamination can spread no further," a female voice stated. "Right now I am more concerned about the wolf and the gargoyle. They are not to be trusted. If it wasn't for The Father's word, none of them would have been brought here."

Jeradon managed to catch part of the conversation from outside as he awoke. He looked around the room once more where Pirian lay on a bed next to him, while a small man inspected him. He looked back over towards the open door as two other figures approached. They were both female, but one sounded older and far more abrupt in her mannerisms.

"Great Gana. It's…it's him," the younger of the two said, her face hidden under a delicate, lightweight hood, her eyes examining the man lying before them.

The older of the two recoiled slightly at her acquaintance's confirmation. "Ah, you're awake," she interrupted, gesturing at Jeradon as she moved into the light.

The woman's gaunt face had been weathered by time and Erth's harsh climate. Her eyes black enough to pierce the soul of any man. Surrounding her face was a strange looking headdress that held her long grey hair back, while a thin, leather cord held a small, charred and twisted object around her neck. The woman who stood with her was still only young, perhaps a teenager; her features difficult to make out under the hood.

They both wore long gowns that hid any definition of figure and their gestures were kept from view. Right away, Jeradon recognised them as Rojin witches. The small facially scarred man who approached them was more than likely a Rojin witchdoctor.

Pausing, he continued to address the older woman. "Their strength is returning, I've administered another injection and they should be ready to leave quarantine by tomorrow. Neither of them have any traces of zetameen, but the boy seems to have a condition."

"A condition...?" queried the older woman.

"It is most likely the reason I found other chemicals in his system. A serum of some kind I believe, not too dissimilar to our own medicines. His sickness isn't contagious, but I am carrying out further tests. If it's a mutation, it just doesn't make sense that he's from Newton. The adult, however, could be Fallen."

"If that's the case then maybe his sin is of benefit to us. The Father has never been wrong. My Select here will help confirm what the gargoyle has told us. Thank you Moku, that will be all for now."

Jeradon watched the witchdoctor hobble away. "My son...?" He attempted to lift himself up from the bed.

The old woman looked over at the boy, pausing for a moment, "The boy is fine. He is sleeping, just as you have been for the past two months."

"Two *months*?" Jeradon rubbed his temples and then opened and closed his hand. His body felt drained. As he pulled his hand down over his head and face, he could feel how much his hair had grown, accompanied by a full beard. "How...?"

"We have kept you asleep intentionally for this period of time. It is all part of the quarantine process. You will eventually be given one final treatment to boost your strength. Please, do not attempt to move, you will find it very difficult and risk further damage to yourself."

Jeradon tried to move once again, but his body was like stone. "How did you find us?"

"You were brought to our attention by the gargoyle. Seems he decided to return home after all these years and bring you to our attention."

Jeradon wondered what she meant, yet was equally curious on the whereabouts of Lomax.

"And his master...the Wolf captain?"

The two women looked at each other before the older of the two replied. "He has been detained, along with his companion."

"Detained?" questioned Jeradon as he sat upright. "The gargoyle helped save his captain's life, along with our own."

"It seems so."

Jeradon paused for thought, surveying his surroundings as best he could. "The wolf, I'm assuming he's Rojin?"

"He was...a long time ago."

"Outcast?"

"I believe you label it 'Fallen'. Just because our city is firmly planted on Erth, that doesn't prevent Rojin from falling too. Looks like The Father finally delivered him back to us."

Jeradon thought for a moment of where he was and assumed he had been brought back to a Rojin outpost. But then there was mention of The Father. "You mean your leader? Your King?"

The older woman took a while to respond to Jeradon's questioning. "King is too small a word and we have many leaders scattered across Erth. He knows everything. Even who you are, Jeradon Horncastle...the Third, to be precise."

"I..."

"Seems you have something in common with the Sea Wolf and the gargoyle, although you and the boy have fallen from a far higher place. You will rest. When you are ready The Father would like to meet the man responsible for slaughtering so many of his people."

VIII

I've been here before, he thought…

A strange thing then happened to the Commander. He was no longer aware of the village, the smell of death surrounding him and the screams of those who fell at his command. Instead he was standing on a grassy plain, a cool breeze ruffling his cloak. The sun shone against his bloodied and corroding armour, and all the while the girl and her mother stood there, never taking their eyes off him.

Either this woman's a Rojin witch…or I've overdosed on zetameen, he tried to convince himself. The woman placed her daughter on the grass as he lowered his gun, nausea washing over him like a tidal wave. For a moment he thought he heard a voice. *You will see all…*

A shot rang out and as it did the man's vision disintegrated. Suddenly he was back in the village. The woman fell forward to the ground, her daughter screaming out and bursting into tears. The Commander dropped his gun, retching as he stumbled forward. Wiping his mouth, he looked up at the other Guildsman who stood where the woman had a moment before; his plasma gun still smoking.

The Guildsman then proceeded to aim at the little girl who lay huddled against her dead mother.

"Lieutenant, stop!" shouted the Commander raising his arm.

The Lieutenant withdrew his weapon and with what seemed like little respect, snapped at his Commander, "This is the last one."

"Back down!"

"But..."

"That's an order!".

The Lieutenant holstered his gun and before long the rest of the crusaders had gathered behind him, looking down at the girl weeping over her dead mother. The Commander stood and stared before addressing his men.

"Anything?" asked the Commander, unclipping his face guard.

A Guildsman stepped forward. "Nothing Commander Horncastle, just peasants, worm farmers and the odd Rojin missionary. Although I believe most of their missionaries and perhaps even their leader are elsewhere."

"Did we actually keep anyone alive long enough to ask questions?" Jeradon's voice was becoming agitated. "Or have we forgotten what we are looking for? Perhaps we're merely using it as an excuse to wipe out as many of these people as we can?" He continued gesturing to the little girl, spitting out the taste that had formed in his mouth.

"Sir...?" puzzled the Guildsman.

"This crusade has taken years and we haven't come across anything that resembles what we're looking for. It could be anywhere. Farmers, you say? Then these people won't even have protronium supplies!"

The Commander's Lieutenant spoke up. "Are you losing faith, Commander?"

"There is nothing here. If there is, it is not our time to find it."

"What are you saying, that we give up?"

"That's exactly what I'm saying. We're searching for

something that may not even exist. It exists in our minds to give us justice to our killing. This is what the Emperor wants."

There was a deadly silence. Never had he spoke with such a negative attitude in front of his men and briefly, he questioned himself. *What am I saying? Has the witch possessed me?* His conscience had never been so loud and clear; it had found a voice, a true voice. For a moment he thought there were voices inside his head, before realising it was the whispering amongst his unit.

Jeradon removed his cloak, placing it over the dead mother; never had he shown so much empathy. He noticed a book gripped in her hand and picked it up.

The Lieutenant unclipped his face guard, retracted his visor and pulled off his helmet to reveal red shaven hair, "Have you gone mad, Commander? Just put the child out of its misery and let's make our way further north as planned."

"The girl stays alive, Lieutenant."

"She's as good as dead then."

"Let the Erth decide her fate, not Newton. If she's lucky, the rest af the missionaries have not travelled far. As for us, we make our way back as soon as possible."

"The Emperor won't stand for this," the Lieutenant shouted as the drop ship began to fire its engines.

"He'll send others to replace us. There are already a hundred other units aimlessly scouring Erth as we speak. We've had our taste of blood long enough, Jakahn."

"No. I want to taste The Father's blood! When we find him, we find the artefact."

Commander Horncastle waited a moment for Lieutenant Jakahn to calm down. "Then you shall do it under your own command." he stated as he turned and made his way aboard.

Nine

There was no pain at all, other than his aching heart.

Pirian watched his mother's face disappear as he slowly began to open his eyes. In shock, he sat bolt upright, lost for words.

The room resembled a cave that had been furnished with strange looking items, which seemed to be growing from the walls. Light shone in from a large opening the other side of the room, leading out to a veranda where his father stood.

He turned and walked over to his son. "How are you feeling?"

For a moment Pirian didn't recognise his father's bearded face and thick hair. "I feel...fine."

Brushing his own hair with his hand, he then looked at the mark on his arm. It had become less prominent and paler in colour. However, as his father inspected it more closely he noticed how much it had spiralled in both directions, in a figure of eight pattern covering most of his son's upper arm.

There was no pain. In fact, Pirian felt there was an odd, ornate beauty about the spreading mark.

Jeradon stroked his beard in concern, trying to distract from his son's condition. "You need to get dressed."

"Dad?" Pirian steadied himself as he attempted to stand up, "What is this place...where are we?"

"We've been brought to the Rojin capital - Yodann, I believe. They've had us in quarantine for the past two months."

"And we've been asleep for two months?" Pirian placed both his hands on his head in shock as his father nodded. Surely his father was mistaken? It only seemed as though a few hours had passed since they were all aboard *The General*. His stomach sank as the realisation of what had happened to them began to take hold. A thousand pictures flashed through his head as he stumbled to the balcony, the view taking his breath away.

Although the land that stretched out before him was not as green as Pirian imagined it would be, the brightness of the sun was enough to lift his spirits. He assumed autumn had arrived early, expecting to see the vibrant colours of a land much like his father's Greenhouses. Instead, the valley was rustic in colour, grounded in all its natural beauty and far more pleasing to the eye than Newton's cold steel.

Beyond the outer walls a huge forest spread as far as Pirian could see, resembling twisted skeletons. There was a distinct lack of foliage, yet it still looked mesmerising. A great river, swept off into the distance pointing towards what looked like a more barren land.

As he gazed along the canyon walls, he could see that the room they were in was one of many small caves. The orange stonework was dry, and weathered by the winds that blew along the valley. Above the buildings were sluggish air machines that looked like giant insects, suspended by leathery balloons. Most were anchored, while others moved slowly over the city.

Pirian closed his eyes and then opened them again. He wasn't dreaming. Holding on to the veranda, he slowly looked over the edge. Below he could see hundreds of other verandas scattered and jutting out along the canyon.

Panicking, he shut his eyes quickly. There was no dizziness, only the fear of looking down as he hesitated, expecting the wall to twist and sway.

"Pirian. Don't overdo it."

"I need to know…" he replied, leaning further forward, his eyes still shut, afraid of the nausea taking control. Opening one eye, he turned his head, unable to look down.

Jeradon lurched forward concerned that Pirian would fall, "You don't feel sick?"

"No. Just my eyes, they're a little unfocussed. I don't think I can look that far down yet. This place…this place has a stronger effect on me than the Greenhouses."

"So it should. Your feet are finally on the ground," replied his father.

"It's like…like I can feel the Erth." Pirian's eyes refocused on the room, sending him off balance. He thought for a moment, still in disbelief that he was amongst the Rojin. "They found us."

Remembering his father's past, he realised what this meant.

"With the help of the gargoyle." Jeradon paced the room. "We have to be cautious Pirian, I have no idea what is going to happen to us."

"But we'll be ok, won't we?"

Jeradon was stunned by his son's naivety. "I'm afraid we cannot avoid my past…here of all places. Now, more than ever, it's caught up with me"

"But that was the past. You've changed, you're who you're supposed to be."

"I'm not sure the Rojin will look on it in the same way. We have been summoned by a man called The Father."

"The Father…?"

"He has been nothing more than a whisper to the Newtonians. Faceless, nameless; we have no idea if it is one man, or one of many. He knows the answers that many have looked for, rumoured to hold the only answer Newton has ever sought. The key to immortality. This 'Father' sees into the very heart of a person; he's become the wind, a legend, a myth. The Guild in which I once served searched the Erth for this man in an attempt to find their precious artefact. They are still looking, but they have never even come close."

"He was never in any of the stories."

"He *was* the stories," replied Jeradon.

Piran looked confused. If The Father was at the heart of all he had read about, then everything he had learnt about the Rojin must have had a far deeper meaning. He was once again reminded of where he was. "I can't believe we are in the Rojin capital."

"Neither can I. It doesn't make sense. Especially them knowing who I am."

"They know? But how?"

"The gargoyle must have told them. Seems it was his ticket back into the city. Vagabond and the Captain are also outcasts; whatever they have done, they'll be treated the same way as us."

"Execution?" asked Pirian apprehensively.

"I won't lie to you, Pirian. The Rojin have methods and they will take a life without a moment's thought. But I am hoping it is far quicker than any Newtonian's torture. They create life, they watch it grow. Yet they know something else about death that detaches themselves from this world. If you are lucky, they will take your head."

Pirian was puzzled, rather than shocked at the thought of a Rojin execution. He'd faced the worst so far and he was sick of death staring him in the face. "I don't understand why Vagabond would risk coming back to the city. It doesn't make any sense, knowing he'd be killed."

"It's because I am of importance to the Rojin. They have their own whisper, their own myth. A man that has gone by many names over the years, while slaughtering their people."

"But you told me people kill when there is a war. That it's

unavoidable."

"If only it were that simple, Pirian. War, death; they are far more complicated than that."

"You were following orders, controlled and under the influence of a drug."

Jeradon managed a tiny smile. His son was wise. Indeed, in the times he led the Guild he *was* following orders while under the influence of the Dosage. It had controlled his thoughts and actions since birth. But this did not make his guilt go away. Without zetameen his memories were crystal clear, his emotions no longer cut off. Everything he had done flooded back the moment he was awakened. If it was simply because of war, Jeradon would have found it far easier to be honest with his son. Sometimes he still wished he was taking the Dosage to help him forget.

"You changed. You're more like them now," added Pirian hopefully.

"If that is what they believe, it is the only thing I can see saving us."

"We're not exactly being treated like prisoners. It's strange, I feel safer here than on Newton."

Jeradon looked at his son as the two women he had already met appeared at the doorway. "You are to come with us now."

Jeradon and Pirian were lead along the valley pass surrounding what they thought was the city. Accompanied by the two women and four armoured guards, wearing similar attire to those that had brought them to the capital; they made their way closer to the ominous enclosed structure before them.

"Forgive me for not introducing myself earlier. It is hard to so willingly give one's name to the killer of our people. You may call me a witch if it comforts you, in the same way I may call you a slaughterer. We often go by the title Missionary, Priest, or in my case High Priestess. My name is Ersula Cordwain…" the Rojin witch, stopped at the boundaries of the city "…And this is our Temple."

They stood before the magnificent building. The central Temple was a city in itself, made up of both inner and outer structures. Great looming towers were spaced out around its walls, while a larger, more dominant tower was positioned centrally. Its lower portions connected to many internal buildings and walkways, leading off into the distance. Bedraggled flags hung down from outside the Temple's great doors, a figure of eight on its side; symbolising their leader's supposed immortality. The huge structure must have been built centuries ago and evoked a distinctive atmosphere, even in the daylight.

There was a tension in the air as the Temple's doors opened and the guards lead them in. Upon entering, they continued to marvel at the serenity of the Temple's entrance hall.

Jeradon's eyes were drawn to the far end of the aisle. In the distance, either side of another large door, were giant stained glass windows depicting all kinds of imagery from Erth's past. Looking either side of him, he could see that the walls were covered in detailed depictions of their people. Up to waist height were symbols, carved within the stonework; Rojin hieroglyphs, including the figure of eight he was all too familiar with.

At head height was a deep band of colourful, sequential images, stretching the whole length of the Temple's entrance hall. Separated by a deep recess were detailed paintings that must have taken a lifetime to complete. Jeradon was in as much awe as his son. The Temple was far grander than anything he had seen on Newton. There was a sense of history, a feeling that these people were proud of their origins and certainly hadn't forgotten their past.

As they walked further into the Temple, Jeradon noticed how awestruck his son was, gazing at the magnificent pillars and statues that dwarfed many of the examples on Newton.

Upon approaching the end of the aisle, two large internal doors loomed in front of them; symmetrical figurines were carved into their surface, reflecting what looked like part of the same story Jeradon and Pirian had noticed on the walls. It was as though he was walking the pages of a book, and that the doors in front of him held further answers.

"The boy must stay here," commanded Ersula.

Remaining calm, Jeradon stood assertively in front of her. "He isn't to leave my sight."

"The boy stays here. Not even a child of Rojin sees The Father."

"Then your Father can wait till he is a man. Then perhaps I will walk through those doors with you."

The younger of the two witches looked up at her elder.

Silence.

"The boy will be safe here. He is of no threat to us."

"But I am?" Jeradon paused. "Do you see an army behind me, Rojin Witch?"

Ersula's eyes flickered black, then shimmered blue for a brief moment. "You are of no threat to us, Jeradon Horncastle. Not even ten thousand men following your orders have made us fear you. You have been awakened. A seed has been planted and along the way you have become nothing more than a broken shell, clinging onto a memory, while you have tried so hard to forget the past. You have seen more than many Rojin have. Your body is free of Zetameen and you are only now beginning to see, to taste…to breathe. You have not followed orders for over a decade and have tried to build something you have not fully understood. Have you listened to the whispers in your head? Your conscience? Your waking life? Is it a voice you recognise? You have lost your identity, Jeradon Horncastle, but at the same time you have discovered who you really are. Listen to those whispers more carefully; they tell you everything. Even how to save your wife."

Jeradon let out an uncontrollable breath, then clenched his teeth. He felt as though he had been emptied like a glass of water. Every notion the witch had picked up on was far closer to the bone than he had ever thought possible. He could not look her in the eye any longer.

"Your son *will* be safe." Ersula had not taken her eyes off Jeradon. "Now please, come."

"I'll be ok, Dad," said Pirian approaching his father's side.

Jeradon looked down at his son. The Temple's strange power, its overwhelming magnitude, seemed intimidating, yet at the same time he knew what his son had meant about feeling safe within the Temple's walls.

"My Select here and these guards will watch over your son. I'm sure he has many questions to ask," said Ersula as the younger of the two stepped forward.

Jeradon glanced over at her, pausing briefly before finally walking through the opening doors.

Pirian watched as the doors slowly closed behind his father.

Standing for a moment, the young female Rojin soon broke the uncomfortable silence.

"It is a great honour to be called by The Father. Especially for an enemy of our people."

"We are as much an enemy of Newton as you are," replied Pirian.

"Then if it comforts you, this may be the reason our fathers are to meet."

Pirian's eyes widened slightly. "I hope that's true."

Underneath the young women's hood, Pirian was sure he saw a slight smile. He looked at the two remaining guards standing motionless either side of the doors, while the young woman continue to study him.

"I have yet to know your name," she asked.

"Pirian. My name is Pirian."

"I am pleased to meet you Pirian, my name is Kira." She paused, motioning to their surroundings. "This all must be very…very 'different' for you."

"Yes." replied Pirian, distracted.

"A boy of Newton. You have never set foot on Erth have you?"

"No."

"Is this why you look so, well…ill?"

Pirian was insulted, even though he was well aware of how pale he looked in comparison to her. "I…I suppose so. We are contained most of the time. Erth is all very new to me."

"I can imagine. Your head was shaved when they brought you here."

"All Newtonian's heads are shaved. It strips away identity. Only those in The Hierarchy grow their hair; it's their sign of power and control."

Kira shook her head slightly. "You *really* are controlled."

"More than you realise."

"Yet you are free of the Dosage?" she asked.

"Yes." Pirian replied, feeling there was no need to say anymore than that.

There was silence for a moment. "I have not heard of this before. I have always imagined your city to be as cruel and twisted as your people's image of the Rojin. That anyone free of the Dosage would be…"

"Outcast." confirmed Pirian.

"Or worse."

"Execution isn't uncommon."

"As I thought. I know enough about your people. I guess it's difficult not to. I am hoping one day that I will be able to help protect our own people further from your flying city." stated Kira.

"I only know a little about the Rojin from books."

"Really? I didn't realise Newton had books."

"It doesn't. It's illegal, but dad had one that he gave me. One that was brought back from one of his expeditions."

"Then no doubt your image of the Rojin is more open minded."

"I'd like to think that." Although the majority of her face was hidden, Kira had given him enough response to comfort him further. "Will I get to see more of your city?"

"That is up to The Father. Right now I don't think that would be such a good idea. People are already curious and once they find out there are Newtonians in the capital, there will be panic and retaliation. This is why you are confined to the inner Temple from now. Our people are already upset enough at the return of Lomax and Vagabond."

"They must have done something very serious." asked Pirian.

"All I know is that they stole something of importance. So important they were sent away and told never to return, unless they brought it back with them. That if they returned without it, they would face execution."

Pirian thought for a moment. "Yet they felt bringing us to your attention was important enough to risk that?"

"There are many questions here and many answers. I'm sure in time you will hear as much as The Father wants you to hear."

The interior of the temple was even more inspiring than the entrance. Jeradon's eyes were averted to another stained glass window at the far end of the aisle. Similar to the first two he had seen, it depicted yet another scene from the Rojin culture. A figure stood in the centre, its hands reaching up towards a strange

JAMES JOHNSON

circular object, depicted in yellow glass, much like the sun.

Steps led up to several figures kneeling either side of another. Although the light through the window lit the main aisle, the figures kneeling underneath were cast in shadow from the lower walls and surrounding statues.

Escorted up the steps by Ersula, Jeradon finally came to a halt several feet away from the lone figures. Not a single breath could be made out amongst them, as they sat motionless in a state of meditation. Ersula knelt and addressed the central figure, whispering in his ear.

Then there was a breath that cut Ersula short, followed by silence as she stepped back awaiting a reply. The atmosphere was calm. The man in shadow had all the time in the world to reply.

Jeradon could sense his glare from out of the shadows.

One more breath and the man rose in one fluid move, as though he had no legs at all. He took a step forward, his bulk silhouetted in front of the glass window behind him. "The Fallen." he stated, "Our enemy, yet...believed to be one of prophetic means." The man gave out a disgruntled laugh as though it was a joke. "A cliché we can no longer brush aside. Prophecies, destinies. Our fate, the fate of the world. Most of us are tired of hearing it. It seems every story comes to this; that at some point there will be one who saves us all. Often he doesn't even know himself. Let alone believe." The man walked forward from out of the shadows and stared into Jeradon's eyes. "What does our enemy believe?"

Jeradon didn't break eye contact. The man was a head shorter, but what he lacked in height, he certainly made up for in presence and build. He had said too much in one go to Jeradon, almost passed off as some trivial matter. Jeradon felt as though he was being tested somehow. For every story told, there was a destined answer to them all; and he had read many stories over the past twelve years. Newton had all but forgotten its history; there was no belief, let alone prophecies.

"I believe in myself and those I love…" he paused, "… Father."

Jeradon wasn't expecting laughter. He wasn't expecting their great leader to laugh at all, or even speak for that matter. The Father was beyond having to use his lips. Apparently he used his mind instead. *This isn't the Father*, he thought.

Of course I am not the Father…, the man replied as Jeradon looked around for the hidden voice. "…My name is Harad Vaseesh and I am merely his eyes, but more often his Voice." Harad continued the traditional way and began to circle Jeradon. "There are many of us here in the capital that still have The Father's interests close to heart. That when he tells us of things, we must believe. The more cynical are simply still learning. I guess believing in yourself is a start, Jeradon Horncastle. Believing in those you love is far more impressive, especially for a soulless Newtonian."

Although he was dressed in simple robes, much like the men kneeling around him, Jeradon noticed that Harad was portly in stature, a rolling figure that looked as though he enjoyed his food and the Rojin beer. A good ten years older than himself, the man's double chin was covered with a groomed beard, his greying, black hair tied back in a ponytail, blond streaks intertwined with gold threading. The sides of his head were shaved revealing an ornate tattoo wrapping from temple to temple.

"What is it you want of me? Surely you should have killed me by now?"

"I guess you still have an ounce of doubt left in you. Maybe you still haven't shaken that narrow minded view that most human nature shares. Indeed, you should be dead a thousand times over for your atrocities; for the people you have slaughtered. Some of us have to look at the more important things happening than just one man. The killer of our people has many faces. You were only one of them; one of many Guildsmen, many leaders, and even many Horncastles. Yet, not one of you had ever become Hierarchy, or even the Emperor of your kingdom in the sky. You have simply been a puppet, with far more controlling strings."

"Zetameen."

"Your reliable Dosage. You haven't been seen for nearly twelve years, or at least that part of you we are more familiar with: the slaughterer of our people. Others simply took over your leadership, but they still never found what they were looking for. We fought them, we continue to fight them, don't forget what efficient, mindless killers we apparently are." Harad paused, he hadn't taken his eyes off Jeradon for a moment. "Your drug may control, but it also clouds judgement and deceives your people. We have been twisted into what Newtonians want to see and fear. What better reason do your people need to use your precious zetameen, than fear? I guess it makes the killing part all the more easy."

"I know all too well about the Dosage. As for stories and prophecies, I am not a religious man. I have very little faith left in anything," replied Jeradon.

"Yet you have brought this on yourself. I think you have more faith than you would care to admit. How else would you have created the habitats; your precious Greenhouses?"

Jeradon watched Harad continue to circle him, "How much do you people know?"

"We know as much as The Father allows us to know. Though most of what has happened recently has been confirmed by the gargoyle."

"The Emperor…?"

"Yes, the Emperor. Whether you killed him or not is irrelevant to us. You have always stabbed each other in the backs in your greed for power. Seems every one of your rulers has fallen at the hands of your own people, that Newton is never truly satisfied as one person replaces the next. Your own downfall, Jeradon Horncastle, began the day you stopped killing. If it is true that you grew these habitats, then we have all the reason to doubt you murdering your ruler. Because only then, after creating something and watch it grow, would you have learned how precious life really is."

"My family was threatened, even the habitats themselves were being destroyed!" snapped Jeradon.

"Hmm…what goes around comes around. This is where the Rojin differ. Where a Newtonian would kill with no feeling, a Rojin would survey the implications. It is important to channel that energy elsewhere."

Jeradon sighed. "It was my *feelings* that took control. My son was in danger, and my wife…she…Perhaps I'd have been better off still under the influence."

"No…you wouldn't have. You were still following your instinct. You had built a great deal to lose. Not just the Greenhouses, but a family. A family you never expected to feel anything for."

"It felt…for the first time in my life; it felt right. That I had to do something more important."

"Taking life or creating life? Tell me, are you still referring to the Emperor's death or studying our culture?" asked Harad out of curiosity. He looked at Jeradon bow his head slightly. "There is much more to this it seems. Maybe you did kill to protect what you had built for so long. Creating life is more rewarding than taking it. You must have had *some* vision to renounce your faith in the Guild. But you were still unclear of why you were following your ideas. Somehow you felt as though you were following a dream instead. A dream that you made up the answers to, even if it meant deceiving your Emperor while you experimented. When you were ready you would have come to us."

How did this man know so much? It was as though Harad was reading him, much like Ersula had. Jeradon was unsure of their intent, unsure of the Rojin power to delve into a person's mind. What was being addressed confused him. It was beginning to feel more and more like a test rather than a trial.

"Come to you? I killed your people, my unit alone slaughtered thousands in order to find what we were looking for. How on Erth could I come to you?"

"We would have found you. We did find you, and in the process you were awakened. It was a shame I wasn't there at the time." the man stopped circling Jeradon and walked back into the shadows, as if to conceal a reaction he didn't want Jeradon to witness. "But if I was there, I would not have lived to see you today. I'd have been slaughtered too, as with the rest of those I had taught. Including my wife…"

Jeradon's stomach turned. As if his guilt wasn't taunting him enough, "Your wife…?"

From the shadows the man answered him, "The woman that died at your feet. The Rojin witch who gave you your visions, your ideas and your dreams, Jeradon Horncastle. Even your nightmares."

IX

Death was all Jeradon could see.

Every night the nightmares would deliver the same visions. He was being tormented; those that had died at his hands playing out in slow motion, over and over again. Men, women and children fell before him as every outpost was burnt to the ground. There was no stopping the slaughter of the Rojin.

The nightmare always ended up in a familiar place, reminding him of the moment he was awakened. Stretched out before him was a golden land, as protronium seeped through the Erth. Gradually the bright yellow amber changed to orange, then blood red. A lone, faceless figure stood on the crimson horizon. The land was then engulfed by a vibrant green and the figure's face became visible. It was his own, before it transformed into his father's; then he recognised his grandfather's as the features continued to morph into, what he assumed, were generations of Horncastles. The likeness was distinctive, yet this was blood that Jeradon could never have known about, even if the Dosage hadn't suppressed his family history.

Finally the vibrant green engulfed the figure, before he would wake abruptly in a cold sweat.

Jeradon knew that if he wanted the nightmares to be over, he should do what was being asked of him.

"As of this moment my Lord, I request to be relieved of command."

Kneeling before the Emperor, Jeradon Horncastle bowed his head, awaiting his reply. The great throne room stretched out behind him. Metalic pillars and Statues of previous Newtonian leaders were bathed in the sunlight that shone down through the glass canopy. Standing as witness to Jeradon's resignation were both Jakahn and Bendarick.

Emperor Surel sat motionless, while two guards stood either side of his throne. His hair was a dark grey, becoming whiter as it reached his temples. As with all the people on Newton his skin was of a pale complexion and wrinkled with age. Jeradon lifted his head, still awaiting his response. Surel's presence was that of an arrogant leader who relied heavily on his Hierarchy to help him make the right decisions. But he knew the signs of being awakened all too well. No one needed to point out being free of the Dosage to Surel.

"Your father would be disgraced. You are the greatest leader the Guild has ever seen, and you wish to walk away from it?" He gave out a disgruntled growl as Jeradon continued to kneel, catching the Emperor's eye. "Disgraced."

"With all due respect my Lord, this is something I have to do. I would have told my father the same."

Jeradon noticed Jakahn twitching, eager to speak up.

Surel put his hand to his chin, leaning forward on his throne. "You think he would have listened? His commitment was unrivalled. You are unfocussed, Commander. Just because you have led my men, you are still not worthy enough to become Hierarchy and no longer use the Dosage." He paused. "You must think I am stupid. I can see the clarity in your eyes - and it seems it is affecting more than your judgement."

Jeradon had left himself wide open, but deep down he didn't care. From the moment he was awakened he had never been shown so much. All he was concerned about was answering the visions swimming around in his mind; for better or for worse.

"My judgement is clearer than ever," he replied.

"Clear enough for you to turn your back on the Guild?"

"I believe so, my Lord."

"And who would take your place?"

"I am sure you have already decided for me."

Surel leant back into his throne looking up at Jakahn.

"I have no doubt your Lieutenant would accept." Pausing, Surel stared into Jakahn's eyes, "I believe he accepted a long time ago. Perhaps the Guild will have more luck finding the artefact under his leadership."

Jakahn stepped forward. "Thank you, Lord Surel."

"There is no need to thank me…Commander." Surel paused, "You have Horncastle to thank for that. Now, please leave us, you have a command to brief."

Jakahn bowed and turned as Bendarick stood motionless. "Are you with me, Lieutenant?" asked Jakahn before he proceeded.

For one moment Bendarick relapsed and thought Jeradon might break eye contact with the Emperor. All he needed was a glance to know what his former Commander was doing. Then the dosage kicked in again, "Yes sir." he replied as they walked away.

Pondering once more, Surel beckoned Jeradon to rise. "What could be so important for you to forget your Dosage and walk away from the Guild, Horncastle?"

"I have…ideas, my Lord."

Jeradon could see Surel beginning to boil. "You have what?" he snapped, "Newton does not credit you to 'think' Horncastle. Ideas are dangerous. This is an outrage! You will take the Dosage and if you refuse I will have no choice but to administer treatment."

"My Lord. The ideas are of benefit to Newton. I believe I have seen the Rojin secret, that the 'idea', the vision I have had, may help to find what we are looking for. Help us understand our enemy."

Surel calmed down slightly. "Help us in what way?"

"How things are grown, which will hopefully lead us to understanding their biological weapons."

Surel's eyes lit up at the notion, "The Darathia."

Jeradon nodded, "Perhaps even their symbiont blades."

"I see. Fight fire with fire."

"This is why I must leave the Guild. I need as much time as possible to begin the work."

"Explain to me. How will this help us find what we are looking for?"

"That is the problem, my Lord. I'm not sure. But the vision I had was so strong, I believe that by growing what the Rojin have, may lead to our people being able to see what I see."

"Visions? You mean ideas?"

"The visions I have had led to the ideas my Lord. It was brought on by one of the Rojin witches we encountered on our last scourge."

"You are testing me, Horncastle. I used to respect you. Now you are telling me you want to learn more about their ways? That you had visions brought on by one of these Erth dwelling scum? They have infected your mind!"

"Indeed. But think about it my Lord, for one moment. If we begin to revert back to growth, this may be how the Rojin probe our minds. If we are able to learn how to do that - if growing a natural habitat here on Newton is the key, then surely it is worth a try. We learn how to read minds, we will find their leader."

Surel's eyes lit up, "Of course. Except you will continue to use the Dosage. Your position does not yet warrant freedom from that, Horncastle."

Jeradon controlled his frustration at the fact Surel had not listened to him entirely, "If you expect me to use what I see - to learn and create what is necessary, then you must allow me to be zetameen free." He paused pushing the Emperor further. "I will also need helpers."

Surel pondered some more. Jeradon could tell he wasn't happy about this. However, the Emperor knew of the benefits and if it meant Jeradon was given the same privilege of Newton's Hierarchy, then so be it. "You will learn their secrets and harness their powers?"

"That is my intention. The plan is to begin work as soon as possible at Alva city."

"How long do you need?" asked Surel.

"How long was the great Fara given for curing the plague? How much time did it take Sir Ivar Gul to levitate this city?" Surel was surprised by Jeradon's sudden knowledge of Erth history. "As long as it takes my Lord."

Ten

There was a sound travelling on the breeze, complex yet somewhat reassuring. It began to rise, echoing within the chambers of the temple. Kira noticed that Pirian was once again distracted as he slowly began to walk down the aisle. One of the guards moved forward to prevent him from making his way any further. Standing in his path, Kira placed her hand on the guard's forearm, then turned and slowly followed Pirian.

The sound was becoming clearer as Pirian's gaze was drawn upwards. He had never heard anything like it; a perfect soundtrack to the images that surrounded him; so much beauty and elegance, as though it was being controlled somehow. He continued to walk the length of the aisle back towards the entrance. For the first time since he had left his mother his mind was filled with happiness, his problems almost forgotten. Then he reminded himself where his mother was.

Kira gazed at Pirian, noticing how new everything was to the young boy.

"That sound…" he said.

"You've never heard music before?"

"Never. I have never heard sounds like that. I can't describe it. Back home, there are many noises Addicts listen to. But never anything as complex as this, just repetitive sounds."

"These sounds are a huge part of our culture. Just one of the many ways we express and entertain ourselves. It helps to take our mind off more serious matters."

Pirian's eyes widened. "I have to hear more. Please, take me to the city. Show me more of these sounds and the other things you speak of."

"That wouldn't be wise."

"It's just until now I've only read about Erth, I never knew that one day I would actually be here - no child of Newton has ever visited this world." Pirian chuckled to himself, "It's weird. Dad's enemy made my dream come true."

"Your Emperor?"

"Yes. Although Newton has a new ruler now. Funny, Dad used to give him orders and eventually *he* ends up as the order itself."

Kira seemed to grow uncomfortable. She turned her back. "Your father, he was in charge of this man?"

"A long time ago yes. Before I was born. He was Dad's second in command."

"This new ruler of yours..." Kira's tone changed, "What name does he go by?"

"Rayal, his name is Rayal Jakahn." answered Pirian.

Kira stood motionless for a moment, before she turned her back, "Tell me more."

Jeradon began to squeeze his own hands in agitation. The vision of the Rojin's wife dying before his feet, was the very first image he remembered when he was awakened; the very image that awoke him from his epiphany.

Harad still stood before him, remaining silent in the shadows, before speaking, "The outpost you attacked; your very last command, happened to be my own. I had nurtured those people during my missions and had made it my home until The Father needed me here. My group and I happened to be spreading the word elsewhere that day."

"Her blood was amongst the small amount that was never

on my hands."

Harad was silent for a moment before answering Jeradon. "Is that right? Does her face haunt you? Perhaps it does. I've almost forgotten what she looks like, even though she meant the Erth to me."

"Her face is not the one I remember. There was a child; a young girl. Your daughter? We...I left her alive."

Harad nodded in response. "Yes, she survived."

"It was my order to leave her be. That was the moment I became aware. Your wife's death was the first thing I saw. The child's face is all I remember, then the dreams. They only show me yellow and green, then everything turns to red." Jeradon paused, his breathing becoming far deeper, "Your wife wanted me to see something...infected my mind with..."

"The truth," answered Harad. "We often have to find the answer to truth by ourselves. We know that you returned to Newton and followed the truth. In order to do this, you deceived your Emperor as much as you could. He became incompetent from his growing sickness."

Jeradon felt wide open. "Newton is controlled by lies."

"Indeed. It took a Newtonian to lie to another Newtonian, so you could learn what the aching desire was inside. You developed a curiosity, a wandering spirit, which led you to give life and grow more into the person you should have been. Your thirst for learning the answers led you back to Erth every time - and finally when Newton feared what you had created, they gave you back to us. Seems irony can be married to fate." There was a long pause as Harad slowly moved from out of the shadow, looking Jeradon in the eye. "The cruellest irony however, is how the man spoken of in our scriptures, turns out to be a slaughterer of our people. The faith of the Rojin it seems, is to be put to the test...more than ever."

"What do you want of me?" asked Jeradon.

"Perhaps it is best to ask The Father."

Pirian had told Kira as much as possible about Emperor Jakahn. There was the burning of the Greenhouses and what he believed to be the framing of his father. He had not mentioned his illness, the weakness had caused him enough problems so far. Taking everything in, Kira hadn't said much in between, she was as curious about Jakahn and Newton as Pirian was about her own culture.

"Gana must have been looking over you." She proceeded to make her way over to a plant that grew out of a wall. Water trickled into a large font, resembling a hollowed tree trunk. Pirian looked up once again towards the overpowering heights of the inner chamber. He had never heard of Gana, but assumed it was their God. Until he had built up the confidence he needed he would not ask any more questions.

Picking up a shell-like cup, Kira scooped water from the font. "You should drink, you must be thirsty sleeping so long. Here." Kira held the shell out to Pirian. The liquid was ice cold and tasted sweet. Gulping the drink back he made his own way over to the plant as he filled the shell once again. "Definitely thirsty," she observed.

He finished another two shells before wiping his mouth. Then, a slight nauseous feeling overcame him. Swallowing, he gagged, swaying slightly. Grabbing the font he regained his balance, panicking as he attempted to turn away. But his troubled arm was stuck to the font.

"Pirian?"

"Stay away." The nauseous feeling had now been replaced by the return of the dull ache growing more painful in his arm. He felt the mark swelling and growing further. Looking down at his hand he noticed it was becoming a similar colour to the surface of the font, his own skin merging into subtle browns and greens of the trunk. His veins throbbed and began to protrude like the vines of a plant. "What...what have you done?" Pirian groaned from the pain as the guards glanced over towards Kira. She once again raised her hand to them so Pirian wasn't antagonised any further. "You've...poisoned me?"

Kira kept quiet and tried to approach him once again to see what was happening. Pirian attempted to conceal his arm, clutching it even tighter.

"We haven't poisoned you, Pirian. What is it? Are you infected? We have to know right away if you are." Kira sounded genuinely concerned, but Pirian was so confused, he was unsure. He felt vulnerable without his father and was angry with himself for letting him go. Now the pain in his arm had returned, only adding to the stress.

Kira stayed a few feet away from him unable to do anything. She looked on as his head tilted backwards. The pain became greater. All the while Pirian thought of his mother. It was almost comforting to imagine her holding him. Feeling as though his arm was about to explode, Pirian placed his other arm into the font. As soon as he did, the pain was no more and his troublesome arm slowly came free, reducing in size.

Stumbling backwards he fell to his knees catching his breath.

Approaching him slowly, Kira looked down at Pirian as he examined his arm. The swelling had vanished, but once again the mark had grown further up and down his arm - from wrist to shoulder. "I'm ok...I'm ok," he said catching his breath. "Maybe...maybe I'm still adjusting."

"Adjusting to what?" queried Kira.

"To having my feet on the ground."

Kira didn't get too close to Pirian for fear of catching something. "You must see Doctor Moku. I'm sure he'll have an explanation."

Maybe the boy and his father should have been left longer in quarantine after all, she thought.

Harad and Ersula escorted Jeradon to the top of the Rojin Temple. The stairs seemed to go on forever as they twisted up towards the top of the tower, before finally spilling out into an ornate corridor, pointing to an open archway. Once again there were paintings, carvings and statues decorating the upper portion of the temple. Either side of the archway were two more guards. Harad and Ersula came to a halt and beckoned Jeradon to go on alone.

"Only you will enter. Whatever you are shown or told is meant only for you." instructed Harad.

As Jeradon entered through the archway he noticed that the large circular room was lined with what he thought were dozens of statues - but he realized they were in fact more Rojin guards.

A large curved window was situated at the end of the room. The glass was knitted into the stonework with coils of plant life and carvings that seemed to grow from out of the walls - much like every other appliance he had seen so far. As Jeradon made his way closer, he could make out the outline of a figure behind the glass; blurred and obscured. With every step that Jeradon took, the room seemed to become brighter as he came to a halt in front of the figure. He looked on in disbelief as the blurred window began to focus - showing a clearer picture of the presence behind.

The figure inside was almost skeletal; frail and shrivelled. Suspended by vines that helped maintain a seating posture, Jeradon could make out that the plants were actually connected to the figure, as though keeping him alive. They shivered slightly - the figure twitching in response as it swayed in the arms of the giant plant. Leaf-like appendages that covered the figure's dignity, were wrapped around his lower portion and also hung down from each shoulder leaving the arms bare. A mass of white hair and beard seemed to be continually growing, moving away from the face. As the growing mass swept backwards, it finally fell to the ground where it was absorbed by the bottomless floor. The vines moved the figure upright and closer towards the glass. The blank face was clearer now, his cloudy eyes unfocussed.

Astonished at the ancient figure before him Jeradon couldn't believe what he was seeing. Barely alive, the fragile man that hung motionless in front of him would have taken nothing more than a sneeze to blow over. He had never seen anyone so weak, so vulnerable. This was the strength of the Rojin - their great leader? The Father was nothing more than skin and bone kept alive by plants and surrounded by dozens of guards.

But the strength of the voice that invaded Jeradon's head was something else entirely. It was one he recognised - the same one that had shown him many things before, the same that had awoken him over a decade ago. Until now he had always thought of the voice as his waking conscience. Eyes wide, Jeradon stood perfectly still as the images flooded into his head. He was unable to differentiate the past and the future.

You will see all, the voice stated once again as Jeradon began to double over. There was too much to take in, but he realised for the first time exactly, why he was still alive.

As quickly as the visions and the voice had entered his mind they vanished. Sweat ran down his face as something opened on the floor before him. A slab retracted, a solid rectangular plinth holding what looked like a stone sword rose to waist height. He examined it closer. It resembled many of the katanac symbiont blades he had come across in the past. Only this one looked dead. More than dead - in fact the sword was nothing more than a lifeless, fossilised husk of its former self. Much like The Father.

Jeradon knew however, that this was why he was here. He had after all, just been shown exactly what to do with it.

X

"It was found with the last group of animals brought into quarantine." stated one of Jeradon's gardeners.

Examining the animal, Jeradon ran his fingers over its shell. "Seems he's been in the wars. Place him with the other reptiles, ten days should be enough."

"It's already been sick. Really didn't like the flight back."

"I see. Just keep him separate in case he contaminates the others."

Jeradon's 'Arks' had brought back many examples of animal and plant life. The first of his Greenhouses, Greenhouse One, was being built at Alva and was still in its early stages and needed as much variety as possible for the environment to prosper. Jeradon's understanding from his dreams was that every living organism he could find would benefit each other and work as a whole. Everything, from the choice of soil to the animals, both prey and predator, would affect the way the habitat evolved. If all went well and the habitat grew strong enough to supply the answers they needed, the plan was to build a Greenhouse at the other two surrounding cities, Beda and Gam.

Finding it very hard to trust any volunteer that Surel had sent to help him, Jeradon was very careful about how much he told the gardeners. One woman in particular was sent directly from Surel's Hierarchy. Although she had not worked her way up enough to be free of the Dosage, it was all the more reason to be mindful of how much was divulged. All his workers were

Addicts, which was the main reason they were so responsive and committed. But Jeradon, at the end of the day, knew where their loyalties lay.

The woman explained what was planned. "Lord Surel has sent me to check up on your progress every five days. Whenever anything significant is found out, you are to report to myself." Her voice was very much like every other Newtonian; a monotone pattern that stood out more than ever since Jeradon had been clean. There was a taste of zetameen in the air as she spoke. Then Jeradon realised he had seen this woman many times before - on the arms of Rayal Jakahn himself. So, this was the mistress he had spoke of, the one he had so much control over.

"That's fine. Maybe we'll also have the pleasure of having Lord Surel survey the Greenhouse?"

"Unfortunately not. His Lordship does not want to risk being contaminated. He is quite happy to survey the reports as requested."

Jeradon wasn't surprised Surel would not come anywhere near the project. However, it seemed sending other people to become 'infected' was fine. "I understand. I will see you in five days then, Neeve. Pass on my regards to Rayal when he arrives back."

Although her personality was non-existent, she was the most beautiful woman Jeradon had seen in a long time. In fact, the feelings he was experiencing were entirely new to him - he had never considered beauty in the past, and the Greenhouse was beginning to show him exactly what it meant.

Neeve bowed her head slightly in acknowledgement.

Jeradon watched her leave. *I wonder who she would truly love, free of control...free of the Dosage?*

Eleven

"All that you have seen and what The Father has told you; please, you *must* keep to yourself. You have been given The Father's blade for a reason. Only you know what must be done with it, in the same way he showed me what was to be done with you," Harad reminded Jeradon.

"I'll do my best, but my son needs far more guidance than me. Right now he is very vulnerable, his mother preys on his mind more than he shows. If we are to stay here, he needs strength, discipline. He has had no formal training - his mother and I couldn't bring ourselves to have him taken in by the Guild. I need to keep him away from death and dishonour."

"Death is unavoidable. We can teach your son how to deal with this. You are simply afraid of him following the Horncastle tradition - that one day he may also be forced to kill?"

"Yes."

"While Newton continues to bleed the Erth dry, killing is unavoidable. Your son, first and foremost, must be taught how to defend himself. The Rojin discipline will teach him the differences between life and death, defence and attack. Even the primal instincts you fear so much."

"I cannot have him pick up one of your swords, yet...." Jeradon's frustration was evident in his voice as he gripped The Father's blade in agitation. "He's still only a child."

"All Rojin are children when they pick their blade. It is how your son chooses to use the sword - a katanac blade will not make him do something he doesn't want to do. You have to understand how differently the Rojin perceive things, Jeradon. Here, a sword is not simply a sword. It is more than an extension of the arm, it is an extension of your mind, body and even your soul. It is as much alive as we are and one cannot live without the other."

"Your weapons are dying, like everything else here. Maybe he'll never have the chance to pick a blade."

"We do not lose hope. He will have as much chance as the rest of the young Rojin," replied Harad.

"And…if I agree, when will his training begin?" asked Jeradon.

"As soon as possible. I will not lie to you, the teachings will be made harder for your son. Others will make it hard for him and yourself, knowing that you are Newtonian, which is the reason you are to stay within the Temple walls. The Rojin capital has been falling apart enough the past decade, your presence is just another test for our people."

"Falling apart? You mean the contamination?"

Harad nodded as Ersula continued. "It's not just our weapons and the land, it seems the people have become contaminated with lies, that we have traitors amongst the Rojin. A couple of Newtonians may be the least of our problems."

Jeradon knew this from what The Father had shown him. He also knew what had to be done about it. He remembered the lifeless body suspended in front of him, the image embodied everything. Jeradon didn't just see a decaying man, he saw a decaying land, a decaying world. They were the very same thing.

They came to a halt on the ground floor of the temple. "Jeradon, we have been shown what we have to do. The Father knows whatever is, is right," said Harad.

Jeradon was silent for a moment before answering. "You

have my permission for Pirian to begin training. In the meantime I must speak with the wolf and gargoyle before you make any decisions on their fate."

Harad and Ersula looked at each other. If this was something The Father had shown or told Jeradon, then there was nothing they could do to prevent it.

They began to make their way back to where Kira was looking after Pirian. Harad replied, "Indeed. Although neither of them will be ready until we have questioned them further. In the meantime I suggest you and your son accompany me around the Temple's inner city."

"Allow your people to question them all you like. As long as no harm comes to them. There was a motive behind what they did all those years ago. Good or bad."

Ersula responded immediately. "Their guilt is of no concern to you."

"As I have said Priestess, if we are to cooperate, you must allow me to carry out what The Father has requested of me."

Ersula pursed her lips, eyes shimmering once again as she attempted to look into Jeradon's mind. But this time there was nothing but a wall protecting his thoughts.

No Ersula...you will leave it be. Have faith, asked Harad as she simply nodded and made her way through the doors.

Jeradon glanced at Harad then followed after Ersula.

Once he approached his son he knew something had happened. Checking his arm he was surprised at how much more the mark had grown. Curiously, Ersula glanced over to Kira.

"Is everything alright?" asked Harad.

"Everything is fine," Jeradon answered. "I'm sure it's nothing your Doctor can't handle."

Harad walked over to Kira as she bowed and pulled back

her hood. "There is to be no mention of where the boy and his father have come from, do you understand? For now keep it to yourself, not even your brother is to be told. I'm unsure of how he'd react."

"I understand, father. But...I believe he'll fit in more than we realise."

From her posture and her hidden features, Pirian had assumed Kira to be much older; at least in her late teens. Her skin was a healthy tan, eyes as dark as her black hair, tied tightly across her scalp. Blonde strands were entwined with multicoloured thread and tucked behind her ears, while heavy black coils hung down from the back of her head. It looked as though she had cut herself in the past; a visible, horizontal mark in the centre of her forehead.

She's beautiful, thought Pirian.

Jeradon had recognised the face immediately. He was more surprised that there was recognition in her own eyes - *she can't have been older than two or three when her mother was murdered.*

"It was important she accompanied Ersula when you had been brought out of quarantine. She had to know it was you that Lomax and Vagabond brought to our attention," said Harad.

Pirian was slightly confused; was there something his father hadn't told him?

"You...remember me?" Jeradon asked, unsure of what was going through Kira's head. Was she to lash out and blame him for her mother's death? How much could she actually remember?

"I remember your eyes...and how they changed. I remember the man who killed my mother and it wasn't you."

"But...your mother..."

"My mother gave you something. She lives on in me and she will see everything she gave to you carried out," she replied before Jeradon had the chance to query anything.

What about my mother? thought Pirian selfishly. He feared that his father was beginning to forget, that suddenly helping the Rojin was more important. What was all this about?

Harad walked up behind his daughter and placed his hands on her shoulders. "We have the same enemy now, Jeradon, we all know what has to be done. The Father has opened all of our eyes, now we must help him. Are you with us?"

"It seems I've been with you for the last decade."

In light of the training that Pirian was about to begin, and the fact Erth would be their new home for longer than expected, Jeradon requested that they be made more familiar with their new environment. Harad, along with his daughter, gave them a tour of the inner city over the next few days, before Jeradon was taken to meet with Lomax and Pirian subsequently begin his teachings.

Pirian knew that the whispers would start as soon as he entered any study. However, Jeradon felt that his son had the right mindset - having been brought up amongst the Greenhouses gave him an advantage. His main concern however, was how unfocused his son could be, distracted due to the separation from his mother.

Harad knew there was something about the boy; his brightness and curiosity wasn't natural at all for a Newtonian. Having already spoke with Moku, he knew full well of his unusual condition.

It was the fourth time since arriving at the capital that they had walked the interstreets. There was a heaving mass of people as far as the eye could see. They could barely get by amongst the abundance of strange creatures and wild folk, making their daily trips to and fro, carrying all kinds of magnificent items. There were hand crafted rugs slung over unnaturally large shoulders and pottery balanced on triple heads. As they made their way deeper into the city there was the smell of meat, while people bought and traded their goods.

Here on the interstreets of the Rojin capital Yodann, deep within the confines of the huge inner temple, everyone was equal.

Only Jeradon and Pirian felt out of place as they followed Harad and Kira, squeezing their way through the crowds.

Approaching a market square, where hundreds of stalls fanned out, Pirian could make out similar sounds to those he had heard at the temple. They made their way closer. Kira grabbed Pirian's hand as Harad parted the crowd, guiding them closer to the front. There before him, Pirian could make out all manner of instruments. There was a huge round box covered in skin and beaten by a huge Rojin mutant, his powerful club-like fists pounding away at the large object. A man blew into a small stick, while another bizarre looking creature with long legs and a stumpy body plucked strings stretched over a finely carved piece of wood. The rest of the noisemakers continued to sing in harmony, reaching a crescendo, before it finally came to an end.

There was applause as the noisemakers left and were replaced by a strange looking man with a painted face and tall, multicoloured top hat. He began by throwing balls in the air and the balls multiplied as they gained height. Finally they caught fire and vanished in a puff of smoke. Pirian was amazed by the Rojin's tricks as he hid under his hood.

The man thanked the crowd as they applauded once again. Next he opened a large case he had brought with him, pulling out a strange little man. It wore a similar multicoloured, raggedy attire to the entertainer. He rested it on his other arm. The creature's face was life-like, yet its expression was vacant as it began to mumble.

"My, we are grumpy today."

"Well…what do you expect keeping me cooped up in that

box?" the little man answered.

Pirian was shocked at the crowd laughing. Even his father smirked slightly. What was so funny about that? The poor little man had every right to be annoyed. The entertainer continued to interact with the little man and the crowd continued to laugh.

Kira noticed Pirian becoming quite upset, a side of her not wanting to tell him what was actually happening and spoil the illusion. "He's not real, Pirian. It's all part of Peakar's act."

"We call it ventriloquism. The voice coming from the little wooden man, is actually Peakar's," added Harad.

That's amazing, thought Pirian briefly. But he guessed for those that could talk with their minds, speaking while having your mouth closed wasn't difficult at all.

Jeradon continued to watch the ventriloquist along with his son as Harad addressed him. "You will be able to question Lomax tomorrow noon. In the meantime, enjoy the show and get some Rojin food down you; I recommend the Abagu steak for you and the boy. He's going to need all the strength he can muster before training."

Two days passed, and by now Jeradon had had several meetings with Lomax. Confined to his chambers and awaiting trial, the Sea Wolf's only punishment for now, it seemed, was no whisky or cigars. His wounds were healing, but it appeared to Jeradon that Lomax was broken inside, still mourning the loss of his crew and his ship. The Father had kept Lomax and his companion within the Temple's walls. Without his symbiont blade close by, his strength was beginning to dwindle.

For the first few visits Jeradon had questioned his past and come to realise that they had more than one thing in common.

"You visited The Father…didn't you?" asked Lomax.

"Just as you did all those years back."

"Yes. I did what was asked of me."

Jeradon lowered his voice. "In the visions there were books. I saw pages being torn from them. There was also an animal of some kind. You took them both, didn't you?"

Lomax turned his head away. "I...I had to take them. I was asked to protect Gana. There have always been traitors amongst us, those that had lost faith. I just didn't think by doing what I had to do...that I would also be labelled a traitor. The Father showed me what would happen - but there was a side of me that doubted it. And everything...all that I was shown has come true. Those pages held important information and I couldn't let it fall into the hands of your people, or even my own. It was only a matter of time until Newton found the answers."

"You couldn't tell anyone?"

"No. It's always been that way. The Father shows you what he wants you to see...and it is for you only."

"The pages reveal the whereabouts of the artefact Newton has been searching for?"

"No. They reveal the teachings of Gana. His true identity."

"Then you were sent away for good reason. What was this animal?"

"I cannot and will not say. If you could not see it, then perhaps that was for a purpose."

"Is all this connected to what Harad has told me from your scriptures?" asked Jeradon. Lomax fell silent. Jeradon thought for a moment and then realised, "The pages were the scriptures?"

The Wolf didn't need to say anything, instead he simply averted his attention.

"Then only Harad knows what they spoke of. The same things he told me when we first met."

"And more," answered Lomax, "Hear yourself. You're a Newtonian and your talking like you have lived amongst the Rojin for years. Scriptures, prophecy...hah...fate. You think The Father knows everything, that he sees the future?" Lomax shook his head and laughed.

"Isn't that what the Rojin believe?"

"I don't know what to believe anymore. It's all just stories to me, something to help give the Rojin hope, and is always open to interpretation. Right now I feel nothing but a pawn. Are we all to be controlled by him? He told me back then, when I believed in The Father, that I was meant to go to sea. But were all of my crew meant to die? Who is he to tell me these things, and who are you to believe? You and your son are Newtonian, enemies of the Rojin and you should always be reminded of that. Just because The Father has managed to find a way into your head, do not think you will suddenly be welcomed by everyone? Why do you think you have been confined to the Temple grounds? You wouldn't survive an hour before someone killed you…and your boy."

Jeradon massaged his temples taking in what Lomax had said. He could see his point of view but he needed to get through to him, "I'm not your enemy, Lomax, I'm trying to help you. Do you know why your sword is so sick?"

"Sea sick. I couldnt' find clean enough soil to look after it, to feed it."

"Yes, but it's also because the protronium has been running low and left the city open to contamination - it should have strengthened by now. Even Yodann's soil is becoming infected. Your land needs protronium to stay alive, to grow. In turn this is what keeps The Father alive. You know what those pages hold. You also know that it will expose the traitors."

"Traitor," corrected Lomax.

The next day Harad took Jeradon and Pirian to the Temple's training grounds, where many Rojin were taught. The building was an enclosed arena, set up with all manner of equipment and obstacles. The outer circles were classrooms where students studied history and theory. There were around fifty students in the class, who Pirian closely watched. Carrying out a series of moves in repetition to the calls of their instructor, every sequence ended with a solid, positive response.

A young man bowed out of his current training schedule and approached Harad. He was in his late teens, his posture was extremely disciplined, fists closed and raised forward slightly. Harad raised his hand and the young man relaxed as he introduced him to Jeradon and Pirian. "This is my son, Karl."

Pirian caught Karl's eyes. Although he was a slender build for his age, he still found him intimidating.

"My brother has just returned home from his Erth Walk. When Rojin reach manhood they are sent away. Not all of them find themselves, some become lost in the wilderness, even die. Those that make it back to the capital, pass their final initiation and finally become Rojin missionaries," explained Kira.

Karl stood motionless.

"Your father feels that it would be wise for you to be trained by us, Pirian," explained Harad. "My son is an example of what you will hopefully achieve in time,."

He had grasped what Harad had said, but he was immediately concerned about mixing with fellow students, as he and his father walked away. "I don't understand Dad. You've barely allowed me to pick up a stick, now you want me trained to fight?" His eyes were averted back down towards the arena and Karl.

Jeradon responded as best he could. "Not just to fight, Pirian. You will be integrated into the training process just as any other Rojin has been. I understand that this will be difficult for you, that the training will not be easy. All you have to do is treat that as part of the lesson. That sometimes in life we have to grow up fast."

"I'm…not sure," he replied, trying to control his frustration.

"You will be fine, Pirian." Kira assured him.

"But…how long will it take?"

Kira looked up at her father who replied earnestly, "Some of the students, including Karl, have been training since they could walk. Initial training from your age will take the next seven years. It is a full schooling Pirian; you will become disciplined in the way of the Rojin and one day you will be thankful for it. However, you will never stop learning for as long as you live."

Even though Pirian had always secretly wanted be a Rojin warrior, the reality of not returning to Newton any time soon was suddenly a reality. "Seven years! But…I…I can't. Dad…tell them, we can't stay here, you can't expect me to do this. What about mum?" Pirian paused as he attempted to read his father's face. "We wouldn't be staying here all that time…seven years while she… we…we have to get back to Newton and rescue her. You know that!"

"This is exactly why I need you to be trained, Pirian. We can't get back to Newton right away. We have to be realistic. You have to make use of the time here and prepare for your journey home."

Pirian's gut began to swim, his bottom lip trembling, "But… I can't do it…"

"You can. You're a Horncastle and I will be there, every step of the way."

Pirian contained his emotions. "You promise?"

"I promise. Now…make that the last time you shed any tears and hold on to that new strength that's slowly growing in here." Jeradon placed two fingers on his son's heart.

It was the first time Pirian had found a smile in a long time.

XI

Free of the Dosage, Jeradon was still surprised he hadn't suffered from altitude sickness at all. Over the eighteen months that followed, the gardeners and Neeve also began to reject it from their systems as they continued to work. Their personalities gradually became more prominent, while also developing a passion for the Greenhouse project itself.

Even though Neeve forgot to file her reports, Jeradon made sure she completed them to prevent suspicion amongst the Hierarchy.

Yet there was one person she was unable to hide anything from.

"Rayal knows. He's gone so long, he sees the difference in me more than anyone when he returns."

"He's frightened of losing you Neeve."

"Are you saying he has feelings?"

"I know for certain he feels pain and hatred and he has no idea how to control it. His wife overdosed; that can wake any man up. Rayal rejected the Dosage when she died. I'm unsure if it was the shock that did it, or if it was a conscious decision; but the loss must have been powerful enough to give him the taste of the real world. Unfortunately this exposed his true nature and he became even more twisted. There is no need for zetameen with people like him. When you're awakened - it exposes who you really are." Jeradon surveyed the landscape that was beginning to finally take shape.

Neeve didn't even feel guilty. Her mind was stronger than it had ever been and for the first time in her life she felt truly free. "There's no need for you to take it either?" she asked.

"No. The difference being I don't have a hunger for power. The Guild, the killing; I believe it wasn't something I was *meant* to do. This is. I don't miss the unit, the command, the drops, the needless searching and killing of innocent people. But there is no escaping those memories; every life I have taken will torment me till the day I die. I will have to live with that." He gestured towards the green open space, "This is the only place that helps to keep me sane."

"I can see why," replied Neeve.

Jeradon pondered for a moment, "Did you know the Guild was brought together by scientists and artisans thousands of years ago? A group of people from each of the twelve surviving cities worked together, to try and make their world a better place. Eventually when they learnt to fly, they developed a drug to prevent altitude sickness. Before long, the drug was sold on the streets and whole cities became addicted. Their addiction was a necessity when the city finally took to the sky. Any individuality disappeared over night, and the Guild became an army in pursuit of power. Every Guildsman to this day has searched for an artefact that may not even exist, but could have even been some kind of illusion, or *delusion* brought on by this drug. It's been every Emperor's obsession since. You see, our rulers remember the myths and the stories, because their minds have remained clean and focussed. Deep down inside them, they have a thirst for the true origins of this artefact - because they remain zetameen free."

"I can see why now…it feels so right. But what of us - what has this place really done to us?"

Jeradon knew what he was about to tell her would be the ultimate test in trust. A test of loyalty and a risk he was all too willing to take. "I discovered that the Rojin use raw protronium to fertilise and grow their habitats and weapons. Where zetameen is distilled protronium and highly addictive, raw protronium is the richest source of energy on the planet. In turn everything you see before you - the rocks, plants, trees, and even the animals, filter the protronium back out into the atmosphere. Here it is caught up in the rain, then drains back into the earth, solidifies and is then reabsorbed. Seems there are many uses for it other than fuel for Newton's engines and vehicles. It's as much a part of Erth's ecosystem than anything else. It's the Erth's blood and continues to bleed until healed."

Neeve pondered for a while trying to take it all in. "So by stopping the protronium supplies we can defeat the Rojin?"

Jeradon was still surveying what he had created as Neeve awaited an answer. "That's almost inevitable at the rate Newton is swallowing up supplies. It will drain this planet dry before it leaves Erth." He paused once again and sighed looking into Neeve's eyes. "And I can't let that happen. What I have here is the ability to cleanse Newton - to wake everyone up from their sleep. You've breathed the air, Neeve; you know what I'm talking about. Newton is far more lifeless than Erth. The rulers of this flying city have done nothing but yearn for power and control. There is nothing to inspire, to help people create something better. No feeling, no passion..."

"No love." Neeve hadn't taken her eyes off Jeradon for a second.

"You took the words right out of my..."

Neeve placed a finger on his lips.

She had listened to everything he had to say, and it was something that would stay in the Greenhouse.

Jeradon's heart began to pound far more than any Dosage induced state could ever comprehend.

It was clear to Jeradon that Neeve no longer wanted to listen.

Instead she was savouring the moment, taking full control of their feelings for once - her kiss alone as she drew him in, helped him realise the very reason he was still alive.

Twelve

Jeradon continued to visit the training grounds with Pirian every day as Harad told them more about Rojin culture.

They were given the honour of witnessing the bonding between the young Rojin and what would become their weapon for life; the katanac symbiont blade. To begin their initiation, several youngsters around three years of age clung to their mother's breast as they were brought before the katanac tree. Surrounded by fountains, the tree stood as a central focus point of the training grounds, where it had stood for centuries. The Rojin had developed a natural understanding and relationship with the tree, this having been the very first seed planted by The Father.

Beckoned on by an adult Rojin, a reluctant and somewhat frightened youngster approached the tree. It was almost instinctive for the child to reach out for what appeared to be small branches growing from the base of the trunk. Then the katanac tree automatically spread its blades from the branches to protect itself.

Harad explained further the philosophy of the symbiont blade. "This weapon is so much more than something that cuts. The blade has the power to send you to the bowels of the inferno or unite your soul with Gana. Some may call it their death stick, others their life. For the Rojin it is important to understand the heart and the terror of the katanac. They must be careful not to let one control the other - but become one instead."

Jeradon and Pirian continued to watch.

The child flinched, pulling back its hand and began to cry. Then, gradually the blades began to retract in response to the child's distress. All but one small blade had vanished, as though the tree was offering it to the young Rojin. Reaching out once again, the child held onto the base, resembling the hilt, the blade then retracted and fell away in the child's hand. The hilt spiked the youngster's palm, joining with the child for the first time and naturally calming the young Rojin after the ordeal.

"Their bloodline will last till the day they die," explained Harad.

Another tradition was connected to the Sisterhood. Harad explained that Kira had already chosen to become a Priestess and her training from now on would be centred around her devotion to Gana and the protection of The Father.

"So she will never marry?" asked Jeradon.

"No. Nor will she bear children." replied Harad.

This made Pirian think a great deal about what kind of future Kira had. Although he was still young, he still assumed it was an important part of being an adult. "That saddens me."

"There is no need to be sad," said Kira. "I will become a mother, but not in the same way you imagine. I will become a mother of the Rojin people. They are my family."

It was clear to Harad that Jeradon understood, but he still noticed a slight disbelief in Pirian's eyes.

Deep in thought, Pirian then asked Kira a question. "So Ersula has never married or had any children either?"

"No. I am her Select, the nearest thing to a daughter she will have. One day I will replace her."

Pirian shivered slightly at the thought of Kira becoming like Ersula.

"She frightens you?"

"A little."

"Her presence is strong. Her mark is even stronger. There aren't many that can resist her power. She can look into the very heart of a person if she needs to and even stop it from beating."

"We have a lot to adjust to other than you reading our minds," said Jeradon as Ersula approached.

"Not all of us can read minds, only those with a strong enough mark and the right training to control it. My father, Ersula and myself share similar abilities which are of great use to The Father and his people."

She paused and addressed Pirian directly, aware that he was about to begin his own training. "So try not to worry about every other student being able to read your mind."

Her words were a comfort, but at the end of the day there was always the risk of more people finding out the truth. "As for the teachers, they will keep to their word. To betray The Father is to betray Gana. It would be a serious crime." She paused and touched Pirian's hand. Blushing, he suddenly realised it was his marked arm and pulled it away nervously, "You won't be able to hide that forever, Pirian."

"You know?"

"Of course. Your reaction to the water in the Temple gave it away. You have a deformity. Doctor Moku thought he was treating a condition. But you cannot treat what you have. Here, amongst the Rojin there is nothing unusual about it. We refer to them as 'marks'. The majority of us have them - those that don't seem more out of place."

"My own mark, it's something I've always had."

"But as a child of Newton you shouldn't have survived a day with the slightest defect."

Pirian's eyes widened, "I'm not a…"

"Freak?" predicted Kira. "Birthmark, deformity or mutation; however you choose to label it, use it positively."

"If anything it should help you blend in even more," added

Jeradon.

"Your father is right. You'll find all kinds of young Rojin that use their marks to their advantage. Even if someone did find out where you are from, no one would believe a Defect could have fallen from Newton."

Between lessons, Pirian would approach those students who showed off their marks. Some were more severe than others and seemed more of a hindrance than anything else. Yet there was never any bullying, it simply broke the ice.

There were two boys and a girl in particular that Pirian had noticed during his first morning's training. He had seen them introducing their symbiont blades to each other, each of which they had given names. Afterwards Pirian decided that he would try and talk to them. Nothing stood out about the girl other than her purple and lilac hair. One of the boys had his back to Pirian as he approached, and he could see that the other two children were waiting for the young Rojin to show them something.

Pirian watched in awe as his face creased down the centre, folded in half vertically, then opened again to reveal entirely new features. Closing back up, the boy's original identity reappeared, his almost amphibious, bug-eyed features blinking back at them.

"A face changer, that's so cool," said the larger boy.

Repeating the process several times, the face changer then stopped and addressed Pirian. "What's your mark?"

"It's nothing much," he replied, pulling up his sleeve. "Just my arm."

They all leaned forward and looked at the mark spiralling around his arm. "It changes colour and shape sometimes."

There was an awkward silence as they all looked at each other, unimpressed. The larger of the two boys pushed out his bottom lip and crinkled his nose looking over at the girl, before adding, "I have an extra one," and unfolded his third arm.

Easing the awkward silence, the girl introduced herself and friends. "My name's Larissa Sou. Faces here is Ched. The one with the arms is Nikanda . We just call him Nik."

"Pirian." he replied, before sipping at his water bottle. Aside from Larissa's confidence - that stoodout as much as her purple and lilac hair, it was immediate that she was the ringleader.

"Where are you from?" asked Nik.

It was difficult not to say Newton and for a moment he began to think of somewhere he was familiar with from his books, but his mind had gone blank. "I'm…my father and I are from…the sea."

All three children looked at each other, before Ched replied. "Your father's a pirate?"

"No…not any more. He's…converted. Thanks to your missionaries."

"I bet you have some great stories?" asked Ched eagerly.

Pirian smiled. "Yeah, you could say that."

Over the course of several weeks, Pirian began to immerse himself in various lessons. At first he found it very difficult to concentrate. He still thought about his mother and realised this was something he had to take control of. The thought that he would not make it back to Newton any sooner was becoming more of a reality, and he was beginning to understand why the training would come in useful.

He genuinely wanted to learn more about the Rojin culture first hand, but his paranoia was beginning to cause him problems. His main worry was that students would find out where he was from. It was bad enough most of the teachers having to know.

Discipline was key to the Rojin. However, where the Newtonian Guild was all about brute strength, power and control, the way of the Rojin was about knowledge, technique and discipline. To the Rojin maintaining a positive attitude was power.

Every morning, up until midday, there were physical training exercises. The techniques explored were very basic, with every emphasis on coordination. The afternoons consisted of various theoretical and practical lessons.

During the History lessons Pirian was beginning to learn vague details about the technical and virtual ages. There was very little information that even the Rojin could draw from, as most of it had become myth.

Ersula was their History teacher. Although Pirian found her intimidating, she seemed to grab the attention of everyone in the room.

"It was also believed that these people reached the stars before causing the great inferno. Although this seems unlikely, it's interesting to see that the Newtonians have ended up nearer to our moon than we ever shall. Perhaps history does end up repeating itself."

In Biology Moku taught the students about botany and also made them fully aware of the contamination. It was close to home and they were all encouraged to come up with experiments and ideas on how to help the less fortunate. Pirian's knowledge of botany from his father came in very handy, and was one of the main things that helped him blend in.

Art was a lesson that really managed to channel his problems. The lesson was taught by the crazy little man Pirian had seen entertaining everyone in the streets, Peakar the Performer.

"Art is personal. It's about seeing things in the most simple of marks. Sometimes the best things can come out of imperfections."

Many students were often lost at what Peakar was saying, or simply took what he said at face value. But Pirian found it very inspirational and couldn't help but realise that Peakar meant many other things.

Pirian was all too keen to revisit a blank sheet of paper, without having to worry about hiding his drawings or feel he was committing a crime. Here his talent was encouraged. Rojin music had already sparked the desire to listen to more and hopefully learn an instrument one day. The more he listened to the sounds during the lessons, the more work he produced.

His drawings captured detail and most of all likeness. When he allowed his marked arm to take control, the images would become more abstract. However, it was a technique that Pirian was new to, and it always felt as though someone or something else was doing the work for him. It was interesting to Pirian how his peers interpreted the final drawings.

By the time Pirian's day was finished it was already dark and Jeradon would make sure he arrived home safely by meeting him outside the temple's training grounds and walking him back to their dorm. Jeradon was fully aware they were under the watchful eye of The Father, yet he still wanted to protect his son as best he could. He had spent most of his time looking into the Rojin's problems after questioning Lomax and was still surprised that the capital had become infected so easily. The traitor that Lomax had mentioned could infiltrate the inner Temple itself, threatening their safety further.

The visions that he experienced after visiting The Father had shown him answers and scenarios that played out in his mind. They were as clear as the moment he was awakened, as though the grass still lay under his feet. For fear of anything happening to it, Jeradon carried the fossilised blade everywhere he went. He'd shown his son, but wouldn't allow him to touch it. Pirian thought nothing of it, since he was used to his father not allowing him near weaponry.

At night the narrow streets within the Temple's grounds were more like enclosed corridors. The darkness created an entirely different atmosphere holding onto every shadow. Looming inner buildings of stone were encased in twisted trees, bent over and grown into the structure, much like giant claws suffocating its victim rather than protecting it.

The dark was quiet. Too quiet.

Jeradon stopped as though sensing a presence. "We're being followed."

"Behind us?"

"No. Above. Carry on walking," he instructed his son, ducking into the shadows. As he kept an eye on Pirian walking further ahead, Jeradon could see a dark figure moving slowly between the twisted rooftops. Slowly it crept forward continuing to follow his son's footsteps. Moving deeper into the shadows, Jeradon kept his eye on the figure. Suddenly it moved at an alarming rate above him, jumping from rooftop to rooftop and closing in on his son.

Pirian didn't hear a sound as the figure loomed over him and then dropped down silently between two buildings.

Jeradon was waiting and could see the figure hesitate and look round for him as it realised he was no longer at his son's side. As the figure leapt towards Pirian, his father was there in a heartbeat. Well aware that his Guild training was rusty, he still remembered enough to grab the pursuer. However, the Rojin was faster and more agile, managing to twist away from Jeradon's grip and kick him to the floor.

In the darkness it was difficult to make out any features at all. But one thing was certain - silhouetted against the street walls and protruding from its dark hood was a snout. *Lomax?* thought Pirian immediately as he charged, reaching for his father. As he dashed forwards the dark figure had already opened out its shredded cape. Pirian was caught like a fly in a spider's web, and the figure simply twisted its arm, entangling the boy further.

Jeradon was up in a shot as the dark figure slowly pulled what looked like a gun from its side and aimed towards his head. He knew what it wanted and without question Jeradon unfastened the strap and placed the long case down on the ground. The figure gestured towards it as Jeradon opened the case to reveal the sword husk inside.

There was a pause, which seemed to last a lifetime to Pirian. He had no doubt his father would trade the sword, but he had no idea their attacker would compromise. Slowly the figure began to back away, it didn't want The Father's sword at all.

"Let my son go," cried Jeradon, realising it was his son the figure wanted.

Pirian was finding it difficult to control his breathing. His arm began to ache and before he knew it, it spasmed uncontrollably and grabbed his captive's arm. The figure gave out a painful, inhuman cry, pulling itself away from the boy's grasp.

Standing motionless, Pirian clutched his arm as the figure scuttled backwards, protecting itself with the gun.

Then there was the sound of footsteps as Harad and his guards approached. The figure pulled itself up off the ground. Turning its head to the side, Jeradon also caught sight of the long snout.

The Rojin guards rounded the corner, symbiont blades already drawn as the dark figure crouched and opened fire on them. Luckily no guards were hit, yet they were distracted enough for the figure to vanish.

Jeradon and Pirian made their way over to Harad and his guards.

"Are you both ok?" asked Harad.

"We're fine," answered Jeradon

"The sword?"

"It's safe. For a moment I thought that was what he wanted. Seems he was more interested in Pirian." Jeradon closed the case and slung it round his shoulder.

"It's a good job your father is around," said Harad.

"Seems my son can take care of himself. Whoever attacked us…whatever Pirian did, was enough to stop him for now."

Harad looked down at Pirian. "Then perhaps you would have been of more use than the guards outside Lomax's quarters before he escaped."

Jeradon and Pirian looked at each other. It seemed that their attacker was none other than the Sea Wolf himself.

Harad sighed. "You may begin to believe what he is capable of once you come with us."

XII

Across from the long dining table, Rayal Jakahn looked at Neeve suspiciously as he ate. A young Viktor robotically shovelled food into his mouth, paying no attention to either of them.

"Why do you look at me like that?" asked Neeve, more aware than ever of his feelings towards her. Conscious of every eye movement he made, she could almost predict what he was about to say.

"You seem somewhat...distracted. More so than ever."

Indeed she was distracted. Neeve was becoming more curious everyday; discovering such simple things as taste for the first time in her life. She was finally in tune with her surroundings, surveying the coldness of their home. Swallowing her food, she screwed her face slightly at the bland taste of the synthetic meal that had been prepared. "I'm fine, Rayal," she replied, catching his eye.

His face repulsed her. Where on Erth had she been? What on Erth was she doing with this loathsome man?

"Well, I do hope you haven't forgotten your Dosage." He gestured towards the capsule at the side of her plate.

She nervously looked down and picked it up.

"Tell me my dear, how is Jeradon getting along? Has he discovered anything of importance yet?"

Neeve toyed with the capsule. "It's still early days."

Rayal laughed, a sly look coming across his face. "Well," he chuckled, "Newton wasn't built in a day."

"I must get a glass of water," replied Neeve, excusing herself from the table.

Rayal sat back in his chair watching her leave. Did she think he was stupid? He knew all too well what was happening to her. There was a part of him that wanted to keep control of her and make sure she was still taking the Dosage, whereas the other part was curious to know the real Neeve. Then he thought of Jeradon. *He's got to her*, he thought.

His blood boiled, his anger slowly building.

Looking over at Viktor he caught a glimpse of his dead wife. There was no one to question him, no one to ask about his time away. His son didn't ask questions, like every other Newtonian. They simply followed orders.

She stared at herself in the mirror. Breaking the capsule, she took a sip of water and washed the zetameen down the sink. Nausea overcame her immediately. Retching she clutched the sink as she vomited.

As Neeve straightened, she jumped from the sudden appearance of Rayal, reflected in the mirror as he stood behind her.

"I suggest you take the Dosage, Neeve. Unless you want to be placed in isolation."

"The Emperor wouldn't allow that, I'm far too useful. Besides, none of this is hindering my work."

"Look at you. You can barely stand."

"It will pass."

"Take the Dosage, Neeve. I will not tell you again. You're sick and we wouldn't want you dying on us, would we."

"That wouldn't be such a bad thing, Rayal. I'd finally be rid of you."

"What did you say?"

"You heard me clearly enough. Now stay away from me."

Rayal stepped closer. He could smell the Greenhouse on her. "Horncastle."

Neeve didn't have to say a word.

Jakahn backed away and laughed. "Go to him then."

"What?"

"Go to him, Neeve. But remember this; one day you will both pay dearly for what he has done. His precious habitats will fall. But first I will watch him build it with every ounce of sweat before he watches it burn to the ground. Then I will take you back. It will be torture not knowing when."

"The Emperor will learn about this," replied Neeve, a tear rolling down her cheek.

"Is that so? What was it you said? Ah yes, 'I'm too useful'. Who else is there left to inform his Guild, search for the artefact and maintain protronium supplies? It's only a matter of time until I become his Advisor, Neeve. I have seen and know far too much for him to cast me aside. I am free of the Dosage, my mind growing in power every day. Then, when the time is right, I will take this city further than it's ever been. To the stars and back again."

Neeve broke down, tears rolling down her face. Rayal took a moment to compose himself. He had become so erratic that he had lost his breath as he spoke. He left Neeve to cry alone.

Slowly her tears turned to laughter as she clasped her hand over her mouth. She knew the sickness wasn't to do with her being free of the zetameen at all

Every mother knew when she was with child.

Thirteen

Slumped against the wall outside Lomax's cell were two dead Rojin guards. Doctor Moku had already checked for any sign of life, spraying and taking samples from the odd looking protrusions that had grown from their wounds. Jeradon was curious about the way the bodies had not been taken control of entirely, and Moku moved aside as he knelt down inspecting the small, plant-like tendrils further.

"There was an attempt at breaking the gargoyle free, but it seems Brom and Stone were alerted in time," said Moku.

"So he's still within the temple?" replied Harad.

The Doctor nodded and looked over at Jeradon and Pirian. "Harad Sur, do you think it's wise…?"

"It's ok, they're of no threat. This man and his son are in The Father's hands - it's what he wants."

Moku didn't question any further and allowed Harad to pass and investigate Lomax's cell.

Pirian had read of Rojin weapons that could turn people into trees and was also reminded of images he had seen of men turned to stone, as though consumed by Erth itself. He then recalled similar weapons in Lomax's quarters, especially the one he pondered over before *The General* sank. *I guess the bullets will pay a high enough price*, he remembered the Wolf saying.

Jeradon snapped off a small piece of the plant, rubbing it between his fingers. "Darathia seeds? An horrific way to pollinate."

Moku nodded. "Indeed. No doubt you have come up against them in the past. It could possibly be a growth rate five, judging by the size of the wounds. That's a fully developed Darathia." Two of Moku's assistants carried the guard's bodies away. "Keep them on ice, I'll inspect them further when I get back to the lab."

Jeradon sniffed the sample. "I never came across a full Darathia specimen for Newton, but I've certainly seen their effect in battle. If I'd managed to grow them, the Emperor would have certainly been impressed. I dread to think what could have happened if they had fallen into the wrong hands. You didn't think of searching the Wolf when you brought him in?"

"We inspected him…" replied Harad.

"We came across several of the bullets and placed them immediately in isolation," added Moku.

"It's quite possible he could have hid more Darathia bullets somehow - he spoke of selling them to the black market when we were on his ship. Perhaps he swallowed one - the transformation process is slower that way."

"I thought Darathia weaponry was extinct, along with those that used it?" asked Pirian.

Harad and Moku were taken back slightly at Pirian's knowledge. "Your son is right," said Harad. "Darathia were originally our Guards, 'Guardeners' as we called them. Before helping us in battle, their guns were simply used for harvesting. When they died out, so did their weapons. They were the first to become infected. Their rarity is the reason they are worth so much to mercenaries, anything from the gun arm to the bullets themselves can be used as biological weapons."

"Lomax must have come across a Darathia gun. I'm just puzzled how he could have grown such a weapon without a host, and then escape so easily considering he wasn't in the best condition," said Moku.

"Who says he escaped?" queried Jeradon.

Moku glanced at Harad, realising Jeradon could be right.

"He escaped before," answered Harad.

Pirian thought back to what they had already been told about Lomax. "He wasn't outcast?"

"No. Lomax and the gargoyle vanished the night we arrested them fifteen years ago."

"Yet on this occasion Lomax is without his companion," added Jeradon.

"A search party will have to be gathered. There is no way out of the Temple. This time he can't run away from his crimes." added Harad.

Jeradon thought for a moment. "I don't believe he is running. Lomax still has something to show us, guilty or not guilty, I will help you look for him."

Pirian was taken back by what his father had said. "You promised…"

Jeradon was finding it hard to explain what was going on in his head. He felt torn between what he had been shown and what he had promised his son. "And I meant it, Pirian. There is every chance Lomax is still in the Temple, I won't be far away."

"Anything could happen. Can't I come with you?"

"No, Pirian. It's too dangerous."

Harad interrupted. "You will need to make your way to the dormitories where the rest of the Temple's students are. You will be safe there. We are unsure of what Lomax is capable of."

"He saved our lives."

Harad didn't answer as Jeradon took his son to one side. "Pirian…"

"I don't understand. Ever since you have seen The Father you seem…different."

Jeradon looked Pirian in the eyes and lowered the tone of his voice. "I'm still your father. The reason I am helping find

Lomax is to find an answer. He knows something that could help us. He may not be as guilty as the Rojin think. Whatever he did in the past is catching up with him and I can't allow the Rojin to execute him. I owe him that at least."

Pirian thought for a moment, "He's protecting something?" He knew he was right by the reaction of his father's face.

"Maybe. But I can't help feel there's more to it than that."

As long as Pirian knew his father was still somewhere within the Temple it was enough to reassure him of his safety. However, the Temple was practically a city itself.

There were secrets hiding in the shadows. Pirian hadn't realised until now how much the darkness could infect the mind; the large open corridors and huge rooms were overpowering for any child, let alone one with an over-active imagination. Before now Pirian had only read of what the darkness could hold on Erth. He had wanted to believe in his stories ever since he could remember. But as he lay in bed with a full bladder, aching for daylight, he hoped most of those stories weren't true. It didn't help with a killer at large, and he hoped the number of guards that were protecting the dormitories were enough to deter anyone.

Over the last two months Pirian had witnessed his pet killed at the hands of a Newtonian thug, the last of the Greenhouses burnt to the ground and his father convicted of murder - all before he had even fallen to Erth. The beasts that he had read about certainly existed, along with pirates, Siran and the Rojin. Pirian would never forget any of his experiences so far, the same way he wouldn't forget his mother. Her presence played heavily on his mind, it was comforting, even though he knew she could be thousands of miles away.

Now there was The Father's presence - felt at all times and adding to the Rojin atmosphere within the Temple. Most of the privileged children who stayed within the dormitories were orphans, of which Pirian had only made friends with a select few. Still finding it hard to believe he was under the watchful eye of The Father, he wondered if there was more to why they were kept confined to the Temple's walls. What of the others outside of the city? Were they treated any differently?

It was hard for Pirian to stop thinking. He continually questioned himself and at the same time wanted to tell others of his situation. Kira had reminded him not to, in case word travelled to the outskirts of the city. An uprising was the last thing they needed right now. These thoughts kept him awake every night, yet surprisingly, when the morning came, he was still fully awake.

Lessons had been cancelled.

Harad, Ersula and Jeradon were searching for Lomax within the Temple's walls, accompanied by Rojin guards.

In the meantime, Moku took it upon himself to examine Pirian further. His face, although heavily scarred, was kind and reassuring, helping Pirian open up to someone other than his father. He looked as though he was a man that had seen a great deal of death amongst his people. And so he had - Moku was much more than just a botanist, he explained to Pirian that he was a chief surgeon; having served many hours on the battlefields. He had saved the lives of his fallen comrades countless times and mentored other Rojin in becoming doctors.

Moku closely inspected Pirian's arm, noticing a distinct change. "Your father tells me you were born with this mark."

"It seems to be growing larger. All it did was itch back on Newton and change shape every so often when I was in father's habitats."

"Interesting." Moku flattened his messy grey hair.

"You don't believe I'm from Newton, do you?"

"I have never known of a person with different eye colour being allowed to live amongst Newtonians, let alone someone who is marked."

Pirian considered what Moku was saying. He went along with what Kira had suggested to be able to fit in with the other children, but now the doctor was beginning to analyse his mutation even more.

"It's just a birthmark."

Moku hobbled over to one of his tables and opened up a large glass container that housed one of the tiny, dying plants that had been growing from the dead guards.

"When you arrived here, no one was sure of what to do with you and your father. Ersula was more concerned about Lomax and the gargoyle turning up after all these years, than listening to anything they had to say. Harad was called for by The Father, and only then did he speak to Vagabond."

"How much did he tell you?"

"Everything. Including how they had found you and what your father had admitted. Harad knew that if your father was indeed capable of killing your Emperor, then it was possible that he would work with us. Hopefully become an advisor to our people, maybe even help us fight Newton."

Pirian bowed his head. "I don't want believe he did it."

"A father will do anything to protect his family, Pirian. The Rojin know that more than anyone." He paused and held up the small plant in front of him. Thin tendrils had twisted at its base and spread outwards towards the top. "Take this plant..." Moku passed it to Pirian. He pulled out a surgical knife from his breast pocket and began to move the knife closer to Pirian's marked arm.

"What are you doing?" asked Pirian as he flinched.

"Don't be alarmed. Just watch carefully," replied Moku as he averted Pirian's glare to the plant he held in his arm. Suddenly it began to twitch and reach towards the knife, as though trying to protect Pirian. At the same time he could feel the mark on his arm begin to throb. Moku withdrew the blade. "This plant too is also trying to protect its family, Pirian. If it wasn't as underdeveloped and confused as you are, it could have killed me straight away."

As Moku withdrew the blade and placed it back in his top pocket, the plant calmed down and Pirian's arm began to settle. "What are you saying?"

"This sample was grown from a scraping I took from your arm when you arrived here. All it needed to grow was good company." Moku smiled. "It is genetically the same as you and almost identical to the Darathia."

Pirian stood, his face screwed up in confusion. "You're saying I'm a plant?" the thought almost made him laugh as he passed the sample back to Moku.

"You are much more than that, Pirian."

"Surely my father would have known…he'd have told me if I was infected."

"If he'd have thought it *was* an infection. Until now it's simply been an insignificant birthmark." Moku placed the plant back in its glass case. "Your father has had suspicions, enough to ask me to see you. Kira mentioned about your reaction to the water at the font. It was your father that brought it to my attention and the incident yesterday with your attacker."

Pirian thought for a moment. "It was protecting me. Whatever this is…this mark - it was protecting me?"

"Your mark was protecting both yourself and your father - protecting its family. The same way your father has tried to protect you, whatever the consequence. I believe it could be a genetic throwback due to being born free of the Dosage. A dormant gene which has resided in the Horncastle blood for centuries, waiting to be set free."

Pirian looked down at his arm. It was now so much more than a birthmark, darker in colour and spiralling from his wrist up to his shoulder. "I suffered from altitude sickness, it's connected isn't it?"

"Plants have to be rooted, Pirian. The sickness wasn't your own. It was your mark's," confirmed Moku.

"It makes sense, the Greenhouses helped. Now my feet are firmly on the ground I feel stronger than ever."

"Then you may be able to help as much as your father can. The Rojin capital isn't getting any better. People are dying, even The Father isn't as strong as he used to be. That is why choices have had to be made beyond his control. The gates have been locked for the last time, he's been unable to help his people outside of the inner Temple's walls. But hopefully there is a way to replenish the whole city, and I believe this sample holds the key."

Pirian began to walk around the laboratory. Within another glass case embedded in soil was an object he recognised. The Katanac blade was protruding from the soil, its posture weak and discoloured. "Lomax's symbiont blade?"

"Yes. So far our guards' blades within the Temple are fine. It seems this one must have become infected having been so long at sea. Being away from its host isn't helping."

Pirian was reminded once again of his father not allowing him to pick up a weapon. All he wanted to do was see if he could help. Lomax's blade would be as good a place to start as any. He placed his marked arm to the glass. "What would happen if I picked it up?"

"It would die," answered Moku. "When it's been picked by a host their bond can't be broken. Lomax's blood flows through that blade. If you were to introduce another bloodline it would perish."

"It's going to die anyway. I'm sure you're not going to give it back to Lomax."

Moku walked over to the container and removed the lid. "Place your hand in the soil." Pirian did as he was instructed.

The first thing Moku noticed were several of the Darathia samples begin to perish. Pirian closed his eyes. When he opened them the blade had strengthened, a healthy bone-white returning to its surface.

The plant filtered what it needed, thought Pirian. For the first time since he'd arrived he felt there was a reason for being here. His confidence grew. "Maybe you're right, Doctor. There is a way I can help your people."

Moku was deep in thought as he picked up one of the dead Darathia samples. "Yes…but at what cost?"

XIII

Freezing gas instantly dissipated from the container the second it was opened.

"Where's the rest of it?" asked a surprised Jeradon.

"Surel gave strict instructions not to allow a complete specimen past Newtonian security," said one of Jeradon's Gardeners.

"I needed a complete specimen. That included the rest of the body, fully developed to a growth rate five -" Jeradon lifted the strange looking limb from the container, " - not just an underdeveloped gun arm. The thing's no more than a three at the most."

"There is a reason for that, sir."

"Which is?"

The Gardener looked uncomfortable. "The specimen was captured by Commander Jakahn personally."

"Is that so."

"He states that the host wasn't one of his own. Therefore he couldn't have brought him back."

Confused by the statement, Jeradon said, "We can see it's obviously no longer one of his own."

"He meant before the host was shot by the Darathia."

Puzzled, Jeradon squinted his eyes.

"He claims the host was Rojin, sir."

"Impossible."

"We have confirmation from their log." The Gardener handed

him the disc.

Snatching it, Jeradon immediately began to view the footage. There was interference on the recording due to the weather. Jeradon could make out the muddy surroundings of a fallen Rojin outpost as the footage from various Guildsmen flickered into view.

The heavy downpour of rain had hindered Jakahn's command for days as he attempted to reach Unit Fifty-Two. Their surroundings had become nothing but a mudslide as the rain ate away at the looming ravines, revealing unstable roots and bringing the trees crashing down on the Rojin outpost.

Jakahn attempted to maintain his footing on solid ground. He had hoped for a fight, but the Rojin, along with the missing Unit were already dead. Most of them had been buried in their trenches. The few bodies that were still visible, pushed along by the slowly moving mudslide, were not Rojin at all.

The creatures were attempting to drag themselves to more stable land, directly towards Jakahn's Unit.

"Darathia," a nearby Guildsman said, lifting his blowtorch and incinerating them.

As the Guild made their way round what resembled a muddy lake, they came across a Rojin body, laying outstretched on the rocky outcrop, half submerged in the mud.

They could all see that the Rojin's arm was deformed. Initially, as they made their way closer, they thought that the deformity was the Rojin's mark. But as he dragged himself further from the mud and began to convulse, they could clearly make out that his arm was in fact a Darathia's. The swelling had reached the shoulder, the forearm developed into its unmistakable gun arm. By instinct it already knew to raise it in defence as the Guild approached.

Jakahn marched forward without hesitation and blasted the

abomination in the chest, preventing the symbiont's complete transformation.

Shocked at the discovery, Jakahn's Unit stood speechless awaiting their orders.

"Your ex-commander needs a specimen. Let's see what he makes of the Darathia turning on the Rojin. Remove the arm, it will still be of use to him."

Fourteen

For three days and three nights Harad, Ersula and Jeradon had taken it in turns to search for Lomax. Security had tightened more than ever, particularly where Vagabond was being held, along with the outer Temple's walls and children's dorms.

It was night when Ersula was taken. The interstreet was cast in darkness, torch flames licking the walls as the shadows danced along the dark corridors. Jeradon and his guards were the first to arrive at the scene as soon as they had heard the screams.

Her injured guards lay around groaning, and the only sign of Ersula's struggle were small traces of blood on the corridor's floors. Darathia bullets had hit nearby walls, their fine roots spread out searching for life, before quickly perishing.

Moments after, Harad joined him and they continued their search for the rest of Ersula's party. It wasn't long before they came across the victims of Lomax's newly found weapon; unmistakable growths withering in the poor light.

"He can't have ventured far. All the interstreet gates are closed. We have the area locked down right up to the central Temple," said Harad.

"There are no other ways past us?" queried Jeradon.

"None."

Jeradon's main concern was his son. If anything happened, Pirian would be alone. Yet if he didn't stop their attacker – whoever he believed it to be, no one was safe. "We leave four guards every one hundred yards until we reach the central

Temple. We stop him tonight."

After reaching their destination, the enclosed surroundings of the interstreets opened out. The mirage high above the valley shimmered. It was a clear night and the stars shone bright. At the main gates there was still no sign of Ersula. The attacker had to be close, yet Harad and Jeradon had no idea how Lomax had managed to elude them at every corner. It was as though he had vanished into thin air.

Brom and Stone waited patiently perched on the spires of the great Temple.

Harad was growing impatient. He sighed and caught Jeradon's eye.

"I can barely hear The Father. If he was as strong as he used to be, he'd have found Lomax for us before any of this had happened. He's growing weaker by the hour."

"Perhaps it wasn't such a good idea bringing Lomax back into the city. Unless The Father knew all too well that he isn't responsible for any of this. Unfortunately we've been left to find that out for ourselves." replied Jeradon.

"At the moment, we're as blind as The Father." Harad sighed and checked his guards' positions. "Lomax was once a great Missionary, you know. He spread the word further than anyone else, back when we had a worthy fleet. Lomax would travel thousands of miles to see who was left. He had a marvellous ship."

"*The General.*"

"No…it was no pirate ship. This was Rojin. A 'Mindship'. *Romulus* was born for the skies - Lomax was once as much sky wolf as sea wolf.

"You still have Mindships?"

"No…only *Romulus* remains. Unfortunately, most of our telepaths were either infected or killed in battle. The sick ones - we were unable to transplant their brains into a sufficient vessel before they died. The contamination infected too many of them - we just couldn't grow any more with our depleted resources. Fortunately, *Romulus* was sealed off in long-term hibernation when Lomax left us. Refusing to believe what had happened, he wouldn't accept any other captain. He was more than just a friend to Lomax - but we all felt just as betrayed."

"The pages - your scripture you spoke of to me."

Harad nodded. "He claimed Gana had to be taken and its secrets lost to prevent them falling into Newtonian hands. The Father was growing weak and Newton was closer than ever to discovering the artefact we have known as The Clock of Ages. Lomax became paranoid after visiting The Father - he didn't trust anybody apart from his faithful gargoyle." He paused, reflecting for a moment, "There is nothing more dangerous than a Rojin that has lost faith. No matter how innocent you think he is, Lomax has been washed by the sea for far too long. Revenge shouldn't even be an option to the Rojin; if it was I'd have killed you myself the moment you entered the city."

Jeradon understood. The Rojin had even trusted to hand him back the Newtonian sword he had acquired from his fall. Something he was glad to have at his side. He'd seen Lomax fight on *The General*, and recently almost become a victim of his Darathia gun.

Jeradon observed the great Rojin statues. If only they were able to help - their intimidating presence was enough to keep anyone away from the Temple. No sooner had he thought this, when from the corner of his eye he swore one of them moved slightly. He squinted to see if it was a trickery of the shadows.

All of a sudden a darker shape fell against the night sky; a blur that hit the giant figurine with such force, it toppled backwards against another statue. Jeradon shouted out to Harad and the guards as they all dived out of the way. The great stone warrior tumbled to the floor in pieces, revealing the gargoyle Brom as he tussled with a shadowy figure. The gargoyle, attached to the figure's back, attempted to crush his neck. Then the figure stood up, grabbed hold of Brom's arms and tried to break free as Stone landed in front of them to assist further.

"Stone, no! Brom! Let him go…it's ok, we have him." shouted Harad, beckoning to the guards to move forwards.

Jeradon held his sword in front of him.

As everyone concentrated on apprehending the attacker, he continued to observe the surrounding statues.

"It's over, Lomax."

A snout was recognisable from underneath the hood as Harad edged closer. Brom released his grip as Lomax straightened himself. Harad peered into the hood in the hope of making contact with the wolf's one good eye - yet, as the face caught the moonlight, he could see there was nothing but writhing tendrils hanging from an elongated mouth.

In a split second the figure lashed out at him.

Jeradon caught the blur of movement as Harad moved with shocking speed for a man so portly. His mark was the fastest Jeradon had seen so far. Extending his blade, he slowed and stood his ground. There was another blur as the figure propelled itself towards Harad, grabbing him by the throat.

Surprised at Lomax's newfound ability rivalling their master's, Brom and Stone attempted to move. Yet they remained cemented to the floor. Fixed helplessly, they witnessed several more figures appear from around the Temple that looked similar to their attacker.

Jeradon ran forward as every guard was fired upon. Reaching the choking Harad, his attacker aimed the Darathia weapon directly at Jeradon with his free arm.

Raising his sword in defiance, Jeradon paused briefly before bringing his sword up in one fluid motion.

The weapon fired at exactly the same moment both arms fell

away. It all seemed to happen in slow motion as Harad fell to his knees, a severed limb still attached to his throat as it continued to strangle him.

The first thing Jeradon noticed, other than the rest of the dark figures surrounding him, was the lack of blood. In fact, there wasn't any. The figure simply raised both appendages and pointed them towards each limb. Suddenly, from each neatly severed arm twisted tendrils grew at an alarming rate. As they met each other halfway the tendrils began to pull the limbs back together. Harad stood back up as the arm reattached itself, not for once releasing its grip from around his throat.

Jeradon sighed and lowered his sword. "Neat trick."

The last thing he witnessed was Harad being dragged away before the figures closed in on him.

Under his covers, Pirian drew by plant light.

The pencil twisted and grew slightly, reacting to the touch of his hand. He was used to it by now, the result was always fluid, organic line work. Whenever Pirian took full control it was images to remind himself of where he came from, such as the Greenhouses and more importantly his mother.

Pulling his covers back, a curious Larissa hovered at the side of his bed, as he quickly placed his pillow over the drawings. "What are you up to?" she asked.

"Nothing. Just…doodling." he replied as Nik's sneaky third arm grabbed his drawings from under the pillow. Larissa and Ched leant over Nik as he scanned through the patterns Pirian had drawn. They stopped at one in particular. Pirian watched their expressions change and tried to come up with an excuse. "I couldn't sleep."

Ched's whole face blinked in shock. "So you felt drawing Newton would help?"

"This is pretty detailed stuff. Have you seen it or what?"

asked a curious Larissa.

Pirian didn't know whether he should answer or not. "Only in books."

"What books? There aren't many. People say it's invisible, that it only shows itself just before it swallows you whole. There are many sky pirates that have never returned," said Larissa.

"Yeah...they say you can see the whole city reflected in the eyes of a Newtonian just before he kills you." added Nik.

Pirian was astounded at their explanations. Yet at the same time he was deeply disturbed. He was Newtonian. There was no escaping that, and he hoped that they didn't see the flying city reflected in his own eyes.

"You're not the only one that has a problem sleeping. We often sneak out though through the underfloors. Fancy joining us? Nik reckons he can get as far as the inner Temple," Larissa smiled.

"You aren't serious. The whole Temple is on alert, Larissa,." replied Pirian.

"Makes it all the more exciting." She leaned forward. "Besides, we just keep an eye out for each other," she assured him as she slowly vanished.

Pirian could hear her invisible laugh while the rest of the children stirred in their sleep.

The laughter quietened when some of the children moaned at being woken. Pirian thought for a moment about joining them. It was no different from hiding on Newton. He'd been doing it all his life, sneaking off on his own to the Greenhouses and hiding in Newton's forests and even the ventilation systems to evade Viktor and his cronies. This time he had some friends to do it with. "Okay...why not," he smiled as Larissa quickly reappeared.

Quietly making their way towards the doorway in the darkness the four children began to make their exit via an underground cooling system that ran under the floor. Larissa, Nik and Ched had used the system for years, pulling up a floorboard or two and slipping through. As they were about to squeeze themselves under, the dormitory door opened, and standing in the doorway was a shadowy figure.

It stood for a moment and entered the room quietly.

All of them froze in terror.

As the figure moved towards them, it spoke. "Any other night and I would turn a blind eye to this in the same way The Father would." They relaxed, recognising Kira's voice. "But tonight you must stay in the dorm. That means all of you, Larissa."

"Ohhh, You're spoiling the fun." she replied, folding her arms.

"Quit it, Larissa," answered Kira sternly.

Pirian caught Kira's eye. "What is it?"

"I didn't know what else to do Pirian, other than come here and make sure you were all safe. I'm sure if my father was here, it would have been easier. Things would be safer." She paused as her brother entered the room and the rest of the children began to wake.

"Kira...not here," said her brother.

"It's alright, Karl," she replied as she began to address the dorm. "Everyone get back to sleep, there is nothing to be concerned about." Groaning once again the rest of the children tossed and turned and then began to settle. Then Kira and Karl took Pirian aside.

"Kira?"

"Ersula was taken. Both our fathers followed and..."

"No."

"They're only missing. There is no evidence to suggest that..."

"I don't want to hear it, Kira. If they are missing then I'm sure we can find them."

"We?" retorted Karl.

"Yes, 'we'. Our parents would do the same for us," replied Pirian.

Kira was taken back by the determination in Pirian's voice. "You can't be serious Pirian. You're just a…"

"What?" he snapped. "A child?"

"A child without any training. Anything could happen to you. We can't babysit you on some heroic quest to bring our parents back." said Karl sternly.

"I'm not asking you to, Karl. Yes, I'm a child, but I'm not going to let that stop me doing what I have to do. I'm not going to let either of you stop me." Pirian looked at Kira. "We all go."

Karl folded his arms in frustration. "For Gana's sake…"

Kira looked at her brother. "Karl, this isn't helping. We need to look for them. We need to find Lomax."

"We'll need a guide that will lead us directly to him," said Pirian. "We find Lomax, we find our parents and Ersula."

"You're thinking of Vagabond, aren't you?" asked Kira.

"Of course. He shares a connection with his captain; he'll be able to lead us right to him."

"No chance. We'd need our father to authorise his release." Karl shook his head.

Pirian grinned. "I think I know a way round that."

Harad, The Father's Voice, was lost.

Karl knew that without Harad to speak for him they would only be challenged by the guards. He knew that Kira's voice was far stronger than his own, yet with her Sisterhood training incomplete, the guards would still not take an order from her.

Kira and Karl were as determined as Pirian to find their own father. For the guards outside Vagabond's cell, it was a great shock to see the face of their leader approaching.

"Harad Sur," bowed one of the guards, then immediately

looked over to the rest of them, "We thought…"

His robe hood was pulled over his head, yet the guards could still clearly see his features. Karl stood behind his father with Kira and Pirian either side. "My disappearance is a decoy - all part of the plan to lure the Sea Wolf out. I will need the gargoyle released to assist us further."

"Sur?"

"You heard me clearly enough. In order to find him, we need the gargoyle to track his Captain. The Father has requested this himself."

The Rojin guard responded immediately and opened the cell door. Harad and his son walked in and commanded the guard once again as Pirian and Kira waited outside.

"Chain him to my son."

There was a jangling sound and before long Harad had exited the cell. Pirian looked on as Karl emerged with a confused Vagabond perched on his shoulder, chains from the gargoyle's bonds dangling down across his chest and attached to his belt.

"Thank you, guard." Harad coughed as his voice broke slightly.

Karl looked over at his sister, maintaining his cool.

"It's…the gargoyle moss. Really gets to the back of my throat," added Harad, coughing once more. "Stay alert guards, we will keep you posted on the situation."

They all made their way to the eastern interstreet and found an unguarded quarter to address Vagabond. Harad stepped forward and looked at the gargoyle as it jumped off Karl's shoulder onto a low statue, tilting its head in curiosity.

Then laughed.

Harad twitched and attempted to bellow, "How dare you laugh!" he croaked.

"I think he saw straight through you, Ched," said Karl.

Ched sighed. His face then blinked and folded out to reveal

his own features. "I just don't see what's so funny. It's hard doing voices."

"You did fine. It was a lot to ask of you." Pirian looked back at Vagabond. "And you can wipe that smirk off your face." The gargoyle sulked, "You know why you're here. You can find your Captain and lead us to our parents."

There was no malice in Vagabond's reactions. This surprised Kira and Karl most of all - only Karl could remember Lomax and Vagabond and they were mainly bedtime stories, as told to many other Rojin children.

They saw that he was certainly less intimidating than Brom and Stone; smaller in stature and less serious. Sitting on the statue a moment longer he looked at Pirian and held out his hand, cocking his head.

Pirian pulled out some scraps from his pocket and threw it to Vagabond who devoured them and put his arm out for more. "Later. After you have helped us."

Vagabond puffed himself up and then took off, Karl immediately following suit, pulling on the chain in an attempt to keep him under control. The others followed. As they reached the end of the eastern interstreet Vagabond stopped and once again perched himself on a statue. Karl could sense there was someone lurking in the shadows, his symbiont blade shivering to life. Edging forward he raised his hand to keep Kira, Ched and Pirian back.

Karl relaxed and then sighed before he snapped, "Come out Larissa."

From behind the statue Larissa Sou sheepishly materialised. Pirian was almost as annoyed as Karl. "What are you doing?"

"Nik and I wanted to know where Ched was. So I thought I'd come and find him."

"Well, you've found him," snapped Karl turning to his sister. "This is ridiculous Kira. Is this going to be a babysitters club?!"

"We're not kids. Who are you to tell us what to do anyway, Karl. You don't even have a mark. Perhaps if you grow yourself another head we'll do as you say!" growled Larissa.

Her feisty attitude disconcerted Karl. Clenching his teeth, he retracted his blade. "I don't need this."

Vagabond sat patiently watching the show.

Pirian broke the tension and surveyed their current whereabouts in an attempt to figure out the direction they were heading. "You're taking us to the inner Temple, aren't you?" he asked the gargoyle.

Vagabond replied with a nod.

"I thought as much. Then that means we need to get into the Temple as soon as possible, before they find out Harad is still missing. It won't take them long to put two and two together."

"So we send Ched back, along with Larissa. Simple as that," said Karl.

"No," replied Kira. "You forget Larissa's 'ghosting' ability. She doesn't just vanish, she can walk through walls, even enable any of us to. Also, Larissa and most of the other children use the underfloors to sneak out at night. They know them like the back of their hands. Even right into the Temple. We need her, Karl."

"You think I didn't do that as a kid? Those cooling systems are pitch black, and with no plant lights we won't be able to see anything!"

"I have torches," answered Larissa.

"You gave this some thought then?" he replied.

Larissa smiled back at Kira. "The thing is, not even Ched and myself have ventured as far as the inner Temple. We wouldn't dare."

"Then let's make this a first. I'm certain that if Vagabond saw through Ched's disguise then Brom and Stone would too. This is our only option," said Pirian.

∞

Barely large enough for an adult to crawl through, the underfloors were simply a series of small tunnel systems carved into the Erth for ventilation. The huge structure of the Rojin Temple and its interlocking buildings relied on them heavily. Guided by Vagabond and the green glow of their torches, they edged their way forward for the next mile.

They came to a number of dead ends, mostly obstructed by bars. Kira knew that they were now underneath the inner Temple and that the bars were there for a reason. When they reached one dead end in particular, Larissa's ghosting ability was called upon. She simply held onto Karl's arm and instructed everyone else to link. Upon doing so, their density altered, enabling them enough to move through the obstruction, but not sink into the Erth.

Pirian shivered as Larissa let go of the chain. Imagining death being a similar experience, it felt as though he'd just fallen into a lake of ice. As his senses quickly came back to him, the first thing he could feel were the small creatures brushing past his feet.

It wasn't long before they began to see a brighter glow in the distance. The tunnel opened out into what could only be one of the many crypts that held the Rojin dead. Torches hung from the small circular room. Grabbing one from the wall, Karl lowered it towards the floor - rats were scurrying back and forth through the tunnel system and around the crypt.

On the walls Pirian could make out many inscriptions detailing the dead. Finely carved stones marking the graves were clearly separated on the walls. What was less obvious was the way out.

Vagabond hung in mid air, avoiding the torch flame that Karl held above his head.

"Now what?" asked Karl. "These crypts are sealed from the outside."

The crypt was circular, bricked up archways equally spaced out around them, each of which had separate inscriptions and carvings; doorways that lead to the tombs of Rojin. Vagabond rested on the edge of one of the arches, holding a hand over the seal and signalling to Karl.

Karl repeated what Vagabond had done. " This one must be the entrance from the Temple, the air is warm."

Pirian watched as Vagabond flew over to another arch, blowing away the dust and cobwebs to reveal symbols and a beautiful stone carving of what appeared to be a man. Pirian recognised the Rojin hieroglyphs; they were exactly the same as the ones he had seen when he first entered the Temple with his father. Upon studying them more closely, the symbols leaped out at Pirian. He could understand every word:

> *The Seventh City cast in Stone*
> *Giant Shadow*
> *A Traitor's Throne*

As they all looked more closely, they could see that the large figure was surrounded by a small city. Perched on his shoulders and flying above him were what looked like hundreds of gargoyles.

"Swift," whispered Kira.

"The Rojin giant. I've read about him." said Pirian. "Rumour has it he was a Rojin whose mark grew out of control."

Kira nodded. "He's a legend, a giant that helped to win many battles. But one day he retired underground where, along with his followers - he discovered one of the lost cities. The only living souls that remained of this city were gargoyles protecting an unknown artefact with their lives."

"The Clock of Ages," Karl added.

"Then this symbol..." Pirian pointed to the central crest of the arch and what appeared to be a carved 'L' tipped on its back. "Seven?"

"This is Gargoy; the Seventh City. Vagabond's home." said Kira.

Vagabond grew restless.

Kira looked up at the gargoyle and continued the story, "These creatures had been locked away for centuries, with nothing but their cherished buildings for company. So, when the Twelfth City attacked, Swift instructed the surviving Gargoyles to take The Clock of Ages above ground, promising he would remain behind, holding their enemy back. The Clock of Ages was handed to The Father, where it remained for thousands of years. It is said that Swift died holding up the very foundations of the Rojin capital when the Twelfth City attacked."

"So this 'Traitor's Throne' is in Gargoy?" asked Pirian.

"According to our history lessons. Lomax must have been using the gargoyle to reveal the location of his city." added Karl.

"Yes. Where he intends to keep our parents prisoner and rule safely underground. He must have deeper motives." said Kira.

Vagabond flew down in front of the tomb. None of them were sure of what he did, but the tomb slowly opened as though answering to the forgotten touch of the gargoyle.

For a moment, they all hesitated at the mouth of the tomb, expecting to see the remains of skeletons. Instead there was a huge, dark cave leading downwards into nothing. "Multiple crypts, tombs within tombs. It's all downhill from here," said Pirian.

"I don't like this one bit." Karl yanked the chain, pulling Vagabond away from the opening. "You better be taking us to your city, or Gana help you I'll crack your stone hide."

Pirian held his frustration. "He's just following his nose as we intended, Karl. The sooner you leave him be, the sooner we find Ersula and our parents."

Karl was apprehensive. "I think he's following his past, and I don't like where it's taking us. He could be leading us into a trap."

"We continue, no matter what." Pirian doubted that Lomax had anything to do with this at all. There was far more to this, and he was sure his father had come close to finding out, which gave him the drive and determination he needed. His father was right; he had to grow up, and now was as good a time as any as he entered the dark confines of the cave.

Pirian, Kira and Karl all wore Rojin utility belts. They had a gas mask and goggles each in case they needed them. Kira carried a grapple and rope, Karl an assortment of weapons, while spare masks were also handed to Ched and Larissa.

Karl unfastened his quiver from his back and handed it to Ched along with the bow. "Just in case."

"Thanks," replied Ched.

"Just stay close. That goes for all of you."

Larissa edged forward, peering into the darkness. The others held up their torches, the blackness that surrounded her was far less imposing in the orange glow. She was the first to step through as Vagabond followed, leading Karl and the rest them further under the Temple.

By torchlight Pirian could now see many skeletons laid out into recesses carved into the cave walls. Their skulls were placed upon their chests, while their withered symbiont blade lay across their lower torso.

"The Rojin believe that to place a man's head over his heart is a symbol of final acceptance. We believe in a final bow. Their own blade opens them, while a Second makes the final cut of the soul. With honour comes the acceptance of death," explained Karl.

"Beheading. Maybe one day I'll understand."

Kira added, "We prefer the term 'Severance'. The head is only the physical cut. We don't see it as execution, but the only way to separate the soul for those that approach death and don't want, or are unable to commit Unity. Those that have already perished on the battle field are returned for Severance."

"Unity?"

"The spirits of the dead survive in the memories of the living. It is a place most souls end up." Kira pointed to herself. "The collective conscience is more than one voice. It can be the voice of your kin and many before them."

"You share Unity with your mother?"

Kira nodded. "She speaks to me all the time, has done since the moment she died. She is part of me now. Newtonians are unable to do this - the Dosage has killed off any memory of their past and connections to immediate family. Their state of mind is a controlled fabrication. Memory is conscience. Conscience is soul. There are many Rojin that have Unity dating back generations."

It was hard to imagine another person living inside his head; he had enough of his own thoughts and memories eating away at him. *No wonder the Rojin are so wise. No wonder they never fear death*, he thought.

As they came to the end of the crypt's tunnel system, they could all see a great a huge open cave. They made their way further down, the stagnant smell of the cavern becoming stronger with every step. Reaching the bottom, the smell became far more overpowering. Karl and Pirian lifted their torches, holding their hand to their masks. Looking upwards they could make out exactly what was causing the smell.

The huge ceiling of the cavern seemed to be adorned with hundreds of dead bodies, hanging from above. On closer inspection Pirian could make out that the bodies seemed to be wrapped in a thin layer of translucent, glistening skin.

Decapitation and burial was one thing, but wrapping the dead and hanging them upside down from the ceiling was something else.

Then they moved.

Larissa looked carefully as the bodies twitched slightly, their slow breathing, interrupted by the odd screech. Doused in orange light, the bodies resembled demons from the inferno.

On closer inspection, Pirian could clearly make out what they were, "Bats…they're huge!"

"Urantah," corrected Karl.

XIV

Jeradon had never held a 'new born' before, let alone delivered one.

In his moment of joy, cruel memories flashed before his eyes; images he thought had been taken away from him since building the Greenhouse. Those that had been blessed with a moment's life were once his victims and he could still see their blood on his hands.

These cruel memories tempted him to take the Dosage once again. He refocused, realising that Neeve and his child were enough to take the pain away.

I don't deserve you, he told himself.

If it wasn't for the Greenhouse, he was certain that Neeve wouldn't have made it. The habitat was the perfect place for their baby to be born, a nursery in more ways than one. To Jeradon his son had come into the world just as effortlessly as the first flowers he had planted. Maybe the Greenhouse was the perfect place to raise him too. Or more importantly, hide him.

Neeve witnessed Jeradon's smile vanish as he thought of the consequences.

She reached out her arms and took hold of her son. "He's perfect."

"Yes…he is. And that's what I'm afraid of. Our son will have to stay here, Neeve - it would be disastrous if he was discovered. He's been born free of the Dosage, and to my knowledge it's never happened in the history of this city."

"Can we not just forget about the consequences for once. Please Jeradon, this is our moment, all three of us. I'm a Horncastle. By the rules of Newton, we're officially married. Our boy has bound us."

"I'm sorry, Neeve." Jeradon held her face in his hands.

"It's okay, I understand. But right now I don't care about what *could* happen. Nothing is coming between us."

"You do realise he will have to stay here. It's early days yet and there may be side effects. We will take it in turns to look after him. Educate him."

"I'm not sure, Jeradon. As much as I love what you have built, we could end up raising a wild child. He could become like the Rojin."

"Neeve, think of all I have shown you. Right now, from what I have seen and all I have learned so far, I would rather him be brought up in an environment similar to the Rojin. Free of the Dosage, free of control. He could be the very answer the Emperor is looking for. The very answer *I* am looking for."

Neeve withdrew and held her son closer. "What do you mean?"

Jeradon pulled away some of the surrounding blanket his son was carefully wrapped in, revealing a tiny arm. "He's a Defect... look, he has a mark. It is slight, yet there is a possibility it could develop into something."

"Our son is not an experiment, Jeradon!" Neeve said angrily.

"No...no, he isn't. I would never look at him like that. But think about it, Neeve. Worst-case scenario is that the Emperor could find out about him. If that happens we will be executed. On the other hand, if this mark develops, if he has potential powers and similarities to Newton's enemy, our son may be seen as a potential weapon against the Rojin. But I believe he's the opposite - he's a weapon against Newton."

Neeve began to weep. "Listen to yourself…our my son is not a weapon. Please Jeradon…you're frightening me. He's just a baby."

Jeradon placed his arm around them both. "I will not allow any harm to come to either of you." Reassured, Neeve smiled and looked into the eyes of her little boy. "What are we going to call him? We haven't even thought of a name."

Yet Jeradon had already been told. A name that he had already seen in his dreams. "He already has one." He gently moved the back of his fingers down his son's face, "Don't you…Pirian?"

Fifteen

Littered across the floor were the rotting remains of Urantah. Their size was three times that of any Rojin, yet most of the bodies were smaller - young that had fallen from their mother's grip. A number of the bodies had been savagely torn apart by something far more threatening, unnerving the group more than ever. The Urantah it seemed, were the least of their worries.

The heat generated by the bodies hanging high above was stifling, only encouraging the surrounding stench.

"I think it's safe to assume these are unbroken for flight. They'll be unpredictable, so keep your voices down," whispered Karl.

Any Urantah that hadn't been broken for flight, could indeed be dangerous. Hidden away underground, they were as wild as they came.

"There must be a way out," said Pirian.

Karl scanned further ahead, noticing a faint amber glow, "Looks as though there is a large opening the other side."

There were many openings, scattered across the cavern, yet moving forwards was the easier route. Vagabond pulled at his chain, urging them on as Karl stepped forward into the putrid mess spread over the cavern's floor.

As they made their way over the decaying matter, giant bugs the size of their forearms scampered over the bones and stalagmites. Ched's face blinked and contorted uncontrollably as he froze in fear. Karl hacked away at them as Ched attempted to raise his bow. His forearm shook and he paused, noticing Karl wave his aim downwards in a gesture not to waste his arrows, or risk being shot in the process.

Kira held out her arm to prevent anyone walking any further, "Wait!" she shuffled forward slightly and looked directly downwards into a bottomless crevasse stretching out beneath them.

Vagabond perched himself on Karl's shoulder as Kira pulled the grapple gun and rope from her pack. The Urantah fidgeted overhead. Larissa looked upwards, noticing several stretch their wings, their faces yawning in the blackness.

Pirian raised his torch slightly, he could make out the detail of their features: huge eyes and snout, their heads resembling that of a bronzed wolf. They were not as grotesque as their smaller cousins, but they made up for it with their imposing size.

Distracted by another movement, Pirian noticed the heat signature of a much larger creature approaching through a large opening in the ceiling. A huge snakelike body coiled outwards from the hole. As it uncoiled, a thousand legs began to ripple across its belly, twitching erratically.

It hung motionless for a moment, dangling overhead.

Pirian froze. He grabbed Kira's arm and pointed upwards. Her eyes widened as the rest of them averted their gaze. Luckily, for now, the huge monstrous centipede hadn't noticed them. Its focus was on the Urantah slumbering away. If the winged creatures were three times their size, then the nightmare edging its way closer towards its sleepy prey seemed ten times larger.

Karl knew that he had to get them across the crevasse immediately, before the creature disturbed the Urantah, or worse, came for them. Frantically he snatched the grapple gun from his sister's hands and fired it. The grapple snagged on an overhanging stalactite the other side of the cavern.

The girls went first, waiting for Ched as he held the rope.

Pirian held his torch higher to inspect the monstrous insect above them. It crawled silently, then rearing on its legs it coiled its body, mandibles ready for the strike. The unsuspecting Urantah opened its eyes and panicked, releasing its foothold in an attempt to drop away from the predator. The centipede struck, swinging its body back to counter the momentum of its prey as it tried to escape.

"Go!" shouted Pirian as he covered his ears at the deafening screech amplifying through the cavern. Ched jumped, swinging across and landing the other side as the two girls dived into a nearby opening. In his frantic rush he let go of the rope as it swung back and forth over the crevasse.

The Urantah swarmed overhead, circling the cavern and coming dangerously near to the ground. Pirian, Karl and Vagabond covered themselves. Karl looked up as he saw the mass of huge, black wings fly towards the swinging rope. As they arched back round for another pass, one was left caught up and tangled. The rope went taut and the Urantah lost its momentum, swinging downwards. Struggling further, it attempted to take flight, all the while pulling against the rope.

The giant centipede caught sight of the entangled prey. Saving its current meal by skewering it on a nearby stalactite, it dropped to the floor below.

As the creature approached, Pirian swung his torch, his only weapon, in front of himself.

Karl's symbiont blade grew in a split second. Even with his training, and surviving his Erth Walk, there was apprehension as he also waved his torch to distract the creature. Vagabond couldn't even fly away if he wanted to.

With an unsettling speed the monster edged closer, rearing its savage legs as the rest of the Urantah flew around its looming mass. Pirian and Karl stared directly into its face, lit up by the torches, oranges and browns glowed even warmer across its girth. The dark patches on its head resembled a giant demonic skull as its mandibles opened wide.

Karl rushed forward, Vagabond having no choice but to follow. As he approached its underside he rolled and slashed outwards to cut the creature's legs. The katanac blade could practically cut through anything, including armoured legs, yet Karl simply didn't have the momentum or the strength to carry the action through.

The creature recoiled as Karl jumped underneath its mass, attempting to slash its underbelly. But this time the creature had not underestimated him, knocking Karl backwards with one of its many legs.

Overhead the tangled Urantah continued to struggle. Distracted, the centipede edged forward, pushing Pirian closer to the edge of the crevasse. Instead of rearing up, the creature came within spitting distance of Pirian. Holding up his torch once again, his arm began to ache. Threatened, his mark locked his hand around the torch.

Mandibles twitched, as an acrid breath poured over Pirian. The flame of the torch grew and without any conscious control, Pirian's arm forced the fire directly into the monster's mouth.

The scream was even more deafening than the Urantah circling above as the centipede reared upwards with an intimidating force. Panicked even more by the noise, the entangled Urantah pulled once more against the rope. The stalactite broke away and as the Urantah flew overhead, the skewer-shaped rock followed, swinging down, directly into the body of the giant centipede.

It fell to the floor in a crumpled mess amongst the bones and putrid mess of its prey, legs twitching for the last time. The Urantah followed, landing awkwardly, its wing breaking under its own weight.

Karl paused for a moment, out of breath, and gave Pirian a surprised look. Then he made his way over to the injured creature, the rest of the Urantah having left their companion behind.

Pirian felt for the poor creature lying there as it attempted to pull itself up off the ground. It screeched with fear as Karl made his way closer.

"What are you doing?" shouted Pirian.

Karl drove his symbiont blade through its skull without a moment's thought. "Putting it out of its misery."

Sick to the stomach, Pirian grabbed Karl by his shirt. "What did you do that for!" he shouted, knowing he could have healed it.

"It had to be done." He knocked Pirian's arm away.

"It saved our lives. That's how you repay it?!"

"I think you had more to do with that," said Karl, as he untied the grapple from the stalactite embedded in the impaled centipede "Its wing was broken. There are many more of these things in the caves." He said gesturing towards the centipede. "I don't wish to hang around here any longer than I have to. I was simply putting it to rest - it's in Gana's hands now."

Frustrated, Pirian saw his point as he looked down at the bat. He just hoped he would never have to do anything like that.

Karl fired the grapple once again, tested it was secure and handed the rope to Pirian. Hesitating, he looked down. His fear of heights was quelled, yet he couldn't help but think of the empty space below. He remembered the morning he awoke in the Rojin capital, his sickness almost cured. Swinging over the chasm was just one more test at overcoming his fear of heights.

He swung across and landed confidently on the other side.

All Kira and the others could make out through the commotion, were two torches frantically moving in the darkness and brief glimpses of the monster. Before long Pirian and Karl were safely across.

Kira hugged her brother, "We couldn't do a thing."

"It's ok. We're alright Kira." saying no more, Karl caught Pirian's eye. There was something his father and sister weren't telling him about the boy. *We should be dead*, he thought.

Pirian's arm had finally relaxed. He noticed Larissa and Ched standing together in the opening, staring at him.

"What in Gana's name are we doing?" piped Ched. "This is madness. If you hadn't turned up, I could have just done my part at the Temple and that would have been it."

"I'm sorry Ched, I shouldn't have sneaked out," whispered Larissa. "Nik and I were just curious what Kira needed you for. It's not often a Vaseesh graces us with their presence."

"Well, now you know. At least Nik had the sense not to come with you. It's not as though we've known Pirian long, and already you're willing to crawl through bat dung, jump crevasses and nearly end up as insect bait for him."

Larissa's voice grew louder. "This isn't just for Pirian. Our leader and High Priestess are missing too, if you'd forgotten."

Kira approached. "Perhaps you should keep your eyes open and mouths closed.".

Ched nodded. "Yeah, and we all love Ersula," he said sarcastically, under his breath. Vagabond flew past leading Karl. "That gargoyle could be leading us straight to our deaths. I've heard all kinds of stories about this Lomax. He could have ki…"

"I don't wish to hear those words," interrupted Pirian behind them as he followed the others, "You're here to help. I *know* my father isn't dead, it takes a lot to kill a Horncastle. It's hard enough not knowing what's happened, let alone where we'll end up. You'll just have to block those bedtime stories out of your head for now."

It was a positive thought. "I hope you're right. None of us have parents anymore, just The Father. I'm sure he's been watching over us, at least," said Ched.

Pirian smiled back. "That's more like it. I believe that too. Ever since we decided to come on this crazy adventure. Even the great Gana you worship is watching over us, I'm sure of it."

Ched and Larissa said no more and continued to follow the others further underground.

Eventually they approached the end of another huge cavern. They could make out the structure of what looked like old buildings buried within the rock - the structures were metallic and had corroded and collapsed under the weight of the stone that had built up around them. It was as though the buildings had been buried and forgotten. Windows and walkways could be made out every now and again, the rock surrendering more detail. Pirian was unsure if the structure was meant to be at such an angle; it was as though the buildings had fallen to one side, before becoming a victim of time. They were familiar to him; almost Newtonian in design.

They walked through one of the windows half buried in the cavern's floor. "We must have walked as far as the canyon. These buildings are part of the archaeological dig. We shouldn't be out here, Kira." stated Karl.

Then Pirian remembered why he felt he had seen these buildings before. There was indeed a canyon and he 'remembered' flying through it, seeing what looked like large concrete and metal structures stitching the walls together. Vagabond perched himself on Karl's shoulder and looked over at Pirian. Closing his eyes, Pirian could see himself through the gargoyle's eyes. The image flickered slightly before he opened his eyes. Vagabond took off once again, leading them further into the old structure.

Once again Pirian closed his eyes. He could now see further ahead. As Vagabond drifted from view around the corner, he could make out what he only assumed Vagabond was seeing. Perhaps he had seen through Vagabonds eyes on his journey to the Rojin capital, *that's why this is familiar?* he thought.

"Pirian?" interrupted Larissa.

His eyes snapped open. "...Sorry. I was distracted for a moment."

Kira placed a comforting hand on his shoulder then walked on.

They began to descend through the inner structure of the buildings that had merged together in a tangled mess of metal and stone. The further they descended, the more the Erth swallowed Pirian, and the stronger he felt.

Reaching the bottom of one of the buildings they could see that the floor had fallen away, leaving a gaping void. Dropping a torch confirmed the void fell hundreds of feet below. A breeze blew up through the structure as they altered their course, making their way through several openings, leading to more caverns and buried architecture.

Descending forever downwards, the caverns were becoming more refined, like large tunnels that had been built centuries before. Where the cave systems had not taken hold, there were many details; such as ceramic tiles closely knitted together along a curved ceiling. Distorted images hung along the curved walls, ripped and faded beyond all recognition. Along the floor they could make out twisted metal that attempted to straighten itself. As they walked on, tracks appeared, guiding them forward.

Pirian knelt down and inspected a large metal frame that had fallen from one of the walls. As he lifted it, sand fell away to reveal an abstract image of broken coloured lines. Looking closer by the light of his torch, he could make out all kinds of strange looking words, similar to the Rojin's ancient tongue.

The others gathered round, unable to shine any extra light on what the images were. They were almost hieroglyphic, reminding Pirian of a broken Newtonian circuit board.

A breeze picked up carrying a distinctive smell, distracting them all from the hieroglyphs.

"Protronium," muttered Pirian as he lifted the torch higher to inspect the tunnel.

The smell of protronium was noticeable to everyone, yet to Pirian it was particularly potent. Venturing further into the tunnel system, they all noticed a large, faded red circular box, hanging from a broken support. What appeared to be some kind of signage was heavily damaged, and the symbols on its surface were once again illegible.

Further on, the tunnel had collapsed, the cave system once again taking hold. As they squeezed through, they began to make out the glistening of protronium ore embedded within the rock, its natural amber fluorescence giving extra light to the darkened cave.

"This is the reason for the capital's location. We've never been short of protronium, but unless the Rojin people continue to mine, the city will fall further into decline," explained Kira. "The Father's voice needs to be heard. We need his guidance, his motivation more than ever."

"The Father holds this city together?" asked Pirian.

Karl nodded. "Yes, in more ways than you realise. As long as he can see through others and spread his voice then the city is safe. We have never been so vulnerable as we are now. There are very few people left beyond the outer walls, farmers are unable to cultivate and provide for their families, animals and plantlife are dying all around us every day. There is only so much room within Yodann's centre and inner walls. Some people have left to fight, others have just vanished and we have no idea where. The Father cannot see or hear them anymore. Even my father has difficulty, the further he ventures from the Temple the less he can hear those close by. Those that still have faith are dying every minute, protecting our people, continuing to spread the word and teachings across Erth. But all they can do now, is try and stay alive out there beyond our city, while the war continues."

Vagabond tugged anxiously at his chain, reminding them of why they were here.

As they pressed on they had come across many buried tunnel systems. There were also rusted boxes protruding from what looked like liquefied stone. Pirian was reminded of the hover trains back on Newton, although these carriages were far different in design. They entered via a small doorway, making their way through the carriage towards another opening that brought them through the blocked tunnel.

The only direction they could go now was upwards. They noticed another doorway leading to stairs, and finally as they reached the top, a further cave system. It seemed that they had now passed through the forgotten tunnels.

The protronium ore was becoming more abundant the further they ventured. Eventually they all came to an outcrop, which looked down over a huge underground lake. Amber in colour, it was obvious that the lake had absorbed much of the surrounding protronium; a vast cavernous hole, rich in supply of their precious fuel.

Vagabond continued to guide them forwards. The smell had become even more potent as they made their way carefully around the outcrop, towards another cave. There was barely any need for torchlight; the cave system they had entered was also rich in protronium ore. For Pirian, the glistening amber was becoming too much, almost making him gag. But it wasn't enough to distract him from pushing on.

The breeze through the cave system was once again beginning to lift.

In the distance, chanting could be heard.

Vagabond pressed on, more eager than anyone else to see his old home.

The voices became louder. Pirian couldn't recognise the language, but it was a distinctive dialect, echoing throughout the caves. Being careful not to be seen, they came to rest at a huge overhang, sneaking up to the edge and peering over.

Everyone but Pirian looked. Closing his eyes he saw exactly what Vagabond observed.

Below, across the vast expanse of what looked like a huge forgotten underground city, were thousands of people. There were men and women of all ages, including children; a mixture of those that carried marks and others that didn't. Protronium ore once again lit the huge expanse, its amber glow reaching as far as the eye could see. Great columns reached up towards the ceiling, knitted into the natural formations of stalagmites and stalactites. A river arched itself around crumbled, stone ruins, similar to the structures they had come across in the cave systems. Huge stone buildings were swallowed by moss and stone, casting ominous shadows along the walls. A huge fallen clock tower lay across the canyon reaching out towards a raised semi-circle; huge bridges enabling access over what looked like a bottomless pit.

In the centre of the semi-circle was the largest statue Pirian had ever seen. A colossus of a man, so large that he was doubled over, the weight of the cavern upon his shoulders. Steps were cut into the gigantic figure, spiralling up its leg, back and arm. Scaffolding stitched its self to stone limbs, ropes and chains hanging down as though the colossus had been caught in a gigantic spider's web. Huge torches surrounded the large underground cavern and spread away into the distance. They all watched as a cloaked and hooded figure stood up from what resembled a large, stone throne at the base of the statue. The figure then walked in front of three large stones that were raising slowly in front of them. Upon the semi-circle surrounding the stones were several more hooded figures. Pirian opened his eyes and took a look for himself.

"Is this Gargoy?" he asked Kira.

"Yes. Looks like they have converted the architectural digs

into a protronium mine. These people, they're from the outer walls."

"That must be the Traitor's Throne," said Pirian.

"And that the traitor," added Karl. "Their chanting, it sounds like ancient Rojin."

Karl kept his eyes on the hooded figures as the stones locked into place. "It has to be an uprising. The Father hasn't been able to answer these people."

The stones began to turn.

Kira gasped, holding her hand to her mouth and preventing herself from shouting out, "Karl…Oh Gana no."

Karl held his sister's face to his chest.

The first stone came to a rest. Facing the crowd Harad was revealed, his wrists and ankles spread outwards and fastened to the surface with stone rings. He barely seemed conscious, a trickle of blood running down his face from a blow to the head.

Pirian didn't say a word as the middle stone finished turning to reveal his own father. He was relieved he was still alive.

Jeradon was obviously fully awake and aware of his surroundings, turning his head as the final stone came to a rest revealing…

"Lomax." stated Pirian.

Vagabond was more restless than ever as he pulled at the chain. Karl yanked him down, a puzzled look on his face, "Then who…?"

Darathia parted, revealing the throne at the base of the statue more clearly. The figure proceeded to pass amongst them, walking more into view, arms spread wide.

Kira's heart sank as her brother held her close. She recognised the figure before anything was said.

Ersula savoured the moment of rapture. "The Father is lost. Not even the man they call the Voice can hear him anymore."

"He's nowhere to be found." stated an agitated Neeve.

Jeradon grew more and more frustrated at the disappearance of his son. "Of all the times he could go missing. We go six years without the Emperor visiting…"

"Jakahn is a powerful voice. Both of us, of all people should know that," Neeve reminded Jeradon.

"But Adviser?"

"Don't be so surprised. He's only one step away from becoming Emperor himself. There'll be nothing stopping him then."

Jeradon brushed his hand over his shaven head. "Surel I can just about take care of. He's out of touch, gullible enough to take onboard what we have to say about the project. Jakahn knows us too well."

Three Gardeners raced up the hill towards Jeradon and Neeve. "No sign of your son." the Gardener caught his breath, "…And the Emperor and his Adviser have arrived."

Jeradon sighed, "Well, we can't keep them waiting. Let them in."

High up in the trees, Pirian could see across the canopy and the valley of fields that stretched out beyond the forest. He had no idea he was on a flying city. To him, the surroundings he had been brought up in the past five years were his home. He more than believed he was on the mysterious Erth his parents' told him about.

Pirian had only recently found the cliffs, which were in fact the walls of the habitat. He hadn't the courage to climb them yet, but imagined one day he would find the strength to do so. Although still so very young, he knew all too well sneaking away from his parents would get him into trouble. But the Greenhouse was far too enticing for him to remain still; it inspired him. As he sat perched in the tree he innocently drew all manner of creatures he had come across.

In the distance Pirian could still make out his parents. He'd heard them and the Gardeners shouting earlier as they looked for him. To Pirian hiding from them all was an adventure.

He could make out his mother and father as several other people who he hadn't seen before approached. Snapping the book shut, he hid it in his secret hide away and descended the tree for a closer look.

"The other two Greenhouses are near completion," stated Jeradon as Lord Surel tilted back his head to breath in the fresh air of the habitat.

"And they are as intoxicating as this one?"

"They are less developed, yet the air is good enough for anyone to breathe."

Jakahn looked agitated. Jeradon could sense his jealousy, he was desperate to say something.

"How close are we to actually finding anything of use in our fight against the Rojin?" asked Surel.

"In terms of...?"

"In terms of these great ideas of yours, which I have allowed you to explore for the past seven years. I am growing tired, Jeradon. For all I know it's these poisonous habitats that have made me sick."

Indeed the Emperor looked ill. His features had become

more sunken and his posture was weaker. Yet it could just as easily have been Jakahn's poisoned advice having an affect on him, rather than his own work.

Neeve saw Jakahn staring at her. She averted her gaze, uncomfortably. She was thinking about her son, hoping that he was hidden away out of sight. She had kept him secret so far. For Pirian to be found out now could be disastrous.

"I seem to remember from Lord Surel's agreement, that you were to find the source of the Rojin's communication. Their reading of minds and use of weapons. The more time you waste, the longer we remain in the dark. We need to fight them with their own knowledge." stated Jakahn. "What of the gift I brought back for you several years ago?"

"I destroyed it."

"You did what!?" shouted Jakahn.

The Emperor intervened. "You destroyed the Darathia specimen?"

"It was far too dangerous. I found out everything I needed to and then burnt it."

Jeradon could see Jakahn's rage building, "This is an outrage. You spend years cooped up in this habitat attempting to find out how to grow their weapons, then when handed to you on a plate you destroy it?"

"You of all people know that the Darathia have turned on the Rojin. They must have somehow lost control, the same way we could. I wasn't going to risk such a dangerous biological weapon to destroy this city. If the Rojin lost control of something they have had such an affinity with for thousands of years, then we'd have no chance."

Surel nodded, knowing Jeradon was right. "I can only hope then that the Darathia will simply contribute to our slaughter of the Rojin."

"For the time being. The Rojin can survive without the

Darathia, yet they cannot survive without the Rojin. However, I believe the Rojin will wipe them out before their numbers are depleted any more by these creatures. Who would you rather we fought?"

"You're right. Perhaps they'll wipe each other out, then we'd have one less job to do," mused Surel. "We have no idea why they have turned on their own?"

"No. Maybe The Father is finally losing control. We have had no luck coming across any more Darathia bullets - their seeds. Perhaps they are simply trying to survive as best they can. They don't rely on photosynthesis, so they could just as well be underground for all we know."

Pirian approached the edge of the forest, knowing he wasn't meant to be seen. Yet there was a side of him that desperately wanted to meet more of his own kind. As he backed away, he bumped into what he thought was a tree.

Turning around he saw it was in fact the dead body of one of his father's Gardeners.

Pirian screamed out as a flock of birds flew out of the undergrowth.

Falling backwards he was immediately grabbed from behind and lifted from the ground.

Neeve was both relieved and frightened for her son's safety as Surel and Jakahn looked over towards the sound of the child's scream. Surel nodded to his guards and they quickly made their way over to the edge of the forest.

A figure emerged holding a child.

Jeradon and Neeve recognised the man as one of their Gardeners.

Jakahn looked over towards them. "Your son, I presume?"

There was silence amongst them as Surel took in the

situation. "Last month, after the third bomb attack we captured three suspects. After hours of interrogation, one of them admitted to being involved. All three suspects were free of the Dosage. Seems they had been having…ideas. Later, we find out under further interrogation that this same suspect is in fact one of *your* Gardeners. Now they have tasted freedom, these people are attempting to shake the foundations of this city with another Resistance. They are uncontrollable and it all stems back to your project!"

"So you're labelling me an extremist now? I had nothing to do with the bombings. These people have obviously gone too far," answered Jeradon.

"Oh we know you had nothing to do with it directly. He was more than willing to tell us how unaware you have been. This suspect was also willing to tell us much more once we had upgraded his medication. He told us of a little boy he had seen deep in the forest, and the possibility that this child had been born in one of these very habitats. Dosage free." Surel snapped his fingers and the Gardener carried Pirian over to him. "Do you realise what this child could be carrying?"

"Our son is clean. He isn't contaminated, or ill," snapped Neeve.

"Perhaps we should address those issues once he actually lives in the city, free from the confinement of this habitat," advised Jakahn.

"What?" replied an enraged Jeradon.

"You know all too well what the other option would be. We reprogrammed your friend here to kill all your Gardeners. I'm sure we can do the same for the boy. No telling what the Dosage would do to him."

Surel interrupted. "This is yet another example of you taking advantage, Jeradon. Your Greenhouses are not breeding grounds. This woman is my Assessor and you have even managed, over time, to influence her. I will have no more of this. By having this child you are legally married, yet having a child free of the Dosage has broken every rule of Newton." Surel turned to Jakahn and the guards. "Quarantine the boy and integrate him into the Underclass along with his parents."

Jeradon was powerless. "What of the habitats?"

Surel glared at Jeradon. "This one I will allow you to work on until you find what we are looking for. The others are to be shut down. Take advantage of your situation one more time and I will burn this place to the ground with your child in it."

Sixteen

"Contamination spreads though our land threatening our capital." Ersula continued to preach. "On top of this the Wolf returns without Gana, yet brings us a Fallen."

The crowd began to whisper amongst themselves, "Yes... not just any Fallen; *the* Fallen. The one supposedly spoken of in our scriptures...the one that turns out to be Newtonian? The Father seems to believe so and has granted him access to more than you will ever have in your entire lives." Ersula held out the sword husk, her voice rising out of control, "Including his very own blade! Is it not enough that he's our enemy? That he is the slaughterer of our people? That his offspring is already amongst us?!"

Walking from out of the shadow cast by the colossus, Ersula's presence was as forbidding as her words. Kira had made the connection the moment Lomax was revealed. She had concocted an elaborate ploy, and Kira was deeply disturbed by her betrayal.

Then she realised Pirian's identity had been revealed.

It was as much a revelation to Larissa and Ched as it was to Karl. They all stared at him before Karl addressed his sister. "You kept this from me?"

"Karl, I'm sorry. We couldn't tell you, not yet."

"We...? Father knew as well?"

"There is much more, Karl, but now isn't the time. We have to help them." answered Kira.

Pirian could see utter contempt in Karl's face. "Karl, please - listen to your sister. The more we argue amongst ourselves, the more time we waste."

"Don't you tell me what to do, you Newtonian scum!" he turned to his sister, "How dare you bring me down here to help rescue a Newtonian!"

"Then do it for father," pleaded Kira.

"The man that can't even tell his own son the truth?"

"Karl..." Kira didn't know what else to say.

Pirian turned to look at his friends. "I'm sorry. I wanted to say, but I was afraid of what would happen."

Ched spoke for all of them. "But you share the mark, Pirian?"

He looked down at his arm, "Yes...I do."

"Then for now that is all we need to know," replied Larissa.

Pirian smiled. "Thank you. But I must ask you to leave, please. Head back to the surface and gather as many guards as possible. Something tells me we'll be needing some help. Tell them that we have found Harad and that he is in trouble." Pirian gazed at them. "Be careful."

Larissa and Ched nodded and quickly vanished back into the cave systems.

"Why would they listen to you?" snapped Karl.

Pirian approached with caution, still unsure of Karl's reaction. "They see the mark Karl, not where I'm from. I've told you, this isn't the time to dispute my origin."

Kira's scream was enough to distract them from the situation as a powerful arm grabbed her from behind. Karl's blade grew in an instant. Five more Darathia appeared from nowhere. Standing his ground Karl charged them, he showed no fear, only concern for his sister. The creatures fired without hesitation as Karl deflected the bullets with his blade, taking the head clean off his assailant. Another Darathia grabbed Karl's blade as he attempted to bring it down upon the creature. With a powerful kick to the stomach he was then knocked to the ground, winded.

Pirian watched as the decapitated head that Karl had removed reached out for its body and knitted itself together. The features of the strange creature were elongated; a dark green in colour, with sunken orange eyes. Encased by its leaf-like hood it could have easily been mistaken for Lomax in the shadows of the night. There were no ears or other recognisable features, they were simply humanoid plants.

His arm had wanted to take control of the situation from the offset, but Pirian knew they had no intention of killing them yet. They would take him to his father and that was all he desired. For now.

Jeradon knew the moment his son was brought before him that it was exactly what the Rojin witch had wanted. She gave a bad name to the missionaries, especially the Sisterhood. No wonder The Father had fallen ill; if she wasn't to be heard, then she would spread lies and deceit amongst those that were more vulnerable, and poison the capital from underneath with her own voice.

She had managed to bring all the missing pieces together once and for all, in the same way Jakahn had planned his own downfall and that of the Emperor. The Rojin capital was wide open to the Newtonian forces and it was only a matter of time until they were found. *They share a similar train of thought. The same motives. Almost as though they were working together.* Jeradon hoped to Gana he was wrong.

"Welcome…welcome to the past." Ersula could see Pirian's curiosity, and was obviously aching to tell him all about her underground city. "Our archaeologists uncovered the Seventh City, thought to be buried during a great battle, fifty years ago. We've all heard stories of the Giant that holds Yodann on his shoulders, that he saved the capital from ruin - it seems it's all true, along with the throne. Gargoy must be thousands of years old and I have learnt a great deal from it, including the resurrection of our Guardeners; the Darathia."

Jeradon knew how unpredictable the Darathia had become. He wondered how Ersula had gained control of them and grown new samples in the first place. "You brought these creatures back…?"

"With seeds I found on the wolf." She turned to look Lomax in the eye, "Hoping to sell them to the Black Market, I assume? They're worth far more to me alive."

So there were more bullets found on Lomax, thought Jeradon, *and Ersula was the one who took them.*

Toying with the charred and twisted object hanging from her neck, Ersula watched as Pirian's gaze was diverted up towards the colossus.

He wondered if this could have been a monument to Swift? Similar to the carving they had seen within the tomb? Or perhaps even Swift himself, slowly turned to stone after thousands of years below ground.

"Newtonians locked their great scientist Sir Ivar Gul away for claiming there were creatures like the Darathia and Rojin giants. They threw away the key; it seemed there was nothing he could write about, other than the theories of levitation and strange beasts, thought to be brought on under the influence of your precious Dosage. But it all came true, we are living in *his* world. Fortunately for the Rojin we have kept hold of our origins, as best we can. You never know when you need to reach into the past for the answers. I am sure though, The Father knows a great deal more about this place and the whereabouts of the Clock of Ages than I *ever* will."

Ersula approached Lomax reaching out her hand and stroking his silver mane mockingly. "I haven't had the chance to thank you yet my old friend, not just for helping to resurrect Darathia -

but for finding the slaughterer and his son. Your loyal companion has a real knack for leading the boy right to me." She leaned in closer. "You may have burnt every page of the scriptures, destroyed every secret to keep Gana's whereabouts safe. But it seems a new page has been found, one that has confirmed the rumours of where the great Gana Kamanuku is located."

Lomax didn't even give Ersula the satisfaction of eye contact. He was tired. Instead he looked blankly at Vagabond perched on Karl's shoulder, until Ersula pulled out several rolled-up pieces of paper and held them in front of him. His reaction was enough to confirm the true identity of Gana. Enough to help them find the only being that could lead them to the Clock of Ages. The very artefact their enemies had been searching centuries for.

"We are one step closer," Ersula said to her followers. The vast crowd's reaction began to swell. "If there is one thing you can truly thank this broken old sea wolf for; is bringing you our enemy, and in doing so has unwittingly helped us find Gana. Only then will we find the Clock of Ages."

Pirian was lost. He had no idea what the insane old hag was preaching about.

It was at that moment she placed the papers into what looked like a large oval light that projected their images onto the ceiling of the cavern. A monstrous flying city lit up the underground ceiling in all its cavernous glory. Several other images followed including a woman that resembled Pirian's mother, before it finally rested on a familiar animal.

The image was all too clear. Recognising the drawings as his own, Pirian couldn't help but whisper to himself, "Cornelius."

Thousands of people averted their gaze towards Pirian's reaction.

There was a deathly silence.

Harad was more concerned how his people would react to Gana

being nothing more than a forgotten animal. But this creature had rarely been seen by the Rojin - to them the animal was a myth, the last of its kind. The tortoise had become symbolic in nature, its true identity distorted though the ages, each Rojin's interpretation becoming further from the truth. The animal had become diluted within their culture, only showing itself in subtle hexagonal patterns and their iconic shields most missionaries carried on their backs.

Ersula was becoming more and more erratic since her astounding discovery. Harad could see the change in her. Rumours of Gana's identity and more importantly his location were all but confirmed. Harad feared what Ersula was now capable of. Approaching Pirian she leaned in towards him - her face wild and even more intimidating.

Before she had chance to quiz Pirian any further, Jeradon interrupted, "There is no need to question us, Ersula. This animal you worship is dead."

Her gnarled lips parted to reveal her wood-like teeth. Her laugh was unsettling. "Dead? Gana cannot die. He is much more than animal, he is immortal and we will find him once again. Tell me the truth, slaughterer, where is Gana?"

Pirian interrupted, "I...I tried to save him. He was thrown from Newton. I watched him fall. There was nothing I could do."

"Indeed you are an outcast, boy. Whoever heard of Newtonian compassion?" snapped Ersula. "Your love, for what you believed to be one of your father's inhabitants, has helped reveal a great secret." Ersula cackled once more, "And it was under your Emperor's nose all along. The one thing that could have lead you to the Clock of Ages."

Harad could feel his head throbbing. He couldn't even remember how he had received the cut to his head. He assumed that the Darathia had done it to him while attaching him to the stone. He was taking everything in as well as he could, and the shock of Ersula's betrayal was enough to bring him to full consciousness.

As Ersula approached Harad, glancing over towards Kira and Karl. "There is no better time for me to find Gana and take control of our people. I will look after them better than any Father and cleanse them with the Darathia seed. As for your children, Harad, I will watch over them more than anyone. Your daughter already has the makings of a great Priestess. She will remain my Select. As for Karl, he will become the greatest of Kings." She edged closer to Harad, whispering in his ear and directing his gaze towards his son. "Can you not see it in his eyes? His burning desire, Harad? Can you not feel his hatred for you at the moment? Secrets can destroy a family. Perhaps you should have told him about our new guests from the beginning?"

"In my own time."

"Hmm. He wouldn't have taken it as well as Kira. Losing his mother to the man you have welcomed with open arms. You don't honestly believe this man, the same man that killed your wife, is the one that will lead our people to a new Erth?" Harad sighed, glancing over to Jeradon. Ersula recognised his own doubt immediately. "You wonder why my faith has been tested? Mine and our people?"

"I'm not wondering anything…I'm finally beginning to realise why The Father never summoned you," replied Harad.

Ersula bit her lip and then beckoned the Darathia to bring forward Harad's children.

"Ersula…?" Kira began to speak, but there was nothing she could say.

Harad could clearly see the anger in Karl. He wished there could have been another way but he knew that seeing a Newtonian, especially the one he believed was behind the death of his mother, would be too much to take.

"I suppose you are wondering how all this started, Harad? In fact, I'm sure everyone here would like to know where it all began to fall apart." Ersula's stage was set. Everything she wanted to say was to be acted out to her new followers. "Well, it's simple. The reason is the same as for most Rojin - most Rojin that have lost anyone in the war, or whatever else you would call the mindless slaughter of our people. All this death for the protection of our precious protronium. It's enough to test the faith of anyone."

Kira interrupted, "But The Father shows us how to deal with this! Not allow these thoughts to consume us. Isn't it this that makes us different from the Newtonians?"

"See how naïve the children of Rojin have become, Harad? Naïve or brainwashed? I sometimes wonder if there is a difference between the Newtonian drug or the power of The Father - entering everyone's head at will, infecting their mind, and helping them forget about what is truly important."

"How dare you compare like that. You're more blind than he is!" snapped Harad as he attempted to pull at the stone rings.

"I dare because I am unable to control my love. My loss, Harad!"

"We have all lost!"

"*My* loss. Mine!" repeated Ersula. "And she never even knew."

"Don't." he whispered pleadingly.

"I will not allow this man to live!" she shouted pointing to Jeradon. "I will destroy this prophecy. But first I will make him watch as I take the life of his child as he did my own!"

Karl glared at Ersula. For the first time there was recognition in his eyes. Kira saw it too, suddenly understanding why she had been watched over all her life. Why indeed she had been selected.

Harad sunk his head. "The Father should never have allowed

this."

"Because I had a child? Whatever is, is right…remember, Harad? I'm sure he intended for all this to happen." Patronisingly Ersula continued, "I think not. For once The Father is truly blind. Without sight and without his precious Voice. I've never heard him! Not once has he come to me! So let me assume he knows nothing."

Vagabond shifted his position to hide behind Karl's head as Ersula approached. Karl began to ask, "You're my…"

"…Grandmother, Karl. And I will not lie to you. This is my own secret that has eaten me away, the one thing that has aged me beyond my years. Both of you will help me find Gana. We will bide our time and take control of the Rojin, creating our own Darathia order to aid us in the war. Then, when we have found the Clock of Ages we will continue by conquering Newton once and for all."

"Father?" queried Kira as Harad looked on wearily. "This isn't what we want. We're Rojin. We won't succumb to bitterness." She looked at her brother, "Karl, please - don't listen to her!"

"Did our mother know?" asked Karl. The reaction on Ersula's face was enough confirmation. "Then perhaps you should have told her," he snapped.

"And still maintain my position within the Sisterhood? You know the rules, Karl; a High Priestess must devote her life to the Rojin order, which means no children. Our people would not have listened to me - they would not have taken my words seriously, having broken The Father's precious rules. But now they will - rules can always be changed."

Karl didn't know what else to say. He glared at Jeradon and Pirian, his suspicions about the boy confirmed. Turning to his sister, he asked, "Why didn't you tell me about them, Kira?"

"They were afraid of the way you would react, Karl." interrupted Ersula. "You take after your mother, and even though you do not share a mark, you have more of my blood in you than your sister. Maybe she will see sense. I am sure you want to see him dead as much as I do?"

"No! This isn't the way." Kira pulled herself away from the Darathia. "He didn't kill our mother! We remember."

"We...?" queried Ersula looking at Karl.

Kira's shoulders pulled back slightly, her posture changing as she closed her eyes. She had found it incredibly hard to keep her mother's presence locked inside, yet her mother's train of thought could almost be as strong as her own. She was more than her conscience and was the main reason Kira had developed such maturity at a young age. "Mother, no..." she whispered before the mark on her forehead opened.

The eye glared at Ersula and Kira's tone changed completely. "Your Grandchildren are not to be used in this way, mother. Jeradon Horncastle has seen more than you will ever see - to the point of redemption. There is another directly responsible for my death, one who *will* answer in time. Jeradon is where he should be and has done all he could because of your granddaughter."

Ersula looked into her daughter's eye, "Mara?"

Harad grew agitated. Although he was aware of his daughter's Unity with her mother, it was the first time he had heard Mara since her death. Never had another's presence made themselves 'aware' through the Unity of their kin.

Even though Jeradon had never heard the woman's voice, he recognised Kira more than ever.

Ersula wanted to reach out and touch her daughter. Her voice was reassuring and for a brief moment Pirian was sure he glimpsed the woman Ersula may have once been. Then she snapped her hand back. "You awakened the slaughterer?"

"No, your granddaughter did. You should be proud of her - you know full well I was born without a mark ...but Kira, her mark was powerful enough to absorb my soul by will alone. She united with me when I was killed, and a chain of events was set in motion the very moment Kira made eye contact with Jeradon Horncastle. Look at the boy, mother. You have seen *his* mark. Can you tell your followers that he is Newtonian? He is a result of everything that was set in motion the day I died."

Ersula pondered.

Lomax was slowly beginning to understand why he had been sent away. The Father knew that he was to be the one that would find the Fallen one. It wasn't just about destroying the pages and hiding Gana. With this newfound enlightenment, Lomax was also beginning to understand what Ersula was thinking. "You won't show them. You're afraid of losing your power over your followers. If you show them his mark then their faith will be restored," interrupted Lomax.

"Then tell me wolf, has your faith been restored? That is all it is - a mark!" she shouted approaching him. "You have no idea how they will react. They are devoted to me. You only have to look at those that have already bitten the bullet."

Lomax growled. "That's the only way you can control Rojin, by having them become Darathia? What happened to you, Ersula? You used to be a woman I could trust."

"I woke up, Lomax. You of all people should be at my side. Look what he's turned you into, an empty shell of a pirate, a lost missionary. You chose to bow to The Father and take what we all needed...the scriptures were all we had left to continue teaching our faith. As for control, these Rojin gladly sacrificed themselves to become Darathia. They have nothing to live for. I simply take their pain away."

"You're insane!" shouted Pirian.

Spinning round in surprise at the boy's insolence, Ersula looked into his eyes, almost afraid to touch him. She attempted to probe his thoughts and saw nothing but his mother's face; the perfect mental block. She could clearly see how much he had grown in the short time of being amongst the Rojin. Agitated, Ersula still held The Father's sword in her hand. "Perhaps it's because I forgot how to laugh." she mused.

Mara interrupted. "We helped him find his true self, free of the Dosage. It is important he lives. You kill Jeradon and the boy - any chance of finding Gana will be lost."

Ersula pulled The Father's blade from under her robes. "So this is why he was given The Father's blade?" asked Ersula.

"The Father was connected to Gana in the same way he was connected to all of us. His blade will show us."

Ersula still held back. "Impossible. The sword is dead and even if it were alive no other person could take control of a symbiont blade unless…"

"…They share the same bloodline." concluded her daughter.

Harad struggled with the truth himself, but having read the scriptures first hand, he knew exactly where his wife was coming from. The Horncastle bloodline had descended from The Father's very first offspring, a captured Rojin, who had become corrupted by the Dosage. Named after Old Town's fallen house of kings. Castle Van Hoarne had become nothing more than a familiarity, forming the basis of a new identity, evolving over thousands of years, and only becoming synonymous with death. Over centuries the zetameen had suppressed their true selves, and in turn their dormant mark.

"Horncastle is nothing more than a slaughterer. We all know what he has done, what generations of them have done to the Rojin. This cannot be," snapped Ersula. "People fall from Newton all the time. This prophecy has never mentioned anything of a slaughterer and nothing of a child."

"Yet isn't it this child you have been so curious about, mother? Isn't it *this* child you have led down here, to the Seventh

City? Your first attempt at abducting him failed. So you thought you would abduct Jeradon instead in the hope the boy would come looking for him, playing right into your hands. You were testing him."

Ersula glared. "Perhaps we should see what happens then if we allow him to hold The Father's blade." Instructing the Darathia to release Jeradon, Ersula approached him as Pirian looked on. "Take it. If you are who you are meant to be, show all these people. For your sake I hope the blade recognises you."

Jeradon knew this wasn't right. He had already handled the blade when it was first entrusted to him. It revealed nothing. The Father had shown him what to do with it, yet he was still uncertain of what would happen. He could see thousands of followers eagerly awaiting his decision.

"Tell me boy, since you have so clearly grown amongst our people, is there any side of you that still sees the blood on your father's hands? Are you fully aware of what he did for his Emperor?"

Jeradon glared at Ersula. Never had he felt so vulnerable, he could see the change in his son and had hoped he hadn't lost sight of what was important. That at least for him, he still had his mother close at heart. "He understands well enough."

"A child coming to terms with the killing of so many people? I find that hard to believe."

"Then why don't you allow him to look?" asked Jeradon as he nodded towards The Father's sword. "If you truly want to test my son, then use what you're afraid of, instead of your poisoned mouth. Hand *him* the sword."

Ersula boiled. "It's a relic. The blade is as dead as he is!"

"Then what are you afraid of?" replied Jeradon, "If there is one blade I will allow my son to hold, it is The Father's. The only way of showing the truth, the only way of testing his strength."

Pirian was taken back at what his father was saying.

Ersula hesitated. She knew of The Father's power and what his sword had been capable of. As with any symbiont blade, it was at one with its host and shared their power. She had to know if the blade still had any dormant life, otherwise her plans would be threatened.

Pirian shouted, "Father, I don't need to do this. I don't *need* to see anything. I've come to rescue you!"

Ersula smirked. "Touching. Touching to see a child try so hard. There is nowhere to go, boy." Pausing, she examined the sword husk once again. "Perhaps you do need to take the blade in your hands, find out how it feels. Then we'll see if you still want to rescue your father."

Still looking at his father, Pirian could see how serious he was. This was no bluff. Jeradon wanted him to take the sword in his hands. His father's only fear was of the doubt in his son's heart; the doubt that he could love a man who had killed so many, once he saw it through his own eyes.

With bound wrists Pirian reached out. His marked arm began to shake and take full control, as though it recognised The Father's blade. Looking once again at his own father bound helplessly to the stone, he attempted to pull his arm back, yet it had a will of its own.

The moment he wrapped his fingers around the hilt, the fossilised stone began to crumble away. Ersula snapped her hand back in surprise as Pirian's arm shook. The Darathia around him shrivelled and died in place of the new life given to the sword. As the blade grew in length, its full strength became apparent. Finally it twisted into shape and began to strengthen. The blade shimmered briefly as Pirian's arm quivered. He collapsed to his knees, an intense pain shooting through his body. Both the blade and his marked arm pulled at each other for control, as Pirian felt himself slowly succumb to the blade's memories.

He slowly felt The Father awaken.

His eyes were no longer his own. A thousand years of memory flooded through his mind, as his eyes began to burn.

Focussing, the first image was a distorted figure that hung suspended before him. Before he could make out who or what it was, the very sword husk he had just brought back to life was raised before him. Picking up speed the images flickered rapidly, his father's memories slowly becoming his own. Those that they had shared in the past few months were a blur as he once again witnessed the sinking of *The General*, the cruel sea and its many beasts. The fall from Newton, his mother's kiss, Jakahn's torment, Viktor's cruelty to Cornelius and the burning of the last Greenhouse. As the memories of his father became clearer, his enemies felt closer than ever as he entered the Emperor's chambers.

Pirian wanted to look away, but was unable to escape the visions pouring out in front of him. He finally knew the truth of where his father had been when the Greenhouse was set alight.

XVI

Much like himself, Lord Surel's chambers were cold and lifeless.

He had been free of the Dosage for over thirty years, developing a natural lust for power, the same as every other Emperor before him. There was no character left; just the greed that all Newtonian rulers shared. Sick and immobile, he had called Jeradon to his chambers one final time, within the early hours of the morning.

Shadows enveloped Surel's feeble body as he sat, propped upright in his bed. He couldn't even move his arms to address his former Commander. "You know why I have called you here?"

"You plan to finish what I started."

"It's been twelve years, Jeradon. You have shown nothing that could lead us to the Rojin. The Last of your Greenhouses will be shut down immediately." Surel's chest rattled as he breathed. "You have taken advantage of your position long enough, your project has done nothing but encourage the Resistance. I allowed only you to be clean and no other!"

"The Greenhouses made them sick, and then eventually better workers. It was the only way they could help me. I cannot work with robots."

"Do you take me for a fool! You have made me look incompetent, I allowed more than I ever should have." Surel wheezed. "Corrupting my Assessor was a very bad move; stealing her from under my Advisor's nose. Then she bears *your* child! I have managed to keep Jakahn under control, but there is something brewing in him Horncastle, there has always been, ever since you were Guild apprentices. I feel he's just biding his time, that he has things planned for you...for all of you. Things I should have seen through myself." Surel coughed and spluttered as he became more irate. "And to make matters worse, we find out your own child was born clean! Do you realise the implications of this? There is already an uprising thanks to your ideas, and fresh fuel has only been thrown on the fire. An Emperor allowing a clean birth! You haven't just threatened your own life, Jeradon, you have threatened mine as well."

"You should never have given Rayal Jakahn power."

"He is Advisor. He has more than proved he is capable of succeeding me. I'm sure he won't make the same mistakes I have made. That is why I granted him permission to close your project once and for all."

"I have to know, Lord Surel...I have to know if my family will be safe."

"You've made your own bed, Jeradon. We'll deal with every one of the Resistance...one by one."

There was nothing more Jeradon could say, the harsh reality of what could happen to his wife and child played on his mind as the Emperor glared at him. He knew all too well what was happening; this was the end but he could not allow it to happen. He clenched his fists and began to leave the chamber. As he reached the doors he paused before walking any further. Jeradon had no intention of leaving right away, no one threatened his family, not even the Emperor.

Ducking back into the shadows just before he reached the two guards, he crept his way back into the chamber towards familiar voices.

Surel's strength had all but vanished. He was yet another ruler of

Newton who had failed to find the artefact and in turn the answer to immortality. The Father would be laughing once more. His time was up, maybe sooner than he thought.

From the shadows of Lord Surel's chamber a voice spoke out. "This should have been done a long time ago, my Lord."

"There is no need to remind me, Rayal. Do what you have to do. I'll be dead before I have to answer to the Hierarchy."

"My son is dealing with the boy as we speak. He followed him to the last Greenhouse."

"Good. Then give him the order to burn it to the ground. Get rid of any evidence. You will finally be free of the Horncastles."

Jeradon was surprised this hadn't happened sooner. Jakahn had his final grip on the Emperor, his advice was heard all too clearly, whatever the consequences. Jeradon's anger boiled for the first time in years. He pulled a knife from his boot and crept along the shadows of the chamber. All he wanted to do was kill the two men before him and protect his family at all costs.

Jakahn looked down at the Emperor, looming in closer. "What of Neeve?"

"Deal with her as you must."

Jeradon could see Jakahn's sneer as he tried to control his rage, pausing before he was about to strike.

"Deal with *me*…as you must." Surel added, knowing all too well how it was to end. The same way every Emperor before him had met their fate; by the hands of their successor.

Jakahn placed his hand over Surel's nose and mouth and pressed down. Just before the Emperor began to struggle, Jakahn was interrupted by his intercom. He released his hand as the Emperor gasped for air, "Yes?" agitated, Jakahn listened to the full communication, "…Good, let him freeze to death. You have training in the morning, get some rest."

"Wha…what is it?" asked Surel.

"My son…he's brought to my attention that the Horncastle

boy is in possession of a book. A more than good enough reason to have gotten rid of him."

No, thought Jeradon…almost losing hope.

"This is your concern now, Jakahn…if you are…going to put me out my misery…do…it now."

"Perhaps we can do it later, my Lord. Prolong the agony somewhat." with that Jakahn left the chamber as Lord Surel wheezed and grabbed his chest. He knew full well that his Advisor already had control over him, raising his feeble arm in response to the outrage.

Jeradon still wasn't thinking clearly. He would deal with Jakahn as soon as he had put the Emperor out of his misery. Moving closer towards him, he paused, sensing yet another presence in the room. Pressing himself against the wall, he noticed a velvet curtain billow slightly. A window was open. Then an arm revealed itself from the shadows enveloping Surel's bedside. A knife was held by a slender hand, rising to strike, and in one swift move Jeradon witnessed the Emperor's throat cut from ear to ear.

The figure came into view. It was female, and as she silently crept back through the open window, Jeradon nearly called out her name.

Neeve!

She had heard as much, if not more than he had. She had done the job both he and Jakahn had intended. There was no going back now, his mind was a blur of situations he didn't fully understand or want to believe. He had been distracted by his hatred, his anger. Was she going to follow Jakahn and finish him off too? He sat for a moment, before moving out of the shadows and looked down at the Emperor's lifeless body. He struggled for a moment to take everything in; distracted by his wife killing the Emperor, Jakahn's motives towards her, the destruction of his Greenhouses, and his son…

Pirian! Thought Jeradon, *how could I be so stupid!*

For a moment he didn't know whether to pursue Neeve through the open window, but decided it would be the best exit, judging the circumstances. Without any further hesitation, he proceeded to make his way to the Greenhouse, hoping he wasn't too late to save his son's life.

Seventeen

Pirian felt the intense pressure on his mind increase. Like an explosion, the visions began to lead further and further back in time. The death of the Emperor became a blur, as he witnessed his own birth, his father and mother developing the habitats, Jeradon's awakening and the subsequent slaughter of the Rojin. He saw the blood on the hands of every Horncastle, the rise of many Emperors, the flying city taking to the sky and a fight between a blind father and his corrupted son. His fall. His survival.

His immortality.

He continued to witness the foundations of the Rojin and the discovery of those who were marked. The seed was planted as Pirian watched the very sword he held in his hand plucked for the first time by the blind man. The blade reacted to its own memory. Then the voice returned that only Pirian could hear.

You have seen all, Pirian Horncastle.

There was panic as soon as Ersula's followers saw the Darathia shrivel and fall to the ground, leaving the riddled bones of their hosts.

Pirian gave out a sigh, the wind had finally been knocked out of him. His marked arm, attached to The Father's blade, began to rise as though it was attempting to lift him up. It continued to nudge Pirian as he snapped out of his epiphany and glanced around making eye contact with his father.

Jeradon barely recognised his own son, who had grown more than he could possibly imagine in that brief moment since he had taken the blade in his hand. Jeradon just hoped whatever had happened to Pirian, whatever The Father had shown him - he had the strength to control it.

Pirian felt nauseous, but this time it wasn't the altitude sickness that had hit him. The amount of death he had seen through generations of Horncastles was unbearable. For a moment he thought death was in his blood, but was reminded that his family, as with all Newtonians, had been controlled and brainwashed by the Dosage for centuries. However, there was still a side of him that had been convinced that his father had given in to the thirst once more. That he was guilty for the death of the Emperor.

Never for one moment had he believed his mother was capable of such a sin. In desperation, she had committed a crime to protect her family. *My mother's love must be the strongest of all*, thought Pirian. *But father's love must have been just as strong to take the fall for her.*

Pirian's arm pulled him towards his father.

"She did it for us, Pirian. She may not have meant for it to come this far - but you belong here now. This is where you've always been intended to be."

"I know…and when I'm ready, we'll find her again." Pirian turned and looked over towards Kira as she approached Harad.

Tenderly she soothed her father's injuries, Harad pulling away slightly, uncomfortable with the fact his dead wife had taken control of their daughter.

"Ma…Mara?"

The third eye blinked and Kira took control again.

Ersula slowly backed away, afraid of her daughter's presence and still in awe of the boy's powers.

Jeradon had stopped Pirian picking up a sword all his

life, from fear of him following a similar path to the long line of Horncastles. Yet this sword was different. You would have thought that there was very little damage you could do with a fossilised blade, in fear of breaking it. But the sword cut through stone with ease as Pirian set Harad and Lomax free, taking care of Kira's bindings in the process. Lomax immediately helped Harad to his feet; a recognition of the wolf he once knew.

Vagabond pulled at his chains as Karl stood motionless, eager to be reunited with his master.

Harad addressed his son. "...Karl...I wanted to tell you, really I did..."

"I don't want to hear it, father."

Ersula, standing alone, surveyed the commotion while some of her followers approached over the bridge. She was unsure of whether they were approaching to help her or gain a closer look at the boy's transformation. Raising her arms, Darathia immediately blocked their approach.

Turning to her grandson, she shouted, "You see what he is, Karl. He's marked. Another that has been blessed other than yourself." Looking into his eyes she began to slowly poison his mind. "You're thinking why should it be him? How Gana is mocking you, allowing a Newtonian to have a power only you deserve."

Karl shook his head. "He can't be Newtonian."

"Then what? Rojin? More Rojin than you? He even holds The Father's blade! He is a threat, Karl. My child, one day he will take your kingdom from under your nose. Is that what you want? Or, would prefer your own throne - Gargoy's perhaps? We can build everything anew down here and be protected at all times."

"She's turning you against us, Karl!" shouted Harad.

Pirian made his way towards him, "Your father's right. We have more important enemies other than ourselves. The same enemy." Pirian reached out his good arm, while he continued to control the power of his mark, which had fused his hand to the symbiont blade.

Ersula released his bindings and presented Karl with his own confiscated sword. "He may have a mark, Karl. But does he have the skill? He has only tasted the Rojin teachings. The one advantage you have over him."

Karl could feel his jealousy build. His grandmother was right, he couldn't allow Pirian to live. He was indeed a threat to everything he believed in - the Rojin throne, his sister, even Erth itself. He may not have been born with a mark or the power of foresight, but it was all very clear to him. Crystal clear.

Kill him, were the only words his grandmother placed in his mind.

Kira shouted out to her brother as he surged towards Pirian.

Generations of training filtered through The Father's blade, Pirian's mark anxious to protect him and use whatever means necessary. It sensed the threat of Karl the same way it had felt Moku's scalpel. Now it could use the blade's very own skills. The challenge for Pirian wasn't in allowing his mark and the blade to take control of the situation, but in preventing it from doing any damage. He didn't want to hurt Karl, but all his mark could see was a threat.

As Karl charged forward, hundreds of Ersula's followers reached the inner platform, racing over the bridge, many falling to their deaths.

Jeradon made an attempt to reach his son and pull him away from Karl's attack. Distracted by the followers that flooded onto the platform, he watched helplessly as Karl engaged in combat with Pirian.

Harad grabbed hold of Kira while she screamed out helplessly to both of them.

Lomax stood his ground, watching Ersula pull a Darathia gun from under her robes and begin shooting her followers. The process of their transformation was faster than anything Lomax had seen before. He looked on in horror as their forearms swelled into huge buds. As they burst open, their own gun arms appeared, the rest of their bodies changing colour and shape immediately; their swelled veins spreading outwards, as though enveloping helpless prey. The victim's faces elongated to a similar shape and size to his own. Lomax noticed that the Darathia immediately turned on the rest of the followers with their own guns and before long many more had transformed. There were no weapons at hand and Lomax could only back away until he was alongside Jeradon, Harad and Kira.

They all looked on as hundreds of followers fell victim. Edging their way closer underneath the colossus statue, Lomax pulled a small coil of chain hanging from a nearby scaffold.

Harad picked up a short scaffold pole, while Jeradon ripped an iron torch holder from the toe of the statue, desperately attempting once again to reach his son. "Pirian!"

Harad pulled him backwards. "Jeradon, stay focussed. We have to find a way round this."

"Pirian *is* the way round this," stressed Jeradon. "Didn't you see it in his eyes? It's like he's seen everything he needs to. I'm frightened for him. The Father may have shown him too much - maybe too much for him to handle. I need to help him!"

Vagabond was caught directly in the centre of the fight between Karl and Pirian.

Pirian's marked arm shook while he attempted to hold it back from killing Karl instantly. At the same time he allowed enough force to block his attack. As their blades parried and made contact, Karl was distracted at how strong Pirian was for a boy so much younger than himself. The Newtonian's skills were incredibly swift, almost effortless as Pirian twisted and turned with perfect footing.

Karl had placed all of his weight behind his own blade, while Pirian's marked arm was all he needed to keep him at a safe distance. As they both made eye contact with each other, Karl noticed that Pirian was pulling his own arm towards him in an attempt to stop his arm taking full control.

"Karl, you have to stop. I can't hold it back. Please!"

The struggle and hesitation between the two boys was all Vagabond needed to pull on his chain. Karl was yanked backwards with such force that he fell awkwardly on the stone floor. There was a snap as his arm broke. Sliding to a halt at the edge of the precipice, Karl immediately attempted to pull himself up, but instead lost his balance and fell from view. Unable to support his weight Vagabond was pulled downwards still attached to the chain. Crashing into the floor the gargoyle scrabbled for a hold, stone claws grating against the stone surface of the platform.

Pirian could see the horror in Vagabond's eyes, as the gargoyle frantically beat his wings for extra hold. His blade retracted, no longer threatened by Karl, and Pirian instantly felt his arm pull towards his father in a need to protect his own blood. Yet it was Pirian who made the decision to dive and grab hold of the chain before Vagabond was pulled over the edge. Karl's weight continued to drag Pirian and the gargoyle across the stone floor. Pulled over the edge of the precipice, he had no free hand to grab hold; the sword hilt still fused to his marked arm.

There was a sudden jolt as they came to a stand still. Vagabond was attached to Karl via the chain as he steadied himself with his wings; Karl swaying back and forth in the darkness. Pirian held onto the chain and looked up at The Father's blade, which had embedded itself into the side of the precipice, saving them all.

There was nothing to see below, apart from the blackness of the void reaching out beneath them, waiting for the loss of grip at any point. Not once did Pirian's fear of heights take hold, thanks to The Father's sword that had just saved them from plummeting to their deaths.

His marked arm began to pull the weight of them upwards, swelling with strength. Vagabond beat his wings and helped to pull Karl closer towards Pirian. "Karl...please. Reach up!"

For a moment he thought Karl was going to unclip the chain from his waist. Instead his sword retracted and he hooked the hilt to his belt with his good arm. Their wrists interlocked and Pirian could feel the strength being lent to the rest of his body as he gained enough momentum to swing Karl above so he could grab hold of the ledge.

Vagabond pulled at the chain as Pirian let go of him, helping Karl just enough to land back onto the platform. Finally Pirian reached out the length of his free arm and grabbed the edge himself. The Father's blade retracted from out of the wall and continued to embed itself back into the stone floor, giving him the leverage and strength he needed to pull himself up.

Karl lay on his back catching his breath amongst the commotion and clutching his broken arm.

"This is what she wants, Karl. Is it really worth losing your life over?"

There was a side of Karl that found it incredibly infuriating to have a young boy show him the truth. He looked round, noticing Ersula standing silent amongst her newly transformed followers who swarmed around her.

Pirian cut Vagabond loose and watched as he flew over to find Lomax.

Many followers had ran back across the bridges to avoid being shot. However, the platform was still taken up with many Darathia and injured followers that were beginning to transform.

Karl held his broken arm and looked over at his grandmother once again. He then frantically attempted to spot his sister and father amongst the commotion.

There were over a hundred Darathia between Pirian and the others. He could feel his arm threatened more than ever as The Father's blade surveyed the situation. Fear struck him. Pirian was barely able to hold his marked arm back from killing Karl. Now the threat was even greater.

One hundred to one.

"You could have at least brought me a cigar," said Lomax, as Vagabond perched himself affectionately on his shoulder. The gargoyle smiled at his master, glad to be back at his side and in his old home.

Kira held onto her father. Harad could see Jeradon's anxiety as he tried to reach his son, but there was no chance - all of them were surrounded by Darathia, with nowhere to go except climb the statue towering above them.

The one person that was preventing their inevitable death moved towards them, parting the Darathia with a simple gesture. Scowling at Jeradon, Ersula was still taken by surprise at his son's newfound ability. She then looked into the very heart of her granddaughter, in the hope her own daughter knew what was happening.

"Who is this boy?"

Kira's third eye reopened. "You know who he is, mother. There is no need to ask. Both Jeradon and his son have brought you closer to what you have been looking for. Inevitably, closer to what we have all been looking for. You have to make a choice and the best advice I can give you is to release everyone here."

"This can't be." Ersula was still struggling with what she had witnessed. She couldn't allow the slaughterer and his son to have any influence over her people. All her teachings, beliefs and everything she had secretly taken control of would be for nothing. She could not allow the prophecy to come true.

"The Father is dead."

Kira's mother took control of her smile. "You couldn't be more wrong. He is very much alive, as he has always been. As long as Gana lives, so will The Father and so will the boy. They are all connected...look at him again, mother - then tell me The Father is dead."

Ersula turned away and looked over towards Pirian and her grandson surrounded by Darathia. Pirian was standing strong, unafraid. She could see his marked arm and The Father's very own blade eager to take down every single Darathia.

Pirian looked directly at her.

The Father could see everything he needed to from where Pirian stood. Slowly he could feel his strength returning, yet held it back as not to overwhelm the boy. Instead of using everyone at hand, The Father simply tapped into Pirian's ability to use Vagabond as an extra point of view.

In the distance there was the sound of an approaching stampede, amplified by the cave systems. Ersula could make out the approaching figures; a small band of Umah riders, accompanied by Rojin guards on foot. Although their best warriors the Umah had become somewhat depleted - stretched thin from their outpost duties, the Temple's guards and select steeds were the best at hand.

Pirian could make out Larissa and Ched sitting on horseback, protected by two accompanying guards. There was no need to endanger the children any more than they needed to once they had shown them the way. As the Rojin approached, Ersula's followers parted, allowing them to reach one of the main bridges. The Rojin were seriously outnumbered, but their main aim was to protect Harad.

As the Commander made his move onto the bridge Ersula stepped forward. "You will approach no further," she snapped as many of her Darathia turned to protect her. The Commander never said a word, as his guards stormed the bridge without hesitation.

"No!" shouted Ersula, noticing the other Darathia follow suit, leaving her prisoners unguarded.

In a split moment, Pirian and Karl were no longer surrounded by so many Darathia. As they engaged the Rojin, both forces met half way at the bridge, several Darathia and Rojin wiped out instantly, falling to their deaths below. Most of the Rojin had managed to use their grapple guns to pull them away from danger, swinging over their assailants and landing on the main platform.

In the blink of an eye they were at Harad's side.

Pirian was concerned at how many innocent people were being killed by the Rojin. They were Darathia, yet their transformation may still be reversible at such an early stage.

As the Rojin guards pushed on over the bridge and onto the central platform, Ersula commanded more of the Darathia to take care of the prisoners.

Lomax was the first to take out an approaching Darathia, whipping out his chain as it coiled around the creature's neck and pulling it over the precipice. Immediately two more were on him. As the Darathia opened fire, Lomax spun round grabbing hold of its gun arm, having no choice but to use the bulk of the creature to help protect him from the second's onslaught of seed bullets. Lomax rolled away as the Darathia slumped to its knees in agony.

Absorbing the bullets, the Darathia began to convulse, then swell and quadruple in size. The second Darathia and Lomax looked on. Vine-like tentacles burst out from its back, wrapping around its body and helping the creature gain more mass.

"I should have thought that one through," muttered Lomax to himself.

The hybrid roared and proceeded to lunge forward, crushing the stunned Darathia as it bolted across the platform with its giant cannon arm extended. Lomax ran towards Harad, Kira and Jeradon finding cover behind the colossus statue.

Pirian could clearly see that Karl was in pain, and his sword arm was barely controllable as it attempted to pull forever more in the direction of Jeradon. There was no chance his arm was going to relinquish the blade, which made it very difficult for him to heal Karl's broken arm.

Karl could clearly see that the Darathia were holding back from Pirian. They had brought the boy as Ersula had expected, yet he noticed even then they were apprehensive. Pirian was either in control of them or they were frightened of The Father's blade. He hadn't fully realised it himself, he was far too concerned about his father and everyone else.

"Karl, we have to get to the others."

"Then what?"

"Stop your grandmother."

Karl's anger began to grow once again. "You may have saved my life. You may want to save everyone else's, but I can't forget where you are from. Just do what you have to do."

Pirian moved slowly forward as the Darathia parted. Karl followed, making his way to the base of the statue where the rest of them were gathered.

"Ersula is escaping above ground," said Harad. "I think the monument leads to another way out. My fear is she will attempt to reach The Father. With most of the guards here, I am concerned for his protection. I can't hear him at all."

"But I can," answered Pirian.

"Use your own voice," added Mara, distracting Harad.

He turned to notice Kira's third eye had once again reopened. He contemplated for a brief moment, before nodding, "Lomax, escort Jeradon and the children above ground. I will take care of this."

"I want to help," shouted Karl.

"Listen to your father, Karl. Come with your sister," asked Mara.

Karl looked around; it was too much for him, he wanted to say as much as his father, but couldn't find the words to address his mother. Just simply do as she requested.

Harad looked directly into the third eye as it blinked nervously, "Mara…"

"Goodbye, Harad. Look after our children the same way you always have - with the heart of a Rojin."

Harad let out a breath as his daughter's eyes opened once again. He held onto her shoulders, "…I…I never had chance to say…"

"She knows, father. She always has," replied Kira.

Karl pondered slightly, managing to force a smile. "We'll be waiting for you above ground, father." He said knowing his father was being protective and that he and his sister's lives were far more important to him than his own.

Harad's children looked back one final time before ascending the statue, watching their father wipe his brow and immediately take on the approaching Darathia. With his famous speed, Harad took out five in the blink of an eye, attempting to reach the rest of his guards. Hearing an almighty roar, the hybrid Darathia loomed in closer, gritting its teeth. Harad could smell its breath, drool hanging from its mouth and splashing on the floor before him. The hybrid had grown larger now from more of its clan having fired upon it. It barely flinched as Rojin pierced it with their arrows. Opening fire once again, the creature raised its arm. Then, just as it was about to bound forward and take them out, Vagabond flew down and diverted its eyes upwards.

Harad watched on in horror as the Darathia giant began to climb the statue in pursuit of Vagabond - and in the direction of Lomax, Jeradon and the children.

There was nothing Harad could do, as the giant Darathia tore into the statue.

XVII

Neeve discarded the blade swiftly, watching it drop into the canal hundreds of feet below. Killing someone had never been so easy. Free of the Dosage she was entirely aware of her actions, yet ironically she didn't feel anything. She simply saw it as doing him a favour, putting him out of his misery. Through love alone, she had committed what she initially thought was a selfless act. Then, slowly but surely, the repercussions began to overwhelm her as she made her way back home.

Entering through a sky hatch, she dropped down into a nearby corridor. She steadied herself, remembering back to what Jakahn had once told her. *You will play into my hands and witness Horncastle fall right before your eyes.* Had she really been a victim of Jakahn's manipulation? Did he know she was lurking in the shadows all along? If only he had stayed a moment longer, then she would have had the chance to kill him too.

But now it was too late. She realised with horror, that even if Jakahn knew that she had committed murder there was no way he would arrest her for the crime. No, it would be far more beneficial for him to have Jeradon accused and finally executed, so she was finally his once again.

Then what would become of Pirian?

Neeve was frightened. Her husband and son were dead already.

What scared her the most was that she would never have the chance to share her news with Jeradon. Steadying herself once more against the cold walls of the corridor, she thought for a moment, before reaching inside her pocket. Opening one hand she looked down at the Dosage capsule, while gently stroking her belly with the other.

"Perhaps your life will be easier this way little one."

Eighteen

Swift's statue utilised a combination of inner and outer stairways, spiralling around the waist and upper arms. Over the years the structure had become heavily damaged and decayed; huge divides between walkways only passable via the abandoned scaffolding, ropes and chains.

Jeradon led the children, followed by Lomax, as Vagabond flew overhead. They made their way through what was left of the structure as quickly as they could, the statue shaking from the giant Darathia's unstoppable ascent. As they reached the neck and shoulder they could make out Ersula and five Darathia poised before a huge gap in the statue's arm.

"Ersula!" shouted Jeradon.

Darathia edged forward to protect her as she screamed defiance at them. "I will listen no more…to any of you! The Father will die tonight!"

The colossus statue shook, followed by a roar as the huge creature approached. Jeradon could see the opening to the exit in the distance - the colossus' fingers enveloping the gateway.

Ersula turned, attempting to make a dash for the opening, while three Darathia remaining to block the others' pursuit.

She hadn't moved far before a huge hand grabbed hold of the statue's forearm, pulling itself up. There was another roar as the creature heaved its weight into full view. There was barely enough room as it struggled to pull itself further up onto the structure. Wrapping its gun arm around the stonework, it released its other arm, clumsily swatting the two Darathia accompanying Ersula, then immediately made a move towards her.

It paused, a quizzical look on its face as it noticed Ersula's necklace. Snorting through its nose, the tendrils around its mouth quivered as huge globules of slime dripped onto the statue below. It reached out its arm slowly towards Ersula as she stood transfixed. Then, with no warning it delicately pulled the necklace from her neck.

It then hit Jeradon how Ersula had kept them from harming her and gained control over these creatures. The charred and twisted object was in fact a withered Darathia bullet. *Of course… they won't harm anyone carrying their seed.*

The huge beast looked down at the small object in the palm of its hand, then at Ersula once again. A deafening roar followed as it realised she wasn't one of its own.

Distracted by the commotion, the remaining Darathia picked themselves up from the floor. Pirian didn't waste anymore time, and taking advantage of the situation, drove The Father's blade towards them.

Instead of penetrating their hides, the blade simply merged, reversing the Darathia transformation. Their original hosts slumped to the ground, their skin covered in severe lacerations and deep, penetrating holes. Unfortunately, two were already dead; the transformation having caused too much damage. Only one remained conscious.

Each time The Father's blade destroyed a Darathia, the giant screamed out, feeling their pain.

The statue shook.

Jeradon could see the stonework of the shoulder cracking as Ersula scrambled backwards towards them. To her horror, she could see for the first time the danger her surviving family were in as the creature lashed out at her grandchildren.

Kira and Karl backed up towards the entrance located at the

colossus' neck. Frantically, Ersula scrambled into the opening for cover as the giant's fist rang home, knocking away a huge portion of the structure.

As the statue shook again, Kira lost her balance falling into full view of the giant Darathia, its hand immediately lashing out towards her.

With no hesitation Jeradon dived in front of Kira. He knew he had enough time to spin and protect her, yet no time to continue moving sideways away from the creature's powerful claws. As they sliced deeply across his back and right hand side Jeradon absorbed the impact as best he could; but this time there was no zetameen in his system to help take the pain away.

Claws retracted and the creature watched as Jeradon fell to the ground with Kira, blood pouring from his back.

"Dad!" Pirian made an attempt to reach his father, Lomax grabbing him to one side as the Darathia aimed its gun arm at the entrance and fired.

As the stone debris blasted through the entrance, Lomax and Pirian dove for cover. Under the severe stress the Darathia was causing, the statue immediately broke away at the shoulder. As the structure crumbled and parted company, the statue tilted slightly. The main bulk of the upper torso pulling away from the shoulder and forearm, the metal lattice within tearing away like stitches, before it finally came to rest.

On one side of the divide lay Jeradon, with Kira and Karl. On the other stood Ersula, Lomax and Pirian along with the surviving follower, who lay unconscious at their feet. Vagabond frantically flew above in an attempt to distract the creature.

They all watched helplessly as Jeradon pulled himself up, the creature looming in for the kill.

"The grapple gun," he asked Karl, holding out his hand. Without hesitation Karl passed it to him. Grimacing from the pain, Jeradon began to close the grapple hooks, immediately firing at the creature. Penetrating the side of its torso, he released the hooks inside the creature and pulled.

"Keep your sister close. Once he's held back, make a move for the exit."

"Are you crazy, ten men couldn't hold it back," shouted Karl.

"I don't intend to."

Pirian could see his father instructing Kira and Karl. They were in full view of the creature. He watched helplessly as Jeradon stood, his right arm limp at his side, blood pouring down it from his back and shoulder.

"When it raises that gun arm…run," instructed Jeradon.

Pirian darted forward once again, in an attempt to reach his father, but Lomax held tight. "Let go. Let go of me!" he shouted. "Dad!" his arm swelled, pulling out towards his father in an attempt to help him. Lomax could feel his strength, and was barely able to hold him back.

As The Father began to quell the boy's emotions, all Pirian could do was watch on helplessly behind his own eyes, caged in his own body.

Jeradon looked back, "Pirian…" it was too late now to say any more to his son, the adrenaline was kicking in, his emotions welling, "Go!" he turned and ran as best as he could across the outstretched forearm of the statue with Karl and Kira, as the creature raised its gun arm once more. Once they had passed the creature, it twisted and turned, shifting its weight and fumbling for a better grip. Meanwhile Jeradon unclipped the rope from the grapple gun and quickly threaded it through the scaffold fastenings.

There was just enough time to reach the exit.

But the gate was closed.

Frantically, they looked around them for the lever. Jeradon could see that it had broken away from the wall and hung from the statue's wrist several metres away. The statue trembled. There wasn't much time left until the stone hand lost its grip entirely from the strain of the broken, suspended forearm. The giant Darathia surged forward as they felt the structure shift beneath them.

In a split second Jeradon pushed Kira and Karl as far towards the closed gate as possible.

Pirian watched in the distance as he saw a figure leap from the statue's hand. Transfixed he watched as his father grabbed the lever, his full weight bringing it down as the gate opened. Distracted, the Darathia watched as the children paused for a moment, wanting to help Jeradon. Karl looked him in the eye, recognising Pirian's earlier actions, a degree of guilt flooding over him as his sister pulled frantically at his arm.

"There's nothing we can do. Come on!"

They ran into the tunnel as the Darathia attempted to squeeze itself through, knocking several torches onto its head in the process.

It was at that moment Jeradon let go.

Pirian watched the distant figure fall from view as the gate crashed down, pinning the Darathia's ignited head. As it struggled frantically, its flaming body only agitated it further, the statue shaking one last time as the forearm broke away at the wrist. The Darathia's exposed half fastened to the structure was torn away, swinging towards the statue's torso.

Pirian fell to his knees, The Father struggling to contain the boy's feelings. Sensing his arm release its hold, the blade retracted.

Ersula looked down at what once again appeared to be a helpless child.

There was a moment of silence, then all that could be heard was the commotion below.

Pirian looked up at Ersula. "You got what you wanted - my

father is dead…there's only *me* left now."

"Pirian," interrupted Lomax as he lifted the unconscious follower, beckoning him away from Ersula.

As they made their way down the statue Pirian could feel The Father distracting him from the pain of losing Jeradon. He could hear him whispering, giving him the strength he needed, yet Pirian was finding it difficult to listen. More importantly, he was finding it more difficult to prevent himself from killing Ersula as they reached the foot of the statue.

The commotion had slowly ceased and the surviving Rojin, Harad and Ersula's followers had surrounded the Darathia.

Pirian glared at Ersula. "Carry on looking witch. I know it's what you want; for me to put you out of your misery. You'd like that wouldn't you…my first kill? Continue the Horncastle tradition."

"All I wanted was for him to speak to me. Take away my pain," she replied as he looked into his eyes. There was a pause. She realised at that moment all of her pain had already been taken away, along with her power.

Now she had nothing left.

Then The Father spoke to her.

This is the first time you will hear my voice Ersula Cordwain… and the last. I have known of your intent for centuries, as I have known of the Horncastle family - especially the boy's father, who has done everything he needed to do. You are all here for a reason and your grandchildren are proof of that; Kira knew exactly who this man was the day she awakened him. She planted the ideas in his head and they grew throughout Newton. Their Emperor believed that he would be able to use it against us, discover our secrets. Yet he was truly blind, hindered by his incompetence. The boy is the result of everything that was grown on the Thirteenth City. I will learn all I need to through him and in turn he through me.

Pirian knelt down, and The Father's blade retracted further. Finally releasing his grip on the hilt, he reached out his hand and touched the follower who lay unconscious on the floor. *We are united. And once Gana is safely back where he belongs we will cure the Erth...the same way we will cure your victim - the same people I have had to abandon because of your poison...your corruption.*

Ersula watched the follower heal before her, his open wounds and lacerations slowly closing. Simultaneously, she could feel the life being drained from her body. Turning her withering form she noticed the remaining Darathia shrivel and perish. Those who were newly transformed healed before her dying eyes, their Darathia skin turning the colour of autumn, before falling to the ground in a pile of rotten vegetation. As they slowly came around, Ersula passed before The Father.

Pirian could see her contorted face, her dark spirit crying out in the hope of finding and possessing Kira who was now venturing towards the surface with her brother. Ersula's spirit was strong, her reach long enough to see her granddaughter one final time. But there was only room for one soul and the final face she saw was that of her daughter Mara. As Ersula screamed out, Mara united souls with her mother, both their presences slowly dissipating to become one with Kira's own conscience. Now, with both her mother's and grandmother's memories, Kira was no more the Select, but the High Priestess herself.

Silence.

Until the boy becomes a man, no prophecy will be answered.

Piran stood motionless as people slowly started to speak amongst themselves.

Vagabond perched himself on Lomax's shoulder as Harad approached them. "Kira and Karl...they are safe?"

"They should be above ground by now. Jeradon made sure

of it."

"I had no doubt in him. I'm sure The Father will be there to thank him personally. As will I."

"You will have to wait."

Harad picked up on what he meant simply by looking him in the eye. The recognition of death was a common thing amongst their people. He watched as the followers attempted to surround their saviour with further curiosity.

Pirian, seemingly ignoring them, made his way over to the fallen, tangled, burnt out carcass of the Darathia giant. There was no host left alive, the body entirely consumed by his healing power. Then he began to walk over one of the bridges. In the distance, amongst those that had perished in the fight, he could make out the broken body of his father.

Apprehensive at first, Pirian wasn't sure he wanted to see his father like this. But Jeradon's face was at peace, helping Pirian to contemplate more easily. Inside there was still a touch of anger, the disappointment in his father leaving him after he had promised to always be there for him. There was nothing he could say, only listen to the voice inside his head.

Whatever is, is right, Pirian Horncastle. Your father died for a reason. I hope you will one day understand. In that moment The Father released Pirian.

The tears came slowly as he knelt at his father's side. Trembling, he reached out his arm and placed it above Jeradon's face, barely touching. He knew there was nothing he could do. There was no voice anymore, and for a brief moment Pirian had hoped that he would have gained Unity with his own father. Instead, his mind and body was preoccupied and Jeradon's spirit was lost.

Harad, Lomax and Vagabond approached.

Pirian was silent. Although he had grown in strength, it was clear from his composure that he was all but spent. He turned and looked at his new friends and family in the hope that for now it would be enough to help him remember what he had to do.

Just as Harad was about to give his sympathy, a familiar voice returned.

You have done well, Harad. Startled for a moment, he continued to listen. *Hear my voice once again and assure our people my strength will return in time. I will allow the boy to grieve for his own father, then you shall prepare him further for what is to come. My sword is now his, yet he must learn how to control it by himself if he is to become the man written about in our scriptures.*

You knew Jeradon would die?

Yes. I have always known...and I have known how *he would die. It is the other reason your daughter awakened him. Her mark of foresight is parallel to my own and she was able to see the future even before she was born. If Jeradon Horncastle had not been awakened, if he had been allowed to continue his life as our enemy, then she would have died there and then along with your wife; there would have been no one to intervene. She knew she was destined to meet Jeradon again and that he would save her own life and brother's in the process. It is one of the reasons he had to return.*

What of Pirian?

Pirian is the result of Jeradon's awakening. He is the prophecy along with his father. Indeed an enemy of the Rojin has fallen. Yet it is his son that will become the man our scriptures speak of. Gana was with him all along and once they meet again they will find the Clock of Ages, cleanse this Erth and destroy Newton once and for all.

Harad thought for a moment. *The boy still has a mother. It is only natural he would want to save her. She is all he has left.*

We are his family now, Harad.

Nothing will stop him finding her again.

262

And this will be the reason he returns to Newton in order to take it from the sky.

Whatever is, is right, thought Harad.

Indeed. Speak to our people. Reassure them that the full strength of their land will also return in time, beginning with the capital. They needn't dwell underground anymore.

What of Lomax and the gargoyle?

They will attend my chambers personally. I have a gift for them.

Harad placed his hands on Pirian's shoulders. "He will receive a true Rojin burial, Pirian."

Pirian remained silent all the way back to the Temple. Following the underground river, Harad led everyone from out of Gargoy. Eventually they exited via the canyon as the river continued east towards the Rojin city. As they approached the outer walls Pirian could already see the difference in the land. Indeed The Father's strength was returning, clearly reflected from how green the surroundings were and how the mirage above maintained its illusion and protection of the city.

The next day, on the outskirts of Yodann, a great ceremony took place marking the passing of those that had died in Gargoy, including Jeradon Horncastle. With their bodies' laid to rest, the ceremony was the perfect initiation of Kira as High Priestess.

Afterwards, Harad gathered his people across the valley with his son and daughter at his side.

"The boy Ersula spoke of is indeed our enemy's son." Harad surveyed the crowd. "If we are to believe Newtonians are simply our misguided brothers, then Pirian Horncastle is truly one of The Father's children. His mark is the result of being born free of the Dosage, the same as all of you. The Thirteenth City is slowly losing the power to control, but not the power to slaughter. While there is still war they will always see a place for blood in this world. Rojin are dying every day, our finest missionaries and our strongest warriors are sent to protect those less fortunate. The Father remains Gana's will on Erth; his strength is returning and once the boy is ready…he will help fight for you all. As long as our people submit to the will of Gana, faith will remain amongst us. Whatever is…is right. It is time to return above ground and take control of your livelihood once more. Help to bring strength back to the land and together we can help fulfil the prophecy. Peace to those that have died and strength to those that willingly protect this city - now they have another to help them believe in their cause."

As Harad concluded his speech, Pirian looked across the open expanse of the surrounding valley, in the company of Lomax and Vagabond. The great river reached out in front of them, thousands of people had gathered to hear the Voice speak to them once again. It wasn't long ago they had listened to the preaching of Ersula, deep underground in the city of Gargoy; but her twisted machinations were all but forgotten. She was a woman who had no intention of believing in Pirian's ability. She had allowed her bitterness to affect her own ideals and he would not allow the same mistake to happen to him. Instead he hoped to turn as much of his experiences, including the loss of his father, into a positive action.

It would have been what Jeradon wanted.

Unsure of his newfound abilities, and everything else Harad referred to; his head was a mess and needed healing as much as Erth itself. He was overwhelmed and felt as though he had taken onboard so much; his mind cracked into a thousand years, his heart broken into a hundred pieces. So much swam around inside his head, he was afraid of forgetting entirely who he was.

For some reason, though, that was quickly being overshadowed by who he was becoming. His father was no longer there for him and his mother was now at Jakahn's side as the Empress of Newton. He had no other choice but to stand on his own two feet.

He pulled himself out of contemplation, almost forgetting he was in good company, "Thank you for finding us, Lomax. If it wasn't for you I wouldn't be here."

"We simply followed what we had set out to do. Although I hadn't expected the Erth, or the sea for that matter, to change me as much as it has done."

"I'm sorry if my father or I ever doubted you."

"No...your father knew, and so did you deep down. He was shown the truth, the same way The Father had shown us what to do fifteen years ago." Lomax held out his sword, as it formed before his eyes. "The Father has seen all this. Your mark has given strength back to my own blade, as well as his own. It has helped restore the little faith I had left in him. We have finally been summoned to his chambers once again. The last time we were there, we were asked to hide Gana and search for the Fallen."

"I guess you found him."

Lomax looked him in the eye. "I believe we did. We just lost ourselves and a lot of lives along the way."

Pirian felt uncomfortable. "I...I feel responsible for their deaths."

"No...never say that, Pirian. Those people were my crew. They were pirates, mercenaries...but I had taught them the will of Gana the best way a faithless Captain could. They were closer to Rojin and they would have known that they had died for a cause at the very least. I need to keep reminding myself of that as much as you do." He turned to leave, "We've all lost. We lose a part of ourselves everyday. The important thing is in figuring out how to put things back together. One day, you'll find Gana for us, and hopefully the Clock of Ages. Just take a look what you and your father have done already." And with that Lomax left Pirian once again in the company of his own thoughts.

He wasn't alone for long before Kira and Karl approached.

"Catch." She threw an apple towards Pirian. "There are plenty more where that came from. The orchards are flourishing already."

Looking at the apple he noticed how healthy and ripe it was, "I'll save it…for later," he replied, placing it in his pocket.

"It's all because of you, Pirian…and your father. You have helped bring strength back to Yodann. Every step you take, brings new life to our land and people."

"Thank you…and thank you for the kind words at the service. I just wish he was here to see all this."

It took a while for Karl to speak. "He wasn't the man I expected. But he was certainly your father. There was little thought for himself…in the same way you saved me. I doubt I will ever forgive the man he was, but I will certainly forgive the man he became." Karl reached out his arm to shake Pirian's.

Pausing briefly, he took hold of Karl's wrist. Flinching, Karl drew his arm back slightly then realised what Pirian was doing. As his arm healed instantly, he truly came to believe in Pirian.

Absorbing the life force from his marked arm Pirian let go of Karl, noticing his arm swell slightly, then his skin shrivel and fall like dried leaves, before finally growing back.

Holding his wrist, Karl opened and closed his hand, checking it over in disbelief. "Thank you." He paused, raising his eyebrow, "Perhaps now we can finish our duel?".

Kira rolled her eyes at her brother.

Pirian placed his hand on the hilt of The Father's symbiont blade tucked into his belt. "I'd like that. I'll need all the practice I can get."

"No cheating this time," replied Karl.

Pirian managed a tiny smile, holding back his emotions as best he could.

"You both have plenty of time for sword practice." Kira brushed Pirian's shoulder affectionately. "I'll be here for you, Pirian...all of us will be."

A single tear fell from his eye as Kira placed her other hand on his cheek.

"I just want to hear his voice again. I don't want to hear The Father's, I want to hear my own father's voice."

"Pirian, look around you. This land has been healed because of yourself and Jeradon's actions. His voice may not be heard, but it surrounds you all the same in what he has helped us achieve so far. All of this, including yourself, is the result of what the Rojin helped him believe in. Something you also believe in. This is simply one of his Greenhouses..." She kissed his forehead. "And one day you will help heal the whole Erth."

Contemplating, Pirian replied wryly, "You're not expecting much from me then?"

Kira smiled. "Spend some time with yourself. When you are ready, our people would like to thank you and your father personally. Then you can continue with your teachings - there is a lot to be prepared for."

He noticed Larissa and Ched close by. They acknowledged him with a nod as Kira and Karl made their way back.

There would be plenty of time to talk *and plenty of time to walk*, he thought realising that the teachings were leading enevitably towards his very own Erth Walk.

"One step at a time." he whispered to himself, his mind drifting to the past.

For a moment he was back in the last Greenhouse; reminded exactly of what his father had achieved. *This is only the beginning* - back in Gargoy, The Father had truly taken control of his situation and rescued him from himself. Although he had now relinquished power over him, Pirian was still able to feel his presence more than ever since he connected through the blade and brought strength back to the Rojin's immortal leader.

Looking up towards the mirage above the city he could make out his mother's face. A strange feeling, he hadn't felt before, slowly began to distract him. He could sense a part of himself growing elsewhere, similar to his connection with The Father. His arm twitched as though it had been rudely awoken, a tingling sensation coursing through his veins. Then there was a faint whisper at the back of his mind. He hoped it was his father; instead it seemed to be someone or even something else entirely. Already it had its own voice, smothered by a familiar control.

Zetameen. Pirian could taste it.

He tried to make out what it was trying to say, *Other?*

No, there was more...

Mother?

Silence. Then the voice echoed inside his head before slowly dropping, almost muffled by a cloud of amber. The Dosage had taken hold...

Brother, the voice whispered back.

EPILOGUE

It would have been very easy for the Sea Wolf to choose the bottle over the boat; perhaps a far quicker way of drowning his sorrows.

In Lomax's eye, The Father could see the loss he had suffered - his crew, even his very soul had almost sunk without trace. He had sacrificed a great deal in their search for the man the Rojin scriptures spoke of and had protected the whereabouts of Gana from the traitor within their midst. Pushed to the ends of the Erth and the very edges of his faith, he and his faithful gargoyle could now finally leave the mercenary life behind and become a missionary once again.

The Father's gift to Lomax was the Mindship he had left behind.

Approaching the vessel, Lomax raised his hand to its underbelly, while Vagabond perched himself on one of its many masts.

"You've been asleep a long time."

"And you have been *gone* a long time," replied *Romulus*. "You look sad...are you here to stay?

"Yes...yes I am," replied Lomax.

"Then come aboard," *Romulus* beckoned lowering his ramp. "You can tell me what's on your mind while I stretch my wings."

"I'd like that, brother...I'd like that very much." Vagabond flew down to accompany him as he walked up the ramp. Before it had even shut behind them, *Romulus* had lifted silently, tilted his nose, then increased his mind to full power aiming himself towards the mirage and out towards the ravaged, distant memory of Erth.

PREVIEW

-NWΣИ𝚪⅃Ꭼ𝚪ᎢHᏟHᎢᏫNⁱᏟᏞᎬꟓ∞ᒐᐱ̄ᗭ̄ᗭ̃̄ᑎ̄̃̄ᗯ̃̄

BOOK II

One

For all the beast knew, it had travelled the full distance of Erth a thousand times over.

It never slept and never stopped to contemplate. This spawn of the inferno merely hunted and devoured any living thing that happened to stumble into its path. There was only a savage instinct - channelled energy that continued to shape its physical and mental state. Its bile and waste expelled from its already decaying body, only added to the desecrated Erth - the creature's stench alone was enough to infect the living.

This beast, this abomination was beyond life and death - a personification of pure evil. It had started life as a chemical reaction, triggered by an unseen energy seven years previously. Born from a protronium rich gyre, deep underground, it had evolved rapidly from a single cell that fused with Erth and putrid, rotting flesh.

After the first day it had continued to absorb the rich surrounding bacteria, and had grown to the size of a mosquito larvae. Now, amber rich fry had become its main source of prey.

One month passed and the glowing, twisted larvae had transformed itself into something far more efficient for its aquatic surroundings. Now a ferocious fish, the creature had already begun to prey on the unfortunate lizards that would drink at the edge of the amber pool.

With pure, distilled protronium coursing through its veins, a year in the gyre had developed its ability to hunt all manner of animals, both below and above the surface of the water. Having beached itself time and time again during its second year, it had absorbed the reptiles' ability to crawl on land.

As its mass increased, the beast's framework continued to evolve at a rapid rate and after three years it was already the size of a wildcat.

Four years - a further increase in fat to aid in the winter months, along with a heavy fur coat. Six eyes and dislocating mandible jaws took up most the size of its head, enabling it to devour larger prey.

Five years - it's first Newtonian kill provided further aggression and increased strength - all the while, an amber source reshaping it from within.

Six years - an unrivalled instinct, closer to intelligence. By now the beast's reputation had taken hold, having been seen by both the Newtonian Guild and Rojin Missionaries. Injecting further fear throughout the land, the abomination was Gana's complete antithesis. Relentlessly, the creature continued to destroy everything in its wake, all the while its body beyond transformation and now closer to death and decay - an amber light caged within a hideous exoskeleton.

After seven years its recognition had brought with it an identity, bordering on myth. Named 'Gana's Brother' by the Rojin; this chimera had now recognised its purpose - the reason it had been born on this Gana forsaken Erth. It wasn't just for the pleasure of the kill, but to hunt down and destroy the one known as Horncastle.

ABOUT THE AUTHOR

Richard 'James Johnson' was born in Derby, England in 1976. After graduating with a degree in Graphic Design from the University of Luton he went on to win a prestigious D&AD first award. Along with his obsession of film, he developed the writing bug at an early age - his passion for storytelling culminating in two illustrated books at the age of twelve. In addition to his work as a writer, he's also an accomplished Illustrator and Graphic Designer, in which he also lectures and leads a degree level course in Nottingham. *The Enemy's Son* is his first novel.

ACKNOWLEDGEMENTS

A huge thankyou to my fellow Erth Walkers over at the official site - your dedication and respect for the story and world I have created so far has been more than encouraging. Over the past year Erthchronicles.com has grown into an admirable community, which I hope will continue to maintain the level of quality we have all set. Thanks to Cornerstones for their more than helpful consultation on the early drafts, John Jarrold for the edit, the mysterious Panama Oxridge - our conversations have helped immensely. Chris and Liam - cheers for the inspiration and your support so far.

Most importantly I thank my parents and grandmother - with all my love and gratitude. You know who the rest of you are - those who put up with the very obsessions that have made my stories and artwork possible in the first place.